THE CALL OF THE WILD

Barbie nodded, not quite ready for speech. Her mental inventory was ringing up a preposterous number of visual pluses. His chiseled features were aristocratic. The high cheekbones, whittled chin, tanned skin and exquisitely shaped patrician nose were painfully beautiful. His dark suit, no doubt terribly expensive, hung perfectly on his frame, buttoned over a soft white shirt.

Was there more to admire? Maybe so, but she had to stop there; he was two feet away with his dark and perfect eyebrows arched. Barbie wanted to run home and pluck hers.

"Barbie?" he repeated with a grin.

She smiled as she met Darin's eyes, which were either hazel or dark green. It was hard to tell the exact color in the dark, especially with all the noises in her ears. *Hubba-hubba* would have been the verbal translation. Or maybe, *My place or yours?*

Barbie
&
THE BEAST

LINDA
THOMAS-SUNDSTROM

LOVE SPELL   NEW YORK CITY

For John, my very own beast.

LOVE SPELL®

April 2009

Published by

Dorchester Publishing Co., Inc.
200 Madison Avenue
New York, NY 10016

ISBN 10: 0-505-52813-4
ISBN 13: 978-0-505-52813-1
E-ISBN: 1-4285-0658-6

The name "Love Spell" and its logo are trademarks of Dorchester Publishing Co., Inc.

Printed in the United States of America.

10 9 8 7 6 5 4 3 2 1

Visit us on the web at www.dorchesterpub.com.

ACKNOWLEDGMENTS

A whole lot of thanks for getting this book into the hands of readers are due to the following people, to whom I will be eternally grateful. My wonderful editor, Chris Keeslar, for making this particular dream come true. My super agent, Jennifer Schober, for helping to see that he did. The Mattel toy company, for creating the Barbie doll in the first place. And my family, those here and those gone, who have always supported my creative endeavors. There just couldn't have been a better group of people on the planet.

Barbie
&
THE BEAST

Chapter One

"Geez, it's really dark out here," Barbie Bradley said, inching her way through almost totally invisible surroundings in Forest Lawn cemetery, searching for anything that might remotely resemble the party they were seeking.

"Duh," Angie Ward grunted.

"You don't happen to have a flashlight, do you, Ang?"

"Oh yes, I have one right here. And while I'm digging in my purse for it, would you maybe like a Big Mac? Some fries? It's all here in this little tiny clutch thingy I'm carrying, because you can't underestimate what you'll need at a party."

Chuckling over her best friend's reply, Barbie lifted her foot to step lightly over something her toe had struck—an object she couldn't actually see, since the owners of Forest Lawn seemed oblivious to the benefits of electricity.

Her foot stopped an inch from the ground. The tightness of her skirt nearly became her downfall. Literally. "Damn," she swore, tripping and righting herself. "Should have worn pants."

"Pants? To a party? Where there are m-e-n? No way, girlfriend. No pants, ever. And what was that you just tripped over?"

"Might have been a tree branch, but could just as well

have been a body part. It is a graveyard, after all. No telling what's lying around."

"Body part?" Angie's voice was nasal and an octave too high, reminding Barbie that her friend didn't like the dark in any way, shape, or form. Angela Ward had grown up without the benefit of the two older Bradley brothers, who had prepared Barbie for all kinds of adventures—fake spiders on the bedspread, flies frozen in ice cubes, ghoulish movies about ghosts and machetes.

Graveyard? Piece of cake for Barbie Bradley, while Angie, even now, and as formidable as she could be at times, had little glowy lights all over the inside of her box-sized apartment. She probably even had a flashlight in that purse and didn't want to admit it.

"I'm not tripping. You don't see me tripping, do you?" Angie asked.

"A miracle, don't you think, in those heels you're wearing?" Barbie teased.

"These heels show my legs off to perfection. Shapely legs are an asset at a party. You can't view shapely legs if there are flat shoes at the ends of them—or if they're covered by pants."

"But four-inch stilettos can be a liability. Especially if stray body parts are skewered on them."

Angie's intake of air was audible. "You are downright catty. What *do* you teach those tenth-graders of yours, I wonder?"

"The hazards of wearing four-inch heels in a graveyard at night, for one thing. The pitfalls of dating, for another." Well, Barbie amended silently, nearly colliding with another lumpy item in her path, she didn't actually teach her students either of those things. But someone should. Modern dating rituals were positively archaic.

"Pitfalls of dating," Angie mused. "Now there's something I never learned in school. I guess I should have gone to college."

"You *did* go to college," Barbie reminded her tall, drop-dead gorgeous, curvaceous, espresso-hued, African-American beauty-technician pal, rolling her eyes. "Beauty college."

"Not the same as your state-college gig."

"I wouldn't go out each day without the benefit of your particular brand of talent, Ang." It was a repeat of their usual back and forth regarding the diversity of their career choices. For the thousandth time.

"Straightening your hair? Anyone could do that."

"Anyone who went to beauty school."

Yes, thank heavens for that beauty school, Barbie said to herself, prodding yet another object with the pointy toe of her sensible two-inch-heeled sandal. Balmy Miami nights like this one, without a good hairdresser's magic? She'd become a citizen of Frizz City. All those frizz jokes in junior high! God, that had been bad. But it also had been one of the reasons for her and Angie getting together in the first place: bad hair days.

Of course, Barbie decided, bypassing the mysterious lump, there had to be men on the planet who wouldn't mind a date with imperfections, just as there had to be men who didn't care for women who primped and pranced around in overly-tight skirts and ridiculous shoes. *Expensive* and ridiculous shoes. As for herself, she preferred a pair of washed-out jeans with a hole in one knee, and a baseball cap to cover her brunette, curly-haired chaos. Until now, she'd heeded Angie's pleas to straighten her hair, but if she relied totally on Angie's fashion advice, she also would be tottering around Forest Lawn in a miniskirt and sling-backed, rather slutty stilettos. Not to mention that her bank account would be depleted at the mere mention of the word *Manolo*.

"Okay," Angie said, voice back to normal. "So tell me

this. If we're educated, talented, young, and fairly attractive, how come we don't have serious dates?"

This rhetorical question had become their mantra of late.

"Men are intimidated by intelligent women," Barbie said, taking a stab at the unanswerable with words that had been on her mind more lately—words she sincerely hoped weren't actually true. Because, heck, if all those other things Angie had just listed were legit, and they were indeed reasonably likeable babes, what was the holdup? Where were the men?

"Intelligent women, huh? Girl, I think you nailed it on the head," Angie said.

"Ew." Barbie looked down. "I hope not."

"I don't mean *that* kind of a head," Angie declared, shuddering. "And don't they have graveyard sheriffs to make sure nothing even resembling a stray head or body part is lying around? I'm sure they do, so you can stop with the creepy images, okay?"

"Okay. But will this be half the fun?"

"Double the fun," Angie grunted. "*Tons* of fun. Lordy, I don't know why I'm still your best friend, Barb. I have a feeling you're liking this dark, spooky cemetery shit. I can hear it in your voice. You've been hardened by all those students of yours. You're not afraid of anything anymore. It isn't natural. I don't know why I let you talk me into these . . . adventures."

"*I* talked *you* into this?"

"Well, okay. Maybe it was that new client of mine," Angie admitted.

"Singles party, the client said."

"Probably guys to die for. She said that, too. Now I'm beginning to think she was yanking my chain. I mean, we are in a frigging *cemetery* here. I thought this party might be better than submitting us to that Dating Game show the country club is putting on soon. Think how embarrassing *that* would be!"

"Hear, hear," Barbie agreed, shivering at the thought. Guys on that show sat on the other side of a big screen where the main contestant couldn't see them, for all intents and purposes invisible. How helpful would that be?

Her toe hit something solid. Glancing up, Barbie decided that the nearly full moon would have been of some use—without the cloud cover. It was a given that the dead people in this place didn't need lights, but women trying to find a party sure did! If in fact there actually was a party . . .

That last *if* gave her pause. A *second* pause, actually—the first being when they'd pulled into the parking lot with the address Angie's client had written down. Odd choice for a party, sure, she had thought. Then again, lots of things were odd these days. Think eyebrow piercings, nipple rings, and five-year-old children with personal cell phones. And there had been twenty other cars in the cemetery parking lot. It was conceivable that a graveyard might be the perfect place for a party, if you could get past the *ick* factor. On the plus side, who would complain about noise?

"Our problem, Ang," Barbie said, slowing, "is that we're too vulnerable."

"You got that right," Angie agreed. "We even bought new clothes for this."

Barbie ran a hand over the hem of her burgundy linen jacket, purchased that morning because it flattered her coloring, not because it was trendy. Her enjoyment of the feel of the paper-light fabric was interrupted by a wayward image of Angie's client laughing her head off about sending them here. Chain yankin', big-time.

"Your outfit is *tres chic*, by the way," Angie said. "Everything in the right place, accentuating the positives. Even if those 'positives' are a tad on the small side." She chuckled.

"Don't even go there," Barbie warned. Obviously her friend wasn't too scared to throw a jab. Why she bothered, Barbie didn't know, since there was nothing to be done about the slightly diminutive size of her boobs, short of having fake ones installed or wearing padded bras that would, if she were alone and naked with a guy, turn into an embarrassment. Sure, her breasts might lean toward the smallish, perky side, yet they were her breasts, the ones both God and Bradley family genetics had given her. Why mess with Mother Nature?

Hearing the crunch of gravel, Barbie moved a little faster, hoping she'd found a walkway they'd somehow missed from the parking lot, wondering how much more of this graveyard wandering they were going to endure. Sixty seconds?

We're on a quest, she reminded herself. But, while she and her friend had both made solemn vows on the first of January to try anything and everything to find good boyfriend/husband prospects, surely the angels monitoring New Year's resolutions would excuse them from trying in bizarro locales. There had to be a loophole.

She wanted to find a man. She really did. Lately she'd had a terrible longing to rest her head on some guy's shoulder, a longing for rainy-day breakfasts in bed, with sex for dessert. She wanted a diamond ring of whatever size and clarity, as long as it was bigger than a bread box and sparkled brilliantly in all light sources. Presented to her, of course (was there any other acceptable way?) by a guy—*her* guy—down on one knee. A Cape Cod house with a white picket fence would be nice, too. A dog in the yard. A baby stroller. Someone to share jokes and baths with. Growing old in the same person's arms—someone who was like a bit of herself broken off from some internal seam.

Yes, what Barbie Bradley really wanted was to find Mr.

Perfect. Problem was, so did every other twenty-something female. Hence, the shortage of candidates. So far, she hadn't come even remotely close to finding Mr. Tolerable, let alone Mr. Right.

Bill Lewis, her ex, hadn't helped much. He had, in fact, set her biological clock back a few ticks. She'd been hopeful he might be "the one." He had flat out told her so, suggesting a rosy future. Then, bam, he'd been hit by the jerk stick. Or else maybe he'd just been a really good liar all along. All those stories he'd told about working late. All those compromising situations she'd caught him in. Bill had been *it* all right—if you started *it* with an *s-h*. The truth was, she had been a sucker for a pretty face.

But this was a new year, and dammit, time was wasting. She wasn't getting any younger. Twenty-something-*else* was right around the corner. Everyone knew that flimsy teddies had to be worn before gravity took its toll. Sex had to be a top priority while a woman was still capable of achieving a rollicking-good orgasm—assuming, of course, that she was indeed capable of achieving a rollicking-good orgasm. Considering such things, in light of her nonexistent experience, meant wallowing in uncharted territory, perhaps in the land of myth . . . but she could dream.

Still, did she and Angie want to rustle up boyfriends this badly? Tromping-through-a-graveyard type of badly?

Uh-uh.

"I think I see a light," Angie said.

Barbie paused midstep, staring out into the dark, and sighed. "Yep. I see it, too."

"Suddenly I'm not too excited by that light, or whoever might be around it," Angie said. "How about you?"

"Nope."

"Do you want to turn back?" Angie suggested, hope ringing in her voice.

"I'm considering it, though you could go on if you want."

"Alone? Not on your life, Barbie girl. My name might not be Midge, but I'm sticking to you all the same."

The mention of the Mattel toy went unchallenged by Barbie. Almost anything could be tolerated between best friends, even poking fun at her doll-inspired name. Maybe her mother had named her after the doll, hoping her daughter would turn out as successful and proper as the plastic blonde, but it had been the bane of Barbie's existence. Mothers should know better. And if anyone else had brought up the Barbie/Midge thing besides Angie, she would have excused herself to stick a finger down her throat. Or theirs.

"If you really want to go, I'll go," Barbie offered.

"No, if *you* want to go, *I'll* go," Angie declared.

"Flip a coin?" Barbie suggested.

"Couldn't see it, it's so bleeping dark. Although . . . this could be a test. Right?"

"What?"

"A test. You know, a survival-of-the-fittest kind of thing. If women actually make it to the party out there somewhere, having traipsed through all the darkness and dead bodies, those women—*us*—will be deemed worthy of all the waiting maleness."

After a hesitant silence in which this theory hung itself, spontaneous giggles broke out between the pair. Girl giggles. Pal giggles. Comfortable giggles that kept right on rolling, same as they had way back in seventh grade.

"That's pathetic," Barbie said, a hiccup later.

"Yeah," Angie agreed. "So maybe we can skip this particular golden opportunity. Besides, that light could be a mirage."

"Maybe," Barbie suggested, "I just scared both of us with all the talk about stray body parts."

"Have to say, though, that I have a new hankering. One that doesn't involve men," Angie confessed. "Not any men who'd be out here, anyway. What man worth a damn would be in a graveyard? Living ones, I mean. We need to try Home Depot. On a Sunday. Or a lumberyard. My new hankering says we go to your place, have some chips and Oreos, and top those off with ice cream. Throw caution to the wind. What do you say?"

"Sounds good to me," Barbie replied, very honestly relieved. The promise of cookies and ice cream seemed a fitting end to the silliness of their current predicament. As a matter of fact, cookies and the mass consumption of them was beginning to seem a fitting end to every situation. "Let's go," she stated firmly. "We don't need this."

Before she could take a backward step, Angie's voice rang out. "Hang on! Barbie, did you hear that noise? Over there?"

There was no way could Barbie see where her friend was pointing, if she was pointing. "Damn. I hope no one heard us," she muttered.

"I hope that noise isn't coming from a severed head," Angie said, tone again high-pitched, as though her own hand might be on her throat, squeezing. "Detached heads don't still have vocal cords, do they?"

"Not unless they're in a Stephen King movie." Barbie didn't actually hear anything. "Most likely it's someone from the party. I'll bet if we can't see them, they can't see us, either."

"Then no one would see us run," Angie said.

"Can you run in those shoes?"

"I'd be willing to give it a try. Can you run in yours?"

"Remember the punch line of that old joke? I don't have to run fast, just faster than you."

"Hmmm," Angie conceded. "It might be a good idea if I took these heels off for a few minutes."

"And step on all those body parts with your bare feet?"

"Geez, Barb!" Angie's subsequent expletive was muffled. No doubt she'd bent over to remove her shoes, chin pressed to her substantial and much-envied bosom. "Did you have to remind me of that joke? Or of Stephen King? That kind of stuff gives me the willies!"

Surprisingly, Barbie couldn't respond to that. Something had encircled her right wrist with a viselike grip, and it couldn't be her friend. Angie would have been worried about breaking a nail.

The suddenness of the touch rendered Barbie speechless. She was pulled sideways, struggled to remain upright with the damn pencil skirt inhibiting knee action, and heard Angie's voice crack slightly. "Okay. Shoes are off. Ready to sprint, Barb?"

Then, "Barbie? Quit playing tricks. Not funny. Say something." Angie's nasal whine returned, following Barbie into the darkness. "Oh crap, oh crap, oh crap. You there, Barbie?"

Barbie was just too stunned to answer.

Chapter Two

The shriek Barbie finally uttered barely made it past her constricted throat and ended up sounding more like a sneeze. She turned, ducked, and got a mouthful of something that tasted like damp Christmas tree. There was no time for a second vocalization. The big hand that had latched onto her was pulling her through a bunch of bushes. She had to wave her free hand to keep from getting scratched, and kept her mouth closed to keep out leaves and God knew what other sort of graveyard debris might get in there. Tugged along at a brisk pace, she had to concentrate, trot on her tiptoes, and pray she wouldn't fall flat on her face.

Whoever had hold of her dove through another batch of greenery. She followed. Clear of that, they hit wet grass. Her heels sank down into the earth, pitching her off balance. She tipped like the famous leaning tower in Italy. *Thook*. Her heels then unstuck, and she hurtled toward whatever person was still attached to her via a firm handhold, thinking as she fell that this grab-and-run had to have something to do with the party—the party she and Angie had decided not to attend. This nocturnal kidnapping routine could only be thought up by party boys. *Men*. Young single men who, having heard her and Angie wavering, were gathering them up before a full retreat.

Considering this, Barbie swallowed a tempting shout for help. She and Angie must have sounded so silly, so chicken, talking about all those heads. They might as well have flapped their elbows up and down and made clucking sounds—

"Oof." She rammed into something hard—her abductor, most likely. The air puffed out of her lungs as she was lifted off the ground and tossed over a meaty shoulder like a sack of potatoes, leaving her legs dangling and her hair in her eyes.

"You have got to be kidding!" she exclaimed. But the guy carrying her didn't react to her exclamation or offer up so much as a single introduction, explanation, or apology for what might easily have been grounds for cardiac arrest.

And wait a minute! Assuming they'd both been abducted, Angie seemed awfully quiet for a person who always had something to say.

Dang, Barbie thought, bumping along upside down on her abductor's shoulder. If this really was the welcoming committee, it didn't bode well for the party. Although her man-wishes hadn't been about finding a male too in touch with his feminine side, neither did she want to be around a bunch of brutes.

All she could see now was . . . well, nothing. She couldn't even make out what kind of jacket the guy carrying her was wearing, though it felt sort of silky as she clung on for dear life. Food for thought: if it was a tux or a nice expensive dinner ensemble, both she and Angie were dreadfully underdressed. Of course, tuxes were rarely worn by weirdos, right?

Relaxing her grip slightly, Barbie shuffled once more through her options. Shout, kick, get to her feet and cause a fuss—all seemed like good ones. Combined, they should just about do the trick to get her free. At the very least, they'd scare the bejesus out of this guy.

Problem was, she couldn't move her legs. The brute must have had an arm over them. Without the use of extremities necessary for a getaway, the only sensible thing to do would be to . . . adapt. Adapt and hope she would someday regain the feeling in her feet.

Really, since the decision of whether or not she and Angie would actually get to the party had been taken out of their hands, she might as well make a concerted effort to remain polite and ladylike in a very unladylike position, obliging these party boys for a few minutes more. Surely she could find the patience, the humor, to deal with a wise guy like this one, short-term? Perhaps talk to him?

Of course, talking required breath, and a broad, muscled shoulder seemed to be cutting off her air. Ditto for Angie, she supposed, whose colorful murmurings should have been audible by now.

Spitting some of the dangling hair out of her mouth, Barbie managed a grimace and the word "Fudge."

She tried again. "Are we going far?" Her voice sounded bouncy and staccato, though the guy's gait was, thankfully, fairly smooth.

"Not far now," a very deep, masculine voice replied from beside her left hip.

Wow. Communication. Good start.

"Ummm . . . you must be very strong," Barbie said. "I don't hear you panting or anything."

"I have my moments," the guy carrying her replied.

"Is this one of them? Because I can walk, you know. Been doing it for twenty-two years now, give or take."

"Ah, but we wouldn't want you to step on any of those stray body parts, would we?" came the wry answer.

Barbie knew wry when she heard it. She was, after all, a

Bradley. Wry was a common Bradley middle name. She tossed back, "But *you're* willing to step on them?"

"I'll miss them."

"Oh? Eyes of a bat, maybe?"

"Bats have radar," he replied.

"A wise guy, huh?"

"I like to think so."

"Nothing wrong with your ego, then," Barbie muttered.

"Had ages to perfect it," the guy agreed, slowing slightly before veering to the right.

After a hesitation, Barbie asked, "Are we going toward the light?"

"Is that a metaphysical question?" he returned.

"Nope. Haven't got a metaphysical bone in my body. I did see a light back there, though. And I am inquisitive. For instance, I'm wondering why you're carrying me."

"I liked your voice."

"You pick up everyone whose voice you like?"

"Those under two hundred pounds."

Very funny. A true wit. So wait, wit meant brains, right? Brains and brawn in the same guy? Surely this was a step in the right direction toward that New Year's resolution.

"I'm also suspicious by nature," she offered.

No comment from her abductor.

"Aren't you going to ask me about the suspicious part?" Barbie asked.

"Nope."

"Damn."

"You'd prefer I asked about it?"

"Conversation might make this situation a bit more civilized," she suggested.

"You're talking about the sack-of-potatoes style of transportation? I'd have carried you differently, in a more civilized manner, but I needed both hands free."

"What for?"

"To open the gate."

"I don't see any gate."

Of course, Barbie didn't have eyes in her butt, and that part of her anatomy was front-facing at the moment.

"We haven't gone through the gate yet," the guy told her.

"Those lights looked fairly close when Angie and I were standing back there somewhere."

"Lights are deceptive," came the reply.

"Well, we can't have deceptive lights, can we?" Barbie did an eye roll. "I mean, who *can* you trust?"

Had the guy laughed at that? Barbie swore she'd heard a rumble. She felt a quick shake of his shoulders. Either he'd laughed, or his stomach growled loudly.

Didn't they provide food at this party?

"You sure this isn't a fraternity bash?" she mumbled, suspicions coalescing into images of beer kegs, sawdust on the floor, and rowdy twenty-year-olds. She imagined platters of Triskets and Cheez Whiz in the can. Kinky abductions without explanation would be just the sort of thing a frat boy might do, while beating his chest with his fists and making Tarzan noises like . . .

"Ungawa!"

"Did you say something?" her abductor asked, slowing.

"I said, 'Ungawa.' "

"That's what I thought you said. Is there something wrong with your tongue?"

"My tongue is fine. The word is a commonly used fratboy password, I believe."

"How do you know that?"

"I'd rather not say," Barbie admitted, "though it could involve old movies on cable."

She was beginning to feel a bit like a rag doll. Thing was, in this position, she couldn't stay tense. If she didn't relax, it would be murder on the abs. "What if I tell you I'm getting seasick, all upside down like this?" she asked.

"I'd wonder if it was the truth or merely a ploy to get me to set you on your feet."

Blowing the hair out of her face, Barbie muttered half to herself, half to him, "Wouldn't want to spoil your nice, soft jacket by barfing up late lunch, is all."

Expecting to hear choruses of those Tarzan vocalizations any minute now, Barbie was surprised when the guy stopped walking. Whoever said that men weren't vain about their clothes?

"Well?" she asked when he made no move to set her down.

"I'm waiting," he told her.

"For what?"

"The volcanic eruption."

"I'm not really going to barf. Not right at the moment, anyway." Shoot. It was a stupid burst of honesty, Barbie realized too late.

"Good." He started off again.

"Doesn't mean I won't change my mind," she warned, lifting her head, trying to look at him.

"Nice of you to warn me," he said. "Very civilized."

Scanning the dark as she tried to keep the hair out of her eyes, Barbie realized it certainly wasn't getting any lighter. They should have reached the party by now. The way she was draped over this guy's shoulder had to be as uncomfortable for him as it was for her; though she'd been going to the gym regularly for the last year, she still had a couple of pounds to lose.

Her fingers were starting to tingle. Blood was rushing to her head. Not to worry, she told herself. She'd read somewhere that being upside down, in the form of head- and handstands, brought blood and nutrients to your brain. This meant, according to what she had read, that a person could think better, feel better, and look perfectly pink cheeked without an application of blush.

Okay, so the last part was her own take on the matter. Still, it remained a fact that a good percentage of people were on either their feet or buttocks most of the day. Maybe it made sense to return some gravity-challenged blood up north.

"You know," Barbie pointed out, not so sure about anything, since she could no longer feel her toes, "this kind of over-the-shoulder stuff went out with the cavemen."

"Did it? Why didn't anyone tell me?" the guy said.

"Gee, I don't know. Maybe you weren't listening?"

"I'm quite a good listener, actually. I heard you mention you're a teacher. And something about Oreos."

"That's called eavesdropping, not listening," she growled.

"You weren't whispering, you know."

"My friend and I were having a private conversation."

"In voices that would wake the dead."

"Oh? Is there a law against talking in a graveyard?"

"Not that I know of, though noise does carry farther than you'd expect. Cemeteries are usually on the quiet side."

"Yeah, I suppose that's why it was chosen for the party."

"Party?"

Not realizing that an upside-down stomach could perform a flip until hers did, Barbie stifled a yelp. There was something in the way he had said that. As if he didn't know about the party.

"You aren't actually going to be sick, are you?" he asked, slowing again.

"Put me down. Right this minute. This position is barbaric."

"You've never dreamed of being swept off your feet?" he asked cockily.

"Oh. That."

The guy laughed again, soft and low and just loud enough

for Barbie to hear, the rumbling sound toying with her attempt at reviving a reality check. Her stomach had, mere seconds before, done an impossible one-eighty, for Pete's sake. She was numb all over, and he was laughing?

Maybe she could kick him with one of her partially paralyzed legs? Then she could mess up his hair. Guys hated hair mussing when they were all dolled up for a party. His hair smelled faintly—and rather nicely, come to think of it—like spice.

As she thought briefly about how pleasant good-smelling hair was on specimens of the male gender, the brawny brute beneath her had the audacity to laugh again, shaking her up, sabotaging her little revenge plan. Thing was, she had to admit, this particular brute had a nice laugh. She liked guys who were able to laugh easily and freely. She liked all the little eye wrinkles on old men's faces caused by a lifetime of merriment.

One thing was certain: laughter was high on her checklist of male characteristics acceptable for further exploration. As was spice-scented shampoo.

So . . . ?

No! Do not go there!

Bad Barbie!

Brutes do not warrant consideration of that sort!

Wildmen are not to be taken seriously! Unless your name is Angie Ward, of course, for whom the word wild, *when applied to a man, would elicit pure, unadulterated glee.*

Which had to be why Angie remained so quiet. She was probably having the time of her life.

Barbie shook her head. To get back on track, trying hard not to sound agitated she said, "I can't say I've ever envisioned this position in my dreams of being swept off my feet. I mean, it's not really very romantic, is it?"

"What's unromantic about it?" her abductor asked.

"Oh, it could have something to do with my rear end being so near to your face. Not to mention the fact that you're wrinkling the clothes I recently spent all my hard-earned cash on, and I won't be able to make a proper first impression."

"You believe that, about clothes and first impressions?"

"Not usually. Hardly ever, really." She added a heartbeat later, "Yet I do hate to iron."

There was now a lightness to the guy's tone. "In that case, I guess I'd better put you down."

"It would be the gentlemanly thing to do," Barbie agreed.

"And I," her companion remarked, "have always striven to be a gentleman."

Chuckling as if amused over some private joke, he bent his knees and bent his back until Barbie could feel the ground beneath her feet. Steadying her with his hands on her shoulders, he waited until she had her balance before letting her go.

Reluctantly? It seemed to Barbie as though he'd released her somewhat slowly. His fingers ran down her arms as if getting in a last feel.

P, for pervert.

Out of habit, Barbie tugged at her little burgundy jacket and straightened her skirt by running her hands over her hips. Waiting for the head rush to subside, she patted her shoulder-length and hopefully still-straight brown hair, making sure it was in order, then squinted in an attempt to see the man who had carted her through the graveyard.

She couldn't see diddly, other than a very tall outline; it was too dark to fill in the rest. And though she was all ears, she couldn't yet hear Angie's protests. At all.

There was no sound of approaching footsteps, no *ching* of glasses or clink of beer steins. There was no sudden blaze of lights, followed by shouts of amusement over her predicament. No *Surprise!* You know . . . *Party time!* Nothing.

Rotating slowly, eyes wide open, as if that would help her to see through the surrounding blackness, Barbie peered out from where the mysterious guy had set her. The only thing she could almost make out was a tall headstone not far from where she was standing. A headstone, as in a gray marble thing with a decaying body beneath it.

Goose bumps reared up then dribbled down her back like pinballs over metallic speed bumps. The tiny hairs at the nape of her neck stood up. Could she have been wrong about this? Had she been insane to humor this guy? Where the heck was Angie?

"So," she said as Old Mr. Suspicion crept into her con-sciousness and rooted there, warning that this mystery guy might truly be some kind of weirdo, even if he did possess a few nice attributes.

She began again. "Where exactly is the party?"

Chapter Three

Darin Russell faced the girl in the dark and put one hand to his throat. Something was clawing at him from the inside out. Something, he acknowledged with a shudder, that he had learned only with great difficulty to get a handle on.

His pulse was racing. The burn of raw nerve endings caused his fingers to curl. A familiar numbness accompanied his attempt at facial expression, and the muscles under his clothes strained at the cloth.

Nothing out of the ordinary here, he thought facetiously—except that these things were happening a bit early.

And wasn't that the damndest thing? Usually it took a full-on flood of moonlight to instigate the twitching, on the nights when a full moon rode the skies.

He glanced up. Cloud cover hid the huge silvery orb that wasn't quite full, he knew well enough . . . yet he had to clench his teeth to keep them from chattering. His free hand had closed more tightly over his windpipe as if to choke off unnecessary sound. All was dark. The dark before the storm. Yet for the lack of light he was truly grateful, because the woman standing next to him wouldn't be able to see the hunger in his eyes.

Easing up on his throat, he smiled wistfully. By his calculation there were twenty-two more hours until the moon would take him. Twenty-two more hours until he would shed this semblance of Darin Russell and become what he was destined to become—a wolf, for frig's sake. Kid you not. A damned wolf.

The thought still gave him pause. Hell, he'd never get used to the idea. Who, after all, would have thought it possible? Who, if they hadn't experienced it firsthand, would believe? But it was true: a mingling of man and wolf blood flowed inside his veins.

Jesus. It was insane, and a physical impossibility, as far as medical sources were concerned. Animals and humans could not share one body. Animals and humans possessed no characteristics that would enable them even to mate or produce offspring. Yet here he was, Darin Russell, a werewolf. An anomaly to beat all anomalies. It was a truly wicked twist of fate.

Was it a nightmare? You bet. Though the realization of what he became each full moon was no longer the shocker it once was. Still, he did often wonder if he'd ever be fully comfortable inside his skin. Hell, as he and the wolf became more familiar, the wolf had begun to assert itself, with no lunar prompting. The wolf was trying to gnaw its way to the surface right now. Sniffing out pleasure, sensing excitement in the air, Wolfy wanted to muscle in, to be a part of this. Wolfy wanted a mate as badly as Darin did.

Stand in line! Darin wanted to shout, right before uttering a swift and silent prayer of thanks for those twenty-two hours he had left.

"The party," he said, sensing the woman's need for clarification, "is in the opposite direction."

"So what are we doing here?"

Darin glanced more carefully at Barbie. That was her

name, at least according to her friend. But whatever her name, she shouldn't have been in a graveyard after dark, promise of a party or not. Women should know better. Dark places were dangerous.

He laughed to himself, even though this wasn't funny. He had decided that Barbie and her friend needed a good scare to make them see the possible perils of Miami after dark. The very *real* possible perils. And because ultimately he was the gentleman he had told Barbie he was—and a worse thing as well, admittedly—who was more qualified to teach them that lesson?

He just hadn't anticipated she'd turn out to be so fun, feel so nice on his shoulder, or that she'd be not nearly frightened enough, in spite of his antics. He could feel her attention even now.

She had felt very nice, indeed. Long legs, smooth and silky. Lean arms. Low, slightly husky voice that floated over everything like an oncoming summer storm.

A wayward pulse like a runaway rocket hit Darin in the chest, along with another thought. Maybe a woman who went through life with a name like hers, with its connotations and association with the Mattel toy, would be sensitive to other people's problems. His in particular? A strange current buzzed through the air all of a sudden. Ridiculous thoughts rode that buzz, like, could this Barbie be the one?

He sucked in his cheeks to withhold sound and warned the looming beast to back off. No. It couldn't be that easy. After searching the world for someone, to quite simply find her in his own backyard? In his lair? Impossible.

Although the night was still, Darin wished desperately for a breeze, a hurricane, anything to whisk his ponderings away. Instead, more thoughts came.

Fairy tales suggested that every person has a soul mate somewhere on the planet, someone fate intended as your partner if you could find them. This seemed a nice idea, this soul-mate theory, but with millions of people in Miami alone, and cities more or less similar in size stretched out all over the world, what were the odds of stumbling across yours?

How about in a cemetery?

In the dark?

The answer was, the odds were just too great to contemplate. There were too many variables, too many people, and too little time to sort through them.

Toss into this fantastical soup the fact that he was nowhere near the normal all-American male, not by a long shot, and that he would require special handling, a truly open mind, and a ton of empathy from his mate, and . . . well, such fairy tales seemed no more than moon gazing.

Soul mates? He and this woman named Barbie? Wishful thinking, and hopelessly naive. Inconceivably romantic, even for him. Nevertheless, his heart was now beating at a million strokes per minute inside of his chest. His body was urging itself to call forth the changes early, was on the cusp of full-blown arousal.

Weird.

The wolf was causing this trouble, really. Wolfy, so close to his time, wanted action, not small talk. Wolfy wanted to nuzzle Barbie's long, swanlike neck. Wolfy and Darin were in complete accord.

Darin paused midthought. Could he actually do that? Change a day in advance? Invite the curse early? Let it out completely? He'd never wanted to before. He had never tried.

Not a good precedent, he decided. Three nights each month of being separated from everyone was bad enough. Going through the physical changes required for the wolf to take his turn would never get easier. And what would Barbie do when her abductor's skin stretched and his bones began to crack? A horrible thought, that! Best to contain the beast until its turn to appear. For now, it was interesting enough to know they both wanted her.

Barbie.

"Is it far?" she—Barbie—asked, her human eyes unable to process the dark, Darin knew. She was trusting him to set the course. He had labeled himself civilized.

Civilized, for Christ's sake.

"We almost there?" she queried. A sensual voice. Very sexy.

"Not even close," he admitted. "I've taken you in a circle."

She chuckled. He heard it, though she tried to hide the sound by turning her head.

Barbie was amused? Not frightened? Could she tell he was interested? Laughter again rose within him, the laughter of freedom, of expectancy, of pleasure and hopeful victory. It was the laughter of the wolf. Dampness gathered on his forehead—a beastly sort of hot flash—and he shook it off with a stern inner warning. He could not give in to the beast now. It would be for the wrong reasons entirely if he did. He must not give in.

"I know for a fact this cemetery isn't huge," Barbie said, sounding only the slightest bit perturbed. "How could there be a long route back to the middle?"

"Looks can be deceiving," Darin replied, his body now feeling odd everywhere, his fingers beginning to ache from the inside out as beastly claws worked their way toward the surface.

Deceiving? And how!

"Really? I never would have thought," Barbie remarked. "They must take their cue from the deceptive lights back there."

"Do I note sarcasm?" Darin coughed to smooth his voice and took hold of Barbie's hand. Soft fingers. No ring on the significant one. Barbie was available.

"Sarcasm is in my arsenal of things to offer," Barbie told

him, tugging back her hand and adding, "Actually, I can't take credit for that line. I read it somewhere and have been hoping I'd get to use it someday."

Darin smiled grimly. Wouldn't Barbie be surprised to find out what he had in *his* arsenal? Wouldn't she be surprised after twenty-two hours fled by, when the moon showed its face, when his body began to tear at the seams with no holding back? She'd be surprised, all right. She'd run like hell, and he'd let her. Heck, he'd push her. Wouldn't he?

All of a sudden, he wasn't so sure. All of a sudden, he wanted to throw his head back and howl. Why? Because the beast knew, as he did, that this woman was special.

Still, howling? Definitely not a good idea. Howling tended to scare people in a very bad way.

Of course, wasn't that what he'd intended in the first place—Fright Night at Forest Lawn, for women lured to this place by bad judgment? Party-boy pranksters were scary enough, whether or not they were human. He took Barbie's hand again.

"That's a little tight," she complained. She was right: his grip was too firm.

"Maybe you'd prefer bumping into a gravestone or two? Bang up those skinny knees?" he said, grinning like a goon in spite of his inner juggling act.

"Hey! Getting personal there!" Barbie warned. "And you couldn't possibly know what my knees are like."

"Don't worry," he laughed. "I like skinny knees."

"They aren't skinny. They're shapely. Very shapely. I inherited them from my mother. I wear short skirts sometimes to show them off."

"Shapely and *skinny*," Darin corrected, almost to himself, thinking how much he'd like to see those legs in the daylight, and how much fun it was to tease her.

"Not!" Barbie argued. "What did you do, cop a feel when I was all sack-of-potatoes back there?"

"I had to hang on to something." Working really hard to stifle a growl and keep human words coming, Darin muttered, "Shit."

This isn't hell, he told himself for the millionth time. This affliction of his was not hell on earth. It was life. It was *a* life, anyway. There was nothing he could do to change it.

"Spilt milk," his parents had told him, stunned to see what the wolf bite in the old forest had done to their child. "No use crying over it," they'd told him quite courageously.

Man, he wasn't sure if they'd treat it so simply if *they* had been bitten. At times the situation was a real bitch. It certainly was hell on relationships. And he wanted a relationship. The little furballs in his bloodstream wanted a relationship. The wolf definitely wanted one. He had waited a very long time for someone with potential, and now Barbie was here, against all odds, by his side.

So, what was everybody going to do about it?

Chapter Four

Barbie took the time to press hair back from her face, seeking a better view of . . . well, nothing, considering the darkness. Scalp prickles signaled a possible goof-up in her choices to this point. A floaty feeling the consistency of fog crept upward from her feet to her legs. A matching lightness filled the space between her ears, the space where her brain should have been—the brain that should have warned her about attending this stupid party before she'd opened the car door.

Stubborn. That's what she was. She hated parties. She'd chosen to ignore the blitz of flashing internal red lights this time. Well, she usually ignored them, truth be told, preferring to label this trait "open-minded." Let this be a lesson.

"Why are we here in this spot?" she repeated, deciding that more useful information would be a very good thing, and that remaining ladylike might not cut it.

"I wanted you to myself," the mystery guy said simply.

It was entirely possible, Barbie reasoned, that such overt behavior was acceptable at these odd parties, and that this guy had simply eaten one Trisket too many. That this was male testosterone running rampant at the thought of all the unattached women freaked out by their surroundings. Could it be something so simple?

"Why?" she asked, wriggling free of his grip, taking a hands-on-hips stance in an attempt to cop an attitude and wishing she had brought a purse. And not just any purse, but Angie's. There would at least have been a compact in there with a lighted mirror, if no penlight. With light of any kind she could have stolen a peek at her abductor. Not that looks made much difference.

Well, actually, looks were a start, she admitted.

"Why me?" she asked, telling herself not to take this abduction personally. Probably anything in a skirt would have done it for this guy.

"I told you. I liked your voice," he replied, fairly straightforwardly, it seemed. But it had to be a crock.

A wayward tendril of annoyance latched on to one of the icy pinballs halting midway down Barbie's spine, a rise of annoyance that was usually bad for anyone on the receiving end. This guy really did not want to mess with her. The Bradley family could attest to what might happen if she were to actually become angered. Think Scots-Irish temper. Think Cuisinart. Think barbed tongue, then add a dash of whirlwind.

"A guy who carts people around on his shoulder like a farmer hauling a sack through a graveyard likes my voice?" she snapped.

"Not people. Women," he corrected.

Barbie could almost imagine him grinning. The cad! His beastly behavior should have triggered a heated response by now. She should have been fully agitated, in fact. But, oddly, her annoyance hadn't risen past a simmer. The whole anger thing had kind of fizzled.

Unusual. Annoyance had never vanished before. Maybe the fizzle was in reaction to the guy's great laugh and easy manner. In spite of everything, he seemed almost likable— in a spicy, silky, strongman sort of way. Besides, hadn't her parents always warned about her temper being a major fault?

"Bro-ther." Barbie gave her head a shake. Reasonably sure that she couldn't have been suckered so easily into something perilous, she had to admit that she really didn't perceive any danger here. Outside of the initial shock, the whole silly abduction could be seen as humorous. To a mental patient.

"You're a farmer, then?" she asked sarcastically.

"Nope. No farmer. Never even seen a farm, actually," he replied—but that was all. The guy was a virtual wellspring of information.

"Insurance broker, maybe?" Barbie asked, deciding to play Twenty Questions.

"What do they cart around?"

"Your money." She tried again. "Car salesman?" Oh please, she prayed. Anything but a car salesman.

"Nope," Mr. Communication replied. "Not even warm."

Not even warm? Barbie tapped her nails on her hip. "Doctor?"

"Nope."

"Lawyer?"

"Nope."

In her head, Barbie went through the old song. *Rich man, poor man, beggar man, thief. Doctor, lawyer . . .*

"Indian chief?" she suggested with a snort.

"Graveyard keeper," he replied, and Barbie felt any remaining questions sink like a torpedoed tanker.

"You're bluffing," she charged.

"Not entirely."

"Which part of not entirely? The graveyard part or the keeper part?"

"I work here, keeping track of what goes on in this cemetery, part-time. It's an odd profession, and not something you hear about every day—but someone has to do it, don't you think?"

Barbie couldn't keep the skepticism out of her tone. "A

graveyard keeper? In a dinner jacket? Odd sort of dress for an outdoor profession, isn't it?"

"I was about to rustle up an evening meal."

"And you thought you'd carry someone around for a while to build up an appetite?"

After flinging those words his way, Barbie bit back a second round of sarcasm. The floaty, tingly sensations she'd been feeling were now hovering around her thighs. Floaty thighs had a way of distracting a person to the point of nearly forgetting which number of Twenty Questions they were on.

Distracted, she lost her desire to harass him. She'd have to work hard to plump back up the balloon of skepticism. Because, truth be told, she didn't feel at all panicky or annoyed. All in all, this whole scenario—the dark, the gravelly voiced guy in a choice suit who obviously had a brain bigger than a Cheeto—might truly be better than what she'd been expecting at this party.

Interesting.

Was it too strange for her to see this odd meeting as opportune? A little sexy? Nope. *Way* too strange. Not opportune.

Don't even think sexy.

"So, you're not the welcoming committee from the party in the opposite direction?" she asked, deciding once again it was time for more information. One year as a high school teacher plus a couple of months with her ex-boyfriend Bill the BS-er really did fine tune the crap-o-meter. Surely she'd know if her companion lied.

"Afraid not," the guy replied.

Barbie waited for the expected, and heretofore absent, attack of panic that every woman in her situation should have exhibited, but it didn't kick in. "You do *know* about the party?" she prompted.

"Yes," he said. "I do."

"Were you at the party?"

"Afraid not. I was keeping an eye on it from a safe distance. Doing my job."

"Yes," Barbie conceded. "Graveyard keepers would have to protect their graveyards from the threat of frat boys with ghoulish appetites. I'm with you on that. Still, I was thinking of possibly attending that party, you know."

"Didn't sound much like that to me," he said. "But I thought I'd pull you out of range—rescue you, just in case."

"That's a bit presumptuous, don't you think?"

"Can I ask why you were thinking of attending the party in the first place?"

"Why does anyone go to a singles party?" she tossed back. "Having a party in a graveyard is strange, I admit, but we didn't know it was in a graveyard until we got here. Dagger Street, end of the block, was the only direction we had. Imagine our surprise."

"You say strange, not spooky," the guy noted. "You're not afraid of cemeteries?"

Barbie shrugged. "My aunt is in one, as are my grandparents. I'd hate to think cemeteries weren't happy resting places for my loved ones."

"Ah."

The guy didn't respond further. While waiting out the silence following this breathy contribution, Barbie had an uncanny desire to touch her abductor. A hand to his arm, maybe. To make sure he wasn't a ghost or a zombie raised from the dead by her comment about stray heads.

Feeling her hands rise, she fought them back down to her sides.

Bad hands!

Also, bad scene, she decided. Certainly a strange one. Time for retreat. Nip this strangeness in the bud. Although this guy hinted at potential and smelled nice, he just wasn't offering up any good answers. There was, despite her willingness to wait and hear real explanations, nothing to be had here.

She truly would have had to be desperate to consider the viability of a graveyard acquaintance, anyway. A terrific voice, a wide set of shoulders, and a nice jacket weren't enough of a foundation for a relationship. There was nothing here to use as a building block for a Cape Cod home with that white picket fence. To think otherwise because the guy seemed reasonably agreeable would be chancy, stupid, and lame. Desperate, even.

Where did graveyard keepers sleep, anyway? she wondered. That question opened up a whole new can of beans.

There was only one thing to do, she concluded: run. Of course, in a tight skirt and heels, running wouldn't be pretty. Dammit, she should have worn pants.

"No more questions?" asked her mystery man.

Barbie took the fact that her feet hadn't moved as a very bad sign.

"I suppose this *is* awkward," he went on, voice all smoky and sincere and doubling up on the velvet quotient. "Maybe you can think of this whole situation as a little intervention. As a Good Samaritan merely saving you some trouble."

Though Barbie squinted harder, trying to see him, her search turned up a big fat zero. It wasn't that the darkness was completely unbroken. Up in the sky came a faint glimmer of stars. The headstone beside them seemed to give off a whitish glow. Still, she couldn't see what she most wanted to see.

"You still here?" the guy asked.

Little electric charges were crackling over Barbie's skin in response to his presence beside her. A heat-seeking missile could have found him, no problem. He was fire in human form, hot enough to cause her hair to curl. She had to ground herself, quickly, before the word *retreat* became a distant memory.

Maybe just one brush against this guy's pecs? After all, darkness worked both ways.

A light touch on her arm made Barbie jump. The guy had beaten her to it. She hadn't been prepared.

"Please tell me you aren't a pervert," she said with a shiver. When her mystery guy laughed again, quite heartily, she asked, "Was that a yes, you are a pervert?" trying to reacquire her Barbie-does-formidable stance.

He sighed. "No pervert, Barbie. Trust me, that party was not for you."

She ground her teeth. Although he was probably right, although she and Angie had already decided that very thing, what right did he have to hurry their decision along?

"The folks there aren't very nice," he added, as if he'd read her thoughts and would explain. "I wouldn't have wanted any friend of mine to attend this particular fete."

This guy she didn't know and couldn't even see would protect her and Angie from a . . . fete? Was that unbelievable bull, or was it . . . gallant? She found herself waffling.

Amid the waffling, her scalp began to tingle, as though little alien antennae were sprouting outward from her brain, trying to get a handle on this guy. Her body was reacting to him on some basic level, suggesting he might be someone she'd want to know. Nice guys were rare in Miami. Especially nice single guys.

No. This new reasoning was stupid. Pure female silliness. Long-awaited hopefulness hijacking her checklist. Her antennae had gone over to the Dark Side. The man was little more than a blur, a sexy voice in the night. If Angie—

Oh God! The sudden remembrance of her friend caused an instantaneous melting of Barbie's sense of sport. Was Angie out here somewhere having a similar conversation? Had Angie tackled her own caveman by now? Her friend wasn't possessed of the Barbie Bradley adventure genes, except when it came to her wish list for—men. Barbie sure hoped Angie had been abducted, too, because if Angie had been left alone, hating the dark and disliking deserted places, she'd very likely be scared stiff. What had she been thinking, playing along with this oddball abduction when her best friend was out here somewhere? A good kick to this guy's shin, something right out of Tae Bo, might do wonders if he planned to keep her here any longer, or against her will.

"Where is my friend?" she asked curtly. "Is someone carting her around, too?"

"It's possible," the guy beside her replied.

"You don't know?"

"An acquaintance of mine seemed interested."

Barbie opened her mouth, closed it, opened it again. How large was this graveyard, anyway? She couldn't hear anything beyond her own heavy breathing. Certainly she should have been able to hear Angie calling if Angie needed help.

"I'd better find my friend," she said stiffly. "Thanks for saving us."

"You're entirely welcome," the guy replied in a tone like warm chocolate fondue. "It's such a shame though," he added, "that we couldn't have met under better circumstances."

"Yes, well, my friend might not be my friend much longer if I don't get back to her. Do you know how hard it is to find a best friend? If you do know, you'll take me to her."

"By all means, if that's what you want," he said.

"It *is* what I want." *Sort of.*

Well, she should have wanted that. She definitely should not have been thinking about the invisible guy's pecs, which were ripped and gleaming, she was sure, somewhere under that jacket. But she was. She shouldn't have been picturing him shirtless, taut skin aglow with a light layer of sweat as he hoisted hammer and nails for a start on that white wooden fence. But she was.

Stupid thoughts! Asinine. For all she knew, the guy had little red horns poking out of the top of his head. Sideburns. That jacket could be plaid.

Yet, her antennae were standing straight up, producing a very strange feeling in and around her eyeballs. Every cell in her body seemed to be at full attention, yammering for a sudden move in her abductor's direction. Even after covering her ears to stifle all that yammering, Graveyard Guy's heat continued to blast away at her mental acuity. There was just something about him.

He took a step. Barbie felt his exhaled breath in her hair behind her right ear, and her entire body ruffled, as if more of it wanted in on that sensation. The guy was invading her space, her antennae told her. He'd issued a physical challenge, upping the stakes, challenging her imminent withdrawal.

And dang, her nipples were puckering. She felt them tighten and strain upward. There was no mistaking what this meant. Puckered nipples were the secret female warning system for pleasurable encounters with the opposite sex, and a direct link to heaven alone knew what else. Puckered nipples were a sure sign that she was enjoying this confrontation, no matter how many excuses she might make.

Standing tall, folding her arms to get the treacherous puckerage under control, Barbie prayed for sanity to intervene. She wouldn't consider the luxury of a frivolous night with a stranger; she had to think of Angie. While she, herself, was having a pleasurable moment, there was a possibility Angie wasn't. What kind of a person would allow their friend to be in pain?

Besides, she couldn't actually jump a guy she couldn't see, could she? There could be no pec exploration. No touchy-feely stuff of any kind. Noway. Nohow. Time to go. But which way? What direction? How would she find Angie out here when she couldn't even see the guy standing next to her?

"Ummm, do you think you might really help me find Angie?" she asked politely.

"I'll help if you promise me something."

The guy's breath skimmed the edge of her cheek. Barbie executed a full body sway. He wasn't just close, but *damn* close. Too close. Way too close. Wonderfully close.

Barbie thumped her head with the heel of one hand to get the antennae to behave. Goose bumps rolled over every sector of her anatomy and kept right on rolling, temporarily blocking out thoughts of invisible paths and lost friends tripping down them in stilettos. Instead her thoughts were of her abductor's chest. Would it be muscular and contoured? Would there be washboard abs? Silky hair?

Treacherous thoughts!

"Promise," he reiterated.

Barbie stammered, "P-promise what, exactly?"

"That you'll forego further graveyard exploration this evening."

"Oh, you don't have to worry about that!" She'd clasped both hands behind her back to ensure that very thing.

When the mystery guy's fingers ran the length of her sleeve, Barbie wobbled as if he'd touched bare skin. The contact was erotic, unexpected—as erotic and unexpected as being rescued by a man who professed to have her safety in mind. Being here with him didn't feel perverted or icky. It just felt . . . hot.

"Come." The guy pried one of her hands free and pulled Barbie forward. But instead of taking one single step in Angie's direction, she found herself pressed up against her nocturnal companion, chest to chest, thigh to thigh. And, um, other parts. Barbie's hands were against his chest at last.

And yes, at least by this quick feel, he had pecs to die for. He wore a silky soft shirt beneath that silky soft jacket.

Lord help her, Barbie didn't want to remove her hands from the guy's upper anatomy. He felt so very good. He smelled so good. He was at least a head taller than she—the pec placement told her this. He was lithe, with just the right amount of muscle. Just the way she liked her men.

Wayward thoughts, Bradley. You make it sound like he's a Happy Meal. "Perverts don't smell this good," Barbie whispered to herself. "If they did, it would be completely unfair."

"Can I take that as a compliment?" her companion asked, chuckling, his arm encircling her waist.

Though this move wasn't particularly dangerous, Barbie experienced a thump down in her nether regions. This thumping confirmed that she still had a nether region—a very good thing, since she hadn't been quite sure.

"You said you'd take me to Angie," she breathlessly reminded her companion, while her nipples again did their thing and her hands slipped downward a little to press against his stomach. His hard stomach. For support.

Heat flew through her. She swayed on her heels, leaning toward the guy she couldn't see. Her antennae were twirling madly. Her stomach did loop-de-loops.

Wow.

His warm breath, his hard-as-a-rock body, the challenging repartee—all those things struck her as honest-to-God promising. One little picket in a large front-yard fence. One baby step toward Tiffany's. Call her nuts, but all of a sudden she wanted this guy to kiss her. She wanted it badly. Yet how could she condone this erratic, hormones-gone-astray behavior for one single second longer?

"Now would be a good time," she said, trying to mean it, "to take me to Angie."

"Okay," he said.

He didn't move. She didn't move. The temperature in the graveyard rose considerably.

"*Now* would be a good time," she repeated.

"Fine."

No movement again, except perhaps that she might accidentally have leaned a little closer. Unintentionally.

"Can I see you again?" he asked, his exhaled question hot as a space heater on her already-flushed cheek.

Red Alert! It had been so long since she'd had any meaningful contact, her body might have been ready for anything. Granted, she and this stranger had some kind of connection. The air between them crackled with electricity. The crackling could even have been the sound of animal magnetism at its extreme. But that would simply mean, she supposed, that this was a case of full-blown lust at first sight, without the sight part.

"See me again?" she whispered lightly. "It's dark. You haven't seen me a first time."

"Maybe I use the Braille method," Invisible Guy replied.

This was so ridiculous, Barbie had to laugh. Her hands, those five-fingered things attached to her arms and sometimes removed from all links to her brain, slipped a bit more in a downward direction, encountering more taut male muscle.

She sucked in a breath, puffed out her cheeks, preparing to comment. Then a sound broke in. Out there, in the dark. In the distance. Sounding like a whisper. A familiar whisper.

It wasn't Angie making pitiful mewling noises, as Barbie had at first expected. Instead, it was a horribly ill-timed and realistic image of her own mother, Mrs. Brenda Bradley, standing in their yellow-wallpapered country kitchen, shaking a finger. Brenda Bradley, aka Mom, upon hearing of this unexpected convergence with a stranger (God forbid!) was moaning and moving her lips in a silent-but-readable *I taught you better.*

Ugh!

The mental image was scary enough to cause Barbie to remove her hands from the stranger's torso and say without further ado, "Please take me to Angie." She was, however, sorry the second she said it. There would be no way to get her hands back on the guy's hot bod. That moment had gone forever.

"Damn. You said the magic word. Now I have to oblige," he—whoever he really was—said.

"Shows you *do* have a civilized bone or two," Barbie remarked, fingers opening and closing in vain.

The guy just chuckled, a low sound, as though he really was having a good time. Then he said, "You haven't answered my question about seeing you again."

"You haven't taken me to my friend."

"I'm thinking about taking you there."

"I'd prefer another verb."

"Such as?"

"Doing it." Feeling an immediate superblush come on with the unintentional double entendre, Barbie added hastily, "I meant going to Angie. Moving. Taking steps in Angie's direction. Not . . ." God, this was embarrassing.

More laughter escaped the stranger, then, "Okay."

"Great. I'd prefer to walk this time, if you don't mind."

Her invisible man backed up a step, slowly, as if he didn't really want to. A reluctance so charming, Barbie almost pulled him back.

"FYI, you're nothing at all like a sack of potatoes," he told her.

"Really? You mean the Braille method works?" she quipped.

It was a stupid conversation to cover an awkward moment. It had been better when they weren't talking.

"So, about seeing you again . . ."

"I don't think so," Barbie interrupted. Why not, why not? her body cried. Her brain answered, Because what kind of relationship can there be if talking is a drawback?

That was before a warm cheek rested against her own. Before the scent of spice became more intense, producing undulations from her thighs to her knees. Before her panties felt extraordinarily tight beneath her tight skirt. And those sensations multiplied as a set of soft lips brushed hers. Not a kiss, just a brush—yet Barbie's body reacted as if she'd accidentally stuck her thumb into a wall socket. As if Forest Lawn had just burst into flames all around them.

Tightening every muscle in her legs to keep from tipping over, refusing to cower or back down, Barbie closed her eyes, parted her lips, and waited for more. Seconds fled. Time stretched. A good kisser could have risen above a multitude of flaws—like the flaw of anonymity.

But he didn't kiss her. Dammit, his lips did not return to hers at all. Instead, his hands closed around her waist. With a heave, he lifted her up, swung her over something she barely felt skim the bottom of her feet. The gate he had mentioned earlier? Maybe a white, wooden one? She was set down gently, almost tenderly.

The guy took her hand again and started off in the dark, now moving with hasty determination. When he spoke, no doubt over his shoulder, Barbie heard him quite clearly say, along with a sigh of impending importance, "Barbie. I have a confession to make."

Chapter Five

"You're married?"

Yeow! Had she said that?

He was moving fast now. Stumbling after him in the dark, Barbie heard a crack and nearly went down. Her damn heel had broken after all.

"No. Not married." His words were muffled. "The confession is that I can see you, Braille comment aside. I guess this gives me an advantage."

At this pace, his guidance was her only means of stability as Barbie trotted on, attempting to keep her one heel lifted.

Up, down. Up, down. Up, down.

"You mean, you can see with your bat radar?" she joked.

"Something like that, yes."

She was skeptical. "So, what do I have on, Bat Boy?"

"A deep, rich shade of red. A short skirt. Matching jacket."

Barbie flinched in surprise, tugging his hand back in the process. Her foot in its broken shoe slipped forward on the grass, her legs went out from underneath her . . . and her invisible savior caught her, miraculously, before she hit the ground. Still, it wasn't the near belly flop that left her speechless. The guy had exactly described her outfit.

The word *pervert* returned as quickly as an inhaled breath.

Pervert. As in, he might have watched them arrive. As in, he might have scoped out the scene and laid a trap. As in, this was a premeditated meeting.

As in, *stalker.*

Her excitement plummeting, Barbie felt her face change from pink to pasty. Could her man radar have been so far off?

"Definitely not," she said. "No seeing me again."

They started walking once more. Up, down. Up, down. She felt a little protest from her left calf muscle.

"Why can't I see you again?" he asked.

"I don't date dates who don't take no for an answer," she replied. *I don't date stalkers.*

There was another unscheduled stop. *What now?*

What now was the mystery man's finger drifting down the side of her face. In reaction, Barbie's pulse did a pirouette. Her heart boomed. Would a stalker bring out these urges? she asked herself. Shouldn't she be able to differentiate between the good and the bad somehow?

"Angie," she directed firmly. "Now."

"Yes," the guy conceded with audible disappointment. She heard him turn. His hand brushed her arm as he did.

Zing! Lightning down south! Everyone out of the pool!

Rocking back on her heels, twirling her arms into space to keep her balance, Barbie yanked the guy back and came up hard against him.

"Uh . . ." she heard him mutter, faintly. "I swore I was civilized."

What? part of her raged. They were up close and personal, and he was giving up? He actually was intending to let her go? Barbie felt the big *P* of Pervert begin to deflate.

"Come on, Barbie," he said. "Watch your step."

His firm grasp on her elbow sent teensy electric charges skittering up toward the bridge of her nose. Like brain freeze when she drank iced tea too fast.

"Oh, I plan to," Barbie remarked with a heroic attempt at control, knowing that this guy had wanted to kiss her as much as she wanted him to. This guy had been hard in all the right places.

He didn't want to take her back. Nevertheless, he was doing as she'd asked, taking her to find Angie.

The things she suddenly wanted to do to him, here in the dark! The things she wanted him to do to her, starting with her lips and working his way down. There was just one little problem. When all was said and done, Barbie Bradley was, aside from all the flirty posturing, a *good* girl. She could count the guys she'd almost nearly landed in bed with on no hands. Kissing, yes—she'd seen plenty of action there. But actually sliding into home base? Never.

Jumping this guy was something Trashy Barbie would do, and to her knowledge, Mattel had never envisioned, let alone created, such a thing. Which was, at the moment, sort of a bummer.

No, the connection between herself and this guy who had hold of her hand was definitely not anything she could pursue. Somebody would have to explain this to her nipples, of course, and break the news to her antennae, which were still spinning. Because if those parts of her didn't immediately stop rebelling against *almost*s and *never*s, if she didn't find Angie quickly and was left alone with this graveyard keeper much longer, with his propensity for quick laughter and his ability to heat up her air space, well . . .

Heck with Mattel. All bets were off.

Chapter Six

Darin found himself feeling unusually fleet of foot. Better get Barbie back to her pal, after all. No telling what might happen otherwise. "Civilized. Shit."

He led her at a jog, with a tight hold on her hand. Barbie kept up, though he could hear her breathing behind him. He wondered if she could feel the excitement in the air, if she could sense the energy rising up through him. Did she know how much he wanted to howl, how much his beast wanted into the action?

"Big step," he said to her, the connection between them searing his flesh. His skin vibrated. Wolfy undulated beneath his bones, moon or no moon. The change would be possible, Darin knew now, if he wanted it. No doubt it was the excitement, the attraction, causing the riot under his skin.

"Almost there," he told Barbie.

"Okay," she said. Was there disappointment in her tone?

"I'm afraid your friend doesn't sound very happy," he announced, adopting a faster pace, knowing he must let her go soon or lose himself.

"Is Angie okay? Was she carted around, too?" she asked, sounding breathless.

"No way to know for sure. Sorry."

When Barbie shuddered, the effect rippled up his arm. She really cared about her friend, he noted, and for that he was envious. Who, other than his tightly knit family, would ever want, or dare, to care for him that much? What woman would tolerate a beast in her bed? All that extra hair on the sheets!

His chest tightened, as did his hold on Barbie. Hell, if he could only explain a few things to her right now, up front and in the dark, so that he wouldn't have to look too hard at her expression when she heard. He might tell her that his ability to see in the dark was real and enabled him to view things no human being could view. He might tell her that her jacket and skirt were of a dark reddish hue that suited her perfectly, and that their details were clear down to the little satin-covered buttons. Buttons that a beast's clumsy, clawed hands could not cope with, but ones his own fingers at the moment could manage very well, thank you very much, given the opportunity.

He might tell her that little edging of white lace showing above the rounded neckline of her jacket was driving him mad. Could there be anything more feminine than a scrap of white lace?

Control slipped further. The tightness in his chest moved to his shoulders.

Must. Run. Faster. Must get Barbie back to her friend.

The objective now was to outdistance erupting emotions, to get a grip on the fact that the softness of Barbie's white lace would most likely never touch his skin and that she would probably turn out to be like all the rest of the women he'd briefly dated: self-centered, careless, in search of the perfect man. Yet, if outdistancing those thoughts was of utmost importance, he ruminated, why then had thoughts of Barbie's little bit of white lace taken over his mind?

"Grrrr." Horrified at the sound escaping his throat, Darin coughed to keep it from Barbie. A sliding movement went through his stomach. The beast!

No! Keep back, I say! Think of something else, Russell. Keep the insanity at bay. Christ, there were hours left until the real change, and he was already acting like a monster. He was thinking monstrous thoughts.

But pheromones were rising on the air like dandelion fuzz; he couldn't avoid them. Both man and wolf had to breathe, and their combined sense of smell was nothing short of miraculous. Pheromones meant excitement. Barbie was excited. He was excited. Their essences were mingling.

His heart thundered. His insides writhed. Not safe, he told himself. One minute more to reach Barbie's friend. They had to make it.

Heck, though, it was too bad the extraordinary nocturnal vision accompanying his condition couldn't penetrate the human skull so that he could see what Barbie was thinking. Not even the beast could help him there. A woman's mind was a foreign and complex thing. Barbie hadn't pulled away, hadn't run, hadn't tugged really hard. Nevertheless, she had refused his offer of getting together again. Why would she refuse? Shouldn't someone with his supernatural abilities be able to figure this out?

Oh no! One of his fingernails began to burn: a claw again wanting to pop. He willed it to chill. Touching Barbie was causing this, he suddenly knew. She was bringing out these feelings. Barbie was liquid moonlight in female form. The smoothness of her fingers, the strawberry fragrance that clung to her skin, but didn't overwhelm—all those things taken to-gether were irresistible.

He glanced back. Barbie's hair was shiny, silky, and slightly curled upward at the ends, where it lay across her shoulders. She had an adorable fringe of bangs across her forehead.

Little wisps of curl at her temple. How good it would feel to lean in and kiss her.

Damn beast! Was it instigating these thoughts? Keep back— I mean it! he inwardly shouted. But the idea of stroking Barbie's hair now haunted him. He wanted it to spill over his neck, tickle his shoulder as they embraced. He wanted to run his hands through it, watch the silken strands slide through his fingers. How long had he waited for someone he could share his plight with? It felt like forever.

At last they passed the fountain. He heard its splash. Seconds more, he told himself. Mere seconds, and Barbie would be safe. Think of the water. No, not Barbie in the water. Not Barbie in a bathtub filled with bubbles. Anything but bubbles.

Too late. There she was, in his imagination, naked, in a bathtub, her dark hair floating on the surface of the water, the contours of her body covered by translucent, bubble gum– scented bubbles. Two firm and flawless breasts rose from the H_2O like perfect little islands. Pink nipples crowned those breasts, the color of the palest rose species and tight with arousal, the paleness a delicious contrast to her tan, caramel-colored skin.

Choking off a cry, nearly forgetting his pledge to behave, Darin found his heart fluttering to an unusual stillness as he raced around the fountain, unable to escape the image. Tub. Barbie. His hand would move slowly over the water, sending tiny, fragile, blush-tinted bubbles spiraling upward to ride the crest of his exhaled breath. Drawn to Barbie's breasts, he'd take one of them in his hand, gently rub his thumb over the peak. Barbie would moan with delight—a throaty response that would make more things than the wolf spring to life.

Holy Mother of God.

With a big gulp of warm night air, Darin hesitated on the cemetery path, staring glassy-eyed at the image his mind had invented. Pure imagination. Not reality. This was only a dream, a longing. *Get it straight!*

Yes, but couldn't it also be a premonition? A door into the future? *His* future? His and Barbie's?

Nope. A little perspective was needed here. This had been a chance meeting in a cemetery, that's all. Nothing more. He should have been laughing at the absurdity of it all, the incongruity. Barbie and the Beast. Little Barbie and the Big Bad Wolf.

He glanced back, swept Barbie around a tall old tree, then came up short—and fully erect. Cusswords rolled over his tongue in a whisper. "Damn. Hell. Shit."

He twirled Barbie around to face him, making sure she remained on her feet and that his hands stayed appropriately placed. "Look at me," he directed, yanking her closer, knowing she couldn't see him no matter how hard she tried; Barbie remained sightless, both in reality and in her ability to perceive the beast lurking within him. "How dare you place yourself in this kind of danger?" he asked. "How dare you take this place so lightly?"

Nearly overpowered by the urge to throw her down on the path, tear off her clothes, kiss her long and hard on that little red mouth and then stroke her everywhere, he sighed audibly. He could not, in fact, touch her that way. Not when a really strong attraction to a woman, the right woman, seemed to produce effects similar to the moon's mojo.

She, Barbie, was looking up at him with large green eyes and an expression that nearly turned him inside out. In fairness to her . . . he'd have to let her go. He couldn't pop out claws and hold her at the same time, and he couldn't tell her the truth. He didn't dare. What person confessed their flaws before getting a foot in the door? Some secrets were meant to be kept.

Swiping at the perspiration gathered on his brow, Darin turned, started away, stopped. Barbie ran right into him.

"Sorry," she said, reaching for her shoe. "If you really work here, you might want to put in a word about lights. Thousand-watt bulbs would be nice. On tall poles."

Darin grinned, shrugged shoulders that refused to relax. Barbie was a nice girl. In truth, it wasn't time for the beast or beastly behavior—not that he could blame this one on Wolfy entirely. Tonight, Darin Russell was mostly a man. Yet tonight, Darin Russell, the man, felt more like a beast than he ever had.

Chapter Seven

Barbie heard a sigh and the word *civilized*. Then she was pushed through more bushes and was off on her own.

The heel of her one good shoe sank down into moist earth. She floundered, righted herself, and remembered to walk on her toes. Forward, she ordered. Not back to the guy. Definitely not back to the guy. And damn if her internal, man-sensing antennae weren't now lying flat on her head instead of waving madly to indicate the presence of her mystery man. He had given up. Given in. Sent her away. In a very unstalkerlike, unpervertlike manner. The mysterious stranger, potential and all, had gone. No expletive she could have invented would have captured the moment, though she tried out a few just the same.

"Barbie?" Angie called out, obviously sensing her presence. Barbie's friend's voice was frazzled, raw, and coated in fear.

Barbie's feelings of guilt doubled. What if Angie really hadn't been carted anywhere by another man? What if Angie had been here in this spot the entire time, alone, waiting? What if, while Barbie Bradley had been enjoying herself, albeit in a very strange way, her best friend had been frightened silly?

"Angie. Here I am."

Angie rushed toward her, missing a collision only because Barbie stuck out her arms. "Jesus, Barbie! Where the hell did you go? What the frig do you think you're doing? You trying to give me heart failure?"

For once, Barbie thought before speaking, which seemed a genuine miracle. How could she explain what had just happened, when she wasn't exactly sure herself? Outside of the rattle of Angie's rising anger, she couldn't hear any twigs breaking or heavy breathing from the evergreen periphery. It was crystal clear now that no he-man had come to rescue her friend from the allegedly unfavorable party, so in this case Angie wouldn't like the truth at all.

Too, how could Barbie, reasonably rational gal that she was, dwell on it? Her own guy had given her a shove. No lengthy good-byes. No good-byes at all! No bargaining. No begging for lunch or a movie, coffee or tea. No further mention of a kiss. The wuss. You'd think he might have asked for her phone number—or presented himself, so that she'd have an easier time with explanations.

How was she supposed to take this? How could she assume the guy was a pervert if he'd refused to act like one? He absolutely had to be a pervert, that's all there was to it, because if he wasn't, and she had allowed him to get away . . . The thought was just too painful to contemplate.

"I'm sorry, Ang. I'm here now."

"Sorry?" Angie boomed. *"Sorry?"*

Okay. Guilt was a terrible thing. As was fibbing. She'd dumped Bill because of his hurtful lies. But this was an emergency. She only needed one small white fib here as a Band-Aid for friendship. Not for herself, but for Angie. God would understand. She had to invent something as unmysterious as possible to satisfy her pal. Under no circumstances short of torture could she mention her nocturnal cartage, since it appeared that Angie had not budged. Besides, she couldn't have been gone long, really. She and the stranger had only trotted in a circle.

"I had to go to the bathroom," she said, crossing her fingers behind her back, because that's what you're supposed to do so that the good powers up in the sky know that you know the difference between a fib and the truth. "Couldn't wait."

"You had to go *out here*?" Angie snapped in disbelief.

"You of all people have the least cause to question that," Barbie pointed out. "I believe you'd have a bathroom installed in your Fiat, if it were possible."

Angie's teeth clamped shut audibly, though she managed a stunted reply. "You might have mentioned this sudden need to go. I thought something might have happened to you."

"All that talk about heads . . ."

"Very funny," Angie chirped. "You left me alone."

"I'm sorry, Angie. Truly. I didn't want to yell back about the lack of facilities or what I was doing. Someone might have heard and come looking."

"Hmph! Lack of facilities? You got that right. I swear I'm never going to do that client's hair again. Or maybe I'll dye it orange. See how she likes that. Singles party, my ass!"

"Amen," Barbie replied. This had been a huge mistake. Except for the strange guy. The thought of a good-bye kiss from him was making her lips tingle.

"Not working with that woman ever again," Angie ranted. "Men to die for? Give me a break!"

"Amen," Barbie repeated, wishing she could cross her arms high enough to cover her chest, where puckered nipples were causing another round of chills. Pesky nipples had a way of bringing attention elsewhere, much farther south on the female anatomy. She didn't want to think about elsewhere. There would be no elsewhere.

"No more singles parties!" Angie all but shouted.

Barbie nodded. "Although we haven't been to one yet, I'm right there with you."

"Graveyards. *Pfft.*" Angie was on a roll, and seemed to have bought the excuse Barbie had given. She hadn't even asked if it was number one or number two.

"Graveyards might even be worse than singles bars," Angie went on.

"Oreos are waiting," Barbie said brightly.

"Oreos are our friends," Angie agreed.

"Can't keep our friends waiting." Barbie tucked her arm inside of Angie's, deciding she had made the best choice after all by returning to her friend. What man actually knew the significance of a moment like this? What man knew the importance of chocolate to the female psyche, or could compete with it? Probably none.

As she and her friend retraced their steps toward where Barbie hoped the car was parked, it seemed that her eyes were adjusting to the dark somewhat. Finally. This was a good thing, and better late than never. Others folks might be lurking in all those bushes, other possible perverts with husky voices, slightly cynical temperaments, and marvelous pecs. Other men who weren't afraid to assert themselves with women in order to gain an introduction.

Ya think?

No! No thinking! It wasn't her fault she'd been the tiniest bit attracted to her temporary abductor, was it? How many men had she actually found in the entirety of her dating career with as much potential? Zero, that's how many. Zippo. Still, her mind warned, since when had kidnapping, even on a temporary basis, been considered endearing? Never. Since when had kidnapping equated to being swept off your feet? Since when had your garden-variety pervert begun to even remotely be considered eligible? Not ever. That was a fact.

She let out a great big sigh and faced those facts. Her wits had made a comeback—better late than never. This encounter had not been racy, sexy, or viable.

"Barb?" Angie called as they hustled along the grassy path.

"Yeah?"

"You did take care where you . . . ?"

Normally Barbie wouldn't have let that question go by without a tart reply. This time she did. She remained acutely aware of the silence of the graveyard. She was aware of the wind in the bushes, and on that same wind, the lingering scent of spice.

Eau de mystère.

"You had some Kleenex with you?" Angie continued.

Barbie sniffed the air. Due to the continued wobble of her knees, and in part to her broken shoe, she only nearly missed a spectacular fall. Thing was, her mystery guy hadn't gone. Not really. She was sure she could smell his scent. She was sure she could feel him there somewhere.

A warm glow heated her solar plexus. She had a sudden desire to press her legs tightly together and vetoed that, since walking would have been a complete impossibility.

"No Kleenex," she told Angie. "Didn't want to litter."

Her thoughts were entirely somewhere else. This inner glow and leftover heart thumping were fueled by the vague notion of the faintest possibility of . . . a possibility. Actual sex, maybe? Finally? Combined, of course (it went without saying), with male companionship. But definitely in that order, considering the way her body was reacting. The golden glow inside was beaming out her needs like a beacon.

Of course, if she needed sex so badly, any schmuck might have picked up on and taken advantage of that. Mystery Guy didn't have to be anything special.

Not special, huh? she thought. Then why did the mere memory of him still have the power to ignite her insides as no other man ever had? Some snag in the rationale there. The dark, the wind, and the entire adventure had been, she had to admit, titillating. Totally. The air still seemed to vibrate with the stranger's presence.

"Earth to Barb," Angie said, out of breath but still racing for the Forest Lawn sign.

"Here, girl," Barbie replied, though she was thinking about being swept off her feet, of spicy scents, of lips whispering in her hair, *Can I see you again?*

"We really do have to hurry," Angie said. "All that talk of . . . and it's my turn to have to . . ."

Beneath the solitary streetlight, Angie's vintage red Fiat came into view, parked where they had left it and still surrounded by other cars. About twenty in all. Where were all those people? Barbie wondered. Moreover, *who* were they, that Mystery Guy would so clearly want to keep her away?

Angie jumped inside of the car and leaned across the seat to unlock the passenger door. Barbie rested for a minute on the Fiat's cool metal frame, head turned to the wind. *He* was out there, beyond the pool of light. He was near.

With mild surprise, she looked down to find her hand rummaging through the contents of her jacket pocket. She came up with a pen. Reciting the word *stupid* over and over beneath her breath, thinking this hand-with-a-mind-of-its-own thing a demonic possession of sorts, Barbie scribbled her phone number on a dry-cleaning business card. She swiveled onto the seat of the Fiat and let the card fall to the pavement.

"I hope that wasn't trash," Angie said. "There's a hefty fine for tossing trash out of a car window."

"That wasn't trash. Trust me," Barbie said, adding beneath her breath, "I'm the trash. Trashy Barbie. That's me."

Chapter Eight

"Your light's blinking," Angie said, tossing her purse on the entry table, kicking off her male-magnet shoes.

Stunned, Barbie stared at the answering machine. Her stomach, queasy all the way home from the graveyard, had tied itself into one big knot. Of course, the blinking light on the machine didn't have to be from the person she was thinking of. What had it been, twenty minutes, tops, since they'd left the old part of town. With stopping at the mini-mart?

"Aren't you going to play it?" Angie padded in bare feet to the kitchen with their shopping bag and dumped the contents onto the green tile counter.

"Not in the mood." Barbie kicked off her own shoes.

"You kidding?" Half astonished, Angie ripped open the bag then leaned across the counter waving an Oreo cookie between her inch-long, fire red fingernails. "You're going to leave that red light blinking? What are you, insensitive?"

Barbie gaped at her. "Insensitive? How do you come up with that?"

"Poor thing's trying to get your attention, doing what it was designed to do, and you're going to make it wait?"

Barbie snorted. "It's a machine, Angie, not a butler."

"See? Insensitive."

"Am not."

"Are too."

"Fine. I'll check the darned thing if it'll make you happy."

Barbie suspended a finger over the playback button. Procrastinating, trying to quiet a heart that flopped around as if it needed a leash, she slowly pressed down.

There was a brief space of nothing, then a voice she remembered as if it had been . . . well, only twenty minutes ago since she'd last heard it said softly, gently, "Thank you."

That's it. *Thank you.* Just thank you. Yet those two words said it all.

Angie, Oreo pressed between her lips, had one artfully shaped eyebrow raised when Barbie looked at her. "You holding back on the explanations?" she asked.

Barbie shook her head, if a little unconvincingly, while trying not to frown. Rumor had it that if you frowned constantly, the wrinkles would be permanent. If such were the case, one more frown ought to do it.

"I don't know who that is," she said. This was, after all, the truth. She *didn't* know who he was. She didn't know anything about him, really, not even his name.

"With a voith like that, you'd want to know who he ith, I'm thinking," Angie suggested without removing the Oreo from her mouth.

"Must have been a wrong number," Barbie said.

The Oreo came out. "Play it again."

"No."

"Come on, Barb, play it again."

"Why?"

"Whoever this is sounds sexy. I need some kind of kick after the night we've had."

Barbie didn't need much more of a reminder of Angie's experience. "Oh, all right." Against her better judgement, her finger headed for the play button. She felt as though this were all a dream. Why had she left that card? Anyone could have picked it up. Anyone could have found it. Perverts galore.

Of course, this wasn't anyone. It was *him*. No mistake about that. Same dreamy voice—smooth, low-pitched, sensual—as if it always spoke from the vicinity of your neck.

She hit play.

"Thank you."

Barbie held her breath.

Angie squealed, took a bite of her Oreo and said, "Play—"

"No!"

"Oh, you are such a party pooper, Barb. Wrong number or not, that's a nice thing to come home to. You sure you don't know who this guy is?"

"Positive."

Barbie peered in the mirror over the sofa to see if her nose had grown longer. Nope. Not yet. But it was only a matter of time, if Angie chose to wear her down. Angie Ward could easily have chosen detective work as a career instead of hair. She handled an interrogation about as well as anyone Barbie had ever seen on Court TV.

Still gazing in the mirror, Barbie patted her hair. Miraculously, it hung neatly to her collar, not too mussed by the carting, after all. She did seem a little pale, though. Was she conspicuously short of breath? What she needed was an Oreo, not thoughts about her caller/stalker/possible pervert.

Making a mental note to purchase a security bolt for her front door first thing in the morning, Barbie sighed. Maybe she'd get a dead bolt the size of Texas. Two of them. With a voice like this guy's, she'd need a good deterrent if he ever showed up on the other side of that door. Something to hold *herself* back.

"Please," Angie said, helping herself to another Oreo, tossing one to Barbie. "Don't erase the mysterious dreamboat. We can listen to it again later, when we're high on sugar."

Barbie separated the cookie's sides, exposing the good part of the Oreo, the white frosting. She stuck her tongue to it and turned the cookie around slowly, counterclockwise, letting her tongue gather all the sugar it could. The icing made her think of the guy's voice. Rich. Sweet. Both icing and the mystery man produced a comparable high, one somewhat forbidden. The pitfalls of Oreos were their calorie content and relationship to diabetes. The pitfalls of picking up strange men were . . . too numerous to consider.

"Milk?" Angie asked, shaking the rest of the package of Oreos onto a blue floral dish and slapping the dish on the counter.

"Make yourself at home," Barbie joked. But when she turned, she caught her friend's expression.

Angie stood with her hands on her hips, staring over the counter. "I'm not only a hair stylist, I'm psychic. I know acting funny when I see it, Barb, and you're acting funny."

Barbie mentally calculated how long she'd have to work out the next day to burn off the cookies she would probably consume that very night, then decided playing the message again would be the only way to appease her friend.

"You *know* that guy," Angie insisted, listening intently.

"I don't."

A best-friend glare passed between them. The one where each person tries to see beneath the other person's skin, all the way to Truth Central. It was critical in this moment not to break eye contact first. Barbie held on resolutely.

"Okay," Angie said, conceding way too early. Nevertheless, she didn't look away. "Maybe you don't know the guy. Silly mistakes happen. Wrong numbers and stuff."

Barbie sagged onto her couch and reattached her tongue to the icing of an Oreo.

"You have some milk in here?" Angie repeated, padding back to the refrigerator.

"Always have milk," Barbie muttered.

"Clean glasses?"

"Dishwasher."

Barbie stuck the two sides of her Oreo back together, minus the icing, and popped the cookie into her mouth whole. Couldn't talk with her mouth full, could she? Angie wouldn't dare expect that.

When she looked up, Angie was all but lying on the counter, inching the Oreo plate toward the couch with a slightly demonic expression on her face.

"What are you doing?" Barbie asked, swallowing a clot of crushed chocolate.

"Plying you with delights," Angie said.

"It won't work. I don't know the guy on that tape."

"You might by the time this plate is empty."

"I won't."

"Damn, you're tough."

"You've got that right."

Show . . . all show, Barbie thought, moving her buttocks away very carefully so Angie wouldn't see how many fingers she had crossed and hidden under there. Everyone knew that crossed fingers absolved you of a multitude of sins. Everyone also knew the children's chant playing inside of her head, too loud for comfort.

Liar, liar, pants on fire.

Some people just never thought it would apply to them.

Chapter Nine

Darin had to run. Nature called—although, altogether different from the usual way the phrase went. Nature caused his skin to prickle and his lungs to ache. The full moon, merely three hours closer than the last time he'd calculated, sang from behind the clouds. The song was old as the ages . . . and twice as freaky.

Hours, she sang. *Only hours until you are mine.*

Darin felt the dryness of the small rectangular paper in his hand. Barbie Bradley's phone number was on that card. Truly, the world was a mysterious place.

It had taken him five full minutes to work up to making the call, and all he'd gotten for the effort was Barbie's answering machine. This wasn't altogether unexpected, but a disappointment all the same. It seemed that Barbie Bradley liked games—as long as they didn't go too far. Barbie Bradley had some substance to her, and possibly a keen imagination. However, he reminded himself, she was more than likely a normal young woman. One who had been issued stern childhood warnings about fraternizing with strangers.

Darin chuckled over that. He was, after all, a parent's worst nightmare. Still, his desire to see Barbie Bradley again was all he could think about. His desire to confirm her as "the one" seemed paramount at the moment, overriding his need for secrecy. The distance now separating them did nothing to dilute the desire.

"Sappy sot," he whispered, borrowing his acquaintance Walter's upper-crust English phrase. "Hooked like a fish. Look at me. And, to my credit, I'm not exactly the worst of the things that actually go bump in the night. Right, Walter?"

He received no answer, because Walter wasn't there. And since his own excitement over finding Barbie Bradley was getting the better of him, the only way Darin could see to ease the excitement and let off steam was with good old physical exertion. Sprinting ought to do it. Feeling the wind on his face and the grass under his feet might help. No cold showers. He hated cold showers.

He took off, racing over the grass, the curb, the asphalt of the parking lot, and several city blocks; then he slowed as he realized that someone might see him and call the cops. A man in a dinner suit and no shoes running for all he was worth, and as if his life depended on it? Dial 911. Wouldn't those cops be surprised to find him, Darin Russell, at the heart of the complaints—if they ever caught up with him—since he was the person the cops usually called when bizarre complaints rolled in?

Hoping to find someone caught, as he himself was, between worlds, between senses, between shapes—that was what had made him take the Miami PD gig, even though cops classified as bizarre anything merely inexplicable. *Paranormal* wasn't in their vocabulary or on their radar. He had been dispatched on two occasions in the past month. Bad news was that so far he'd had no success in the supernatural department. Most monsters were of the purely human variety. Tempers, alcohol, drugs, stress, and tightly packed cities seemed to bring out the worst in people. Maybe he should bite them all. Show them what trouble really was, and then how to overcome it?

Well, he'd thought he knew how to overcome his furry little problem. His plan had been to become a loner. To stay away from crowds and a full moon. But now, he had a sudden craving for company. And the practice of biting others to get them to grow up wasn't viable. There were so many of those people, he doubted his teeth would last. Nor would everyone be cool about the wolf thing. Some animals you just couldn't tame. If a bad guy were inadvertently initiated, then what? Darin made a mental note to ask Walter.

Of course, worries of bad wolves did little to prevent Darin's wondering if somewhere out there, in all those buildings, on all the streets, there wasn't one other person with a similar affliction. If a wolf had made him what he was, surely that wolf or the wolf's buddies had made others. A werewolf female, maybe? Imagine!

Which brought him back to Barbie Bradley. What would she do if she found out about the sudden infusion of furballs into his genetics?

"Ah, crap," Darin barked. "I can't think logically about this. Why don't you answer your phone, Barbie?"

City blocks blurred as Darin again ran. Very few cars passed. Finally he stopped beside a lamppost, barely breathing hard but wondering why he cared whether or not Barbie answered her damned phone. Other women found him attractive. Other women would appreciate his call.

"Yeah. Hosts of women," Darin remarked aloud. "Outside of a few character flaws which unfortunately include claws, fangs, and a furry hide, I'm a pretty great guy." He bent down and flicked a piece of glass from his bare baby toe—a hazard of running barefoot, though his wolf genes wound heal the tiny wound in about five seconds. "Some of the women I've dated were very fine," he continued, straightening. "Some of them I even dated more than once!"

But never for more than a month, his conscience nagged. And never seriously. His cyclical disappearance always freaked them out. His secrets drove them crazy. Plus, none had been "the one." He knew that.

"Why should I fake interest merely for the sake of sex?" he asked the lamppost he leaned against. Then he laughed aloud. Talking to inanimate objects. What next?

The sound echoed faintly between the tall narrow buildings as he laughed again. "That last bit didn't sound very manly, did it? I mean, what man doesn't like sex any way he can get it?"

The lamppost didn't have a reply, so Darin explained: "The truth, though you must promise to never tell anyone, is that I prefer not wasting time. What's the point of the typical date ritual when I'm not a typical date? Where's the fun, when I would scare those women to death with a popping button here, a bit of fur there, or canines that get in the way of French-kissing?"

Shaking his head, he strolled around a corner. Beneath a floodlight designed to keep a typical city's predators at bay, he stopped again, suddenly, and dropped to a feral crouch. His skin crawled, the initial warning system every predator possessed that warned of prey—in this case, Barbie Bradley. She lived in one of these buildings. On this block. In one of these little apartments, behind dark windows in the rows of stucco and pale brick. What were the odds of that, and of finding her so easily without really looking? It had to be a sign.

"Where are you, Barbie?" he called softly as his skin danced pleasurably over his bones.

He glanced up past the rooflines at the sky. His senses were sharpening, yes, but not entirely due to the moon. This skin ballet was more on account of being near to a chosen female, a mate recognized by both man and wolf.

A chill wafted up his neck, followed closely by a rush of heat. The other female in his life—the round, silver one gleaming ominously behind the clouds—had to wait her turn. The beast might be yipping at the door, but it hadn't yet come through. Though his humanness was slipping, there remained a ray of hope. He still had a few hours to find the woman he sensed so strongly.

Wanting a woman this badly was a totally new sensation. He had tracked her here, to this block, without realizing how he'd managed it. He'd never even come close to feeling like this before, and had to act, had to speak to her before the opportunity passed. Barbie Bradley was special. Even a beast had a right to happiness, right? Surely there was room in the everyday world for a man such as himself to find love?

"Barbie."

The slow slip of her name through his teeth was like mink on bare skin. The fine hair on his arms bristled. Fine hair? For now. Time was not on his side. Soon enough, when the moon performed her unusual trick, his body would alter. Light brown fur would spring from follicles. His face would morph. Speech would be impossible. He wouldn't be able to talk tomorrow night, if Barbie waited that long to pick up her damned phone. He wouldn't be able to see her for the next three nights. Even if he could trust her to maintain interest in him for that time, he was like a kid in a candy store who couldn't reach the jars on the counter. Now that he'd found his mate, he didn't want to wait or be restrained. He wanted satisfaction *now*.

"Have to reach her," he whispered with another glance at the sky.

Real connections in this day and age were transient. Yes,

he had to reach Barbie while he could still communicate, while he maintained some control and she her interest. He had to reach her before his transformation began. And, damn!—he had to reach her before he went out of town on that police gig he'd accepted. That would postpone his time with Barbie for a couple weeks more. If she would just answer her phone. If she would only give him a chance. He had a very short window of opportunity in which to make her see reason.

"Damned bloody moon!" he snarled. "Damned bad timing!"

He sagged against the warm brick of a building. "Don't think about that," he told himself. "Think positively. If this is meant to be, Barbie will answer."

What he had to do was concentrate real hard, see if he could sniff her out. He could actually knock on her door. Either that, or else he could call his buddy at the police department for a favor. Her address? The police were always happy to oblige someone they trusted. And if the police trusted him, so could Barbie—at least for a few hours more.

This isn't presumptuous, Darin assured himself. Barbie was interested; he had felt the spark. There remained a very good possibility their meeting in the cemetery had been preordained, even. Destined. Somebody up there in the big sky and endless universe was smiling upon him at last, and though he'd never believed in that before, hell, if there were such things as beasts and other darker beings that went bump in the night, why not divine intervention of some kind? Why not believe that Barbie was the one to accept what he was? Fate was perhaps more than wishful thinking. Maybe there were such things as miracles. Maybe dreams could come true.

Not one peep. Barbie hadn't uttered one peep when he'd temporarily abducted her. This suggested an inner confidence in her ability to perceive and separate danger from adventure, he guessed. Unafraid. She'd joked about cemeteries, with no odor of fear emanating from her, only those crazy female pheromones. She was perfect.

Stop, he told himself. He couldn't really know her for sure, could he? Other than this strangely powerful attraction between them, he had no idea what Barbie was made of. Hopefully she wasn't just sugar and spice and everything nice. With luck she was a bit more. . . . Well, he wasn't so keen on slime or snails, himself. But puppy dog tails were mandatory.

He eyed the street, blew out a sigh. Good thing he hadn't lost his sense of humor over all this.

Good thing Barbie Bradley had one.

Chapter Ten

Barbie's face was plastered to her pillow in a major sugar hangover. Too tired to move, other than to glance briefly at the dial on the clock radio, she muttered, "It's midnight. I'm not going to answer this phone, so you can stop calling."

Riiinnngggg.

She covered her ears with the pillow.

Riiinnngggg.

"Hey! Wake up the neighbors, why don't you?"

Riiinnngggg!

Barbie picked up the receiver, dropped it, then managed to retrieve it again and place it to her ear.

"Your new message is quite funny," said the voice on the other end of the line.

Bolting upright, Barbie fumbled with the pink princess phone again, then put one hand over her heart to make sure it didn't leap out of her chest.

" 'Hello. Barbie doesn't know you and has thought better of this, so please stop calling.' That's not a proper message," her mystery man chided in his sexy bedroom voice.

Barbie cleared her throat. "Then what is it?"

"A challenge."

"It wasn't meant to be a challenge." Or maybe it was, Barbie admitted silently. Could it have been, without her knowing?

"Why did you leave your number, if I wasn't to call?" the stranger asked.

"Moment of weakness. Women have them. I'm a woman."

"I know."

Gulp. Of course he did. He'd done all that feeling around in the graveyard.

"It's midnight," Barbie said.

"Not my fault. You had the phone off the hook for a while."

"It took me an hour to make that message."

"Then you picked up anyway?"

"Yep," Barbie admitted with a shrug. "And if you tried for an hour, you sure must like challenges."

"What I am is persistent."

Uttering a silent cheer over the fact that he had tried for an hour to reach her, Barbie then slid into inner chastisement. *Remember the stalker theory!*

Her mystery guy continued. "Am I the only one here who wanted to see the other again?"

Barbie considered. In point of fact, she hadn't been able to concentrate on anything else since Angie left. She had eaten ten cookies. Ten! A zillion calories. A month in the gym. All because of this arrogant stranger with his iffy persona.

"Okay," Barbie said tentatively—right before wondering if it was anatomically possible for a person to kick herself in the ass.

"Okay what?" the sexy voice queried.

"For the sake of my figure, we can see each other again."

"I don't know if I follow the first part, but I like the second. When?"

"Next weekend. Friday. In public. In a busy place. Lots of

lights. Lots of people. *Alive* people. No graveyards, no light-less places, no carting. Very little touching."

This, to Barbie, sounded not only reasonable, but like a normal date.

"Lots of rules going on there," said the voice.

"I stand by them implicitly, just so you know."

There was a hesitation on the line, then, "All right."

Barbie fell back onto her pillows, grasping the receiver. "All right? You agree?"

"Can't get rid of me that easily, Barbara."

"Barbie."

"Not a nickname?"

"My mother liked the doll. A lot."

There was chuckling on the other end of the line. Barbie hadn't forgotten how nice this guy's laughter was, nor how much she liked the sound. It seemed to flit across her skin through the phone lines, light, earnest, and rumbling. Not at all wicked. Not too cynical. Hearing it, she blew out a sigh, settled into her pillows with the phone cradled to her ear, and said, "You didn't tell me your name, as I recall."

"Maybe I should say Ken," the voice suggested.

"You do and I'll hang up."

"What if it really is Ken—as in Kenneth?"

"It would be way too cute. I couldn't stand that much cute. I've grown up with Mattel jokes, you know."

"Lots of jokes?" he asked.

"Too numerous to mention. Anyway, Ken, it's rumored, has been recently replaced by Blaine—an update, it seems, for the youth of today. Of course, I suggest we don't take this information too seriously, as Ken and Barbie are true soul mates. Blaine is merely a feeble attempt at modernization."

Realizing what she was saying, Barbie covered her mouth with her free hand and clunked herself on the head with the phone. *Motormouth.*

Her caller just chuckled. "Seems we're safe, then," he said. "My name is Darin."

Barbie perked up. "As in the singer, Bobby?"

"Named after the singer, yes. But my *first* name is Darin. Last name is Russell."

Points there, Barbie thought to herself. Darin Russell knew who Bobby Darin was, and he knew about Ken. Plus, he hadn't made any more Mattel jokes. How bad could he be? She pulled the covers up beneath her chin.

"Friday? Is that what you said?" he asked.

"I . . ." Barbie's mind was a great big blank as she struggled to justify what she was doing, and as she fought off the image of how her mother would disapprove of the words *graveyard guy*. The date would be in public, though, so it was probably all right. If Darin Russell tried anything strange or forward, other folks would help out when she yelled.

She wondered though, as she listened to his soft breathing, whether the toy company had ever made a Rebel Barbie, because that's what she was feeling like right at that moment, by taking him up on his offer.

"Shall I pick you up?" he asked.

"No. We can meet," she hurried to say.

"May I suggest somewhere?"

"Sure." *Maybe. If it's not too pervy.*

"A restaurant on Third. A Gypsy place. Have you been there?"

"A Gypsy place?" Barbie repeated. "No, can't say I have." But inside, her heart was racing. Would people who frequented a Gypsy place come to her rescue if necessary, or be too busy dancing on the tables naked?

"Good," Darin Russell said. "It'll be an adventure."

"Another one?" she muttered.

Quietly she kicked herself, because he had succeeded in manipulating her into a date on foreign turf, when she'd been prepared to refuse any date at all. What had happened to that? What had happened to fortitude? Adherence to a plan? She'd rehearsed her refusal over and over, in case he did call, hence the hour with the phone off the hook. Her waffling now was surely due to the evening's unusual glucose consumption. And now she had to be nervous until this date actually took place. Would the mini-mart have enough cookies to tide her over for a week?

"Wait. How about tomorrow?" she said. "Instead of Friday."

"That would actually be today, I think," Darin Russell said after a pause. "Since it's now after twelve."

"Yep. Luckily there's no school on Sunday, so I won't have to worry about getting up early the morning after." Gee, that might be misconstrued, Barbie realized right after she said it. Yet if she tried to clarify the matter, it might only make things worse.

"Tonight," Darin Russell repeated, as if thinking about it.

"You game?" Barbie sensed hesitation on her male pursuer's part. She didn't know if she should push farther and see if he cracked.

"Would lunch be better?" he suggested. "Full daylight? Plenty of crowds?"

"Possibly, but I do need a little time to prepare," Barbie said. "Also, I have things to do." Barbie, you little dickens, she thought. That's what is known as taking the big bad bull by the horns and not letting him make the rules. And on the plus side, she was avoiding a ton of interim weight gain. Win-win.

"All right," Darin conceded, though slowly, almost tentatively. "Tomorrow. I mean, tonight. Nine o'clock all right?"

Nine was her usual pj's-and-a-book time. But then, what was more important, anyway? A book, or a guy beside her in his own pj's? Better yet, a guy beside her in no pj's at all!

Oh, right, she quickly amended. Like she'd know. Like she'd ever come remotely close to having a guy in bed. Like that was even a possibility now, with this wildman stranger. No good girl should invite a wildman into her immediate vicinity—especially her apartment!

"Gypsies don't get moving until nine," Darin explained. "Food's not even in the ovens until eight forty-five. It's a dark place. Cool. Lots of ambience."

"Do I wear bangles?" Barbie asked.

"The more bangles the better, I'm thinking," he agreed.

"Aren't Gypsies the ones who hang all that garlic everywhere?"

"You don't like garlic?"

"Sure. But then there won't be any vampires in the place," she joked.

Another few seconds of silence passed before Darin Russell replied. "Nine it is, then. Oh, and a skirt and heels would work, along with the bangles—just in case you had jeans in mind."

Jeans? Did he think she wouldn't know how to dress for a first date? Smiling, Barbie eyed the jeans dangling over her chair. "Swanky Gypsy place, is it?"

"Very old-world," he replied. "No sneakers allowed. Dinner jackets are the norm. You all right with that, Barbie?"

"Perfectly all right." But she wondered if a swanky place might allow baseball caps along with the bangles, since she couldn't get Angie to do her hair without an explanation about any of this.

"Do you want to know anything else?" Darin asked.

Your chest measurement, maybe? Your medical records?

Instead of those things, Barbie asked, "Do you like movies?"

A laugh came over the line. He was clearly astonished

she'd asked that particular question, and not something more serious. Then he said, "I do like movies. Especially old black-and-white stuff."

"Another question?" Barbie inquired.

"Shoot."

"Why *me*, Darin?"

His voice seemed to get a bit more serious, though she supposed she could have been imagining it. "Nice voice. Nice body. Sense of humor. Loyal. Good friend. Adventurous attitude. Skinny knees," he said.

"Hey!" she protested.

"I just wonder if you're beautiful."

"Sorry," she snapped. "Plain as pie. I rely purely on charm. And I thought you could see in the dark."

"Well, no worries about the looks," Darin Russell assured her, laughing. "I have enough for the both of us."

"You're humble, too," she noted.

"To a fault."

"I knew you couldn't really see out there."

"Oh, but I could."

"Then tell me something, Bat Boy."

"You're a brunette."

Barbie paused, taken aback, then said, "You saw me by the car. I knew you were watching."

"Yes, but I knew about your hair color before that, and that your lipstick was red."

Now, why would he notice a lipstick shade? Barbie wondered. Why would he even mention it? Was it something to do with coloring? She recalled Angie's bit of grooming trivia: no red lipstick for blondes. Some sort of skin-tone incompatibility. But since she was a brunette, it should be fine on her. And what sort of man noticed that sort of thing? Unless Darin Russell was . . . gay?

Lord almighty. Not gay. Nope. There was nothing gay about this man. This hunk of flesh had been all hetero man, front and back. She was most sure about the front.

"Your mouth smelled like cinnamon," he elaborated. "The scent was right up there with feeling up your knees."

"Which are not skinny. I believe I mentioned that," she remarked.

"So you did."

"Anything else you want to tell me?" Barbie asked. Noting another teensy hesitation, she held her breath. Would his next words be a compliment or a critique?

"I don't think so," he said. "Except that I would like to say I think you might be a great person to know, and to share a life with."

Share a life with? He'd said that as though he really meant it! Like they had skipped all the middle stuff, all those fairly important details, and gotten to the entrée before the salad course. For a minute Barbie was speechless. Her tongue wouldn't work. Her breath was suspended.

"See you soon, then?" Darin said.

That mesmerizing voice seemed to glide through the phone wires, through the receiver and into her ear, and down, down, down, to . . . *that spot*. The spot her mother had warned her about, the spot Mattel's Barbie didn't come with. It was a spot Barbie now had no doubt she herself possessed, one that was throbbing insistently at the moment, begging to be noticed. Begging for attention. Heck, she was panting. Her knees were vibrating. Forget not telling her, she might need to stash Angie at a side table as a chaperone for this date. If a phone call from this guy could hit that spot, think what being near the guy might do!

Maybe Angie could lounge out of sight with binoculars and a direct line to the Miami PD. She wouldn't be a chaperone, really—more like backup. And crap, she hadn't told

Angie anything yet. How was she going to break this to her friend? With all her fibbing, she was turning into her ex, Liar Bill. Maybe falsehoods were contagious.

"I'll be there," she heard herself say. "I'll take a cab, since I haven't gotten around to buying a car."

"Good night, then," Darin whispered, and before Barbie could protest or add anything or change her mind, he disconnected.

Her pink princess phone slipped from her hands, crashing onto its plastic cradle. Barbie stared at it for a long minute before mumbling, "Well, that's that."

Of course, it was, in actuality, a long way from *that*. She had a made date with Graveyard Guy, as in a guy who patrolled graveyards for a living. She was going to a dark Gypsy place on a date. And to top it all off, she'd just experienced phone sex without meaning to. Every one of her body parts was humming Darin Russell's tune. She closed her eyes, pressed her thighs together, and whispered, "Barbie Bradley, you have really gone and done it this time."

Still twitching, she lay back on the bed and covered her head with her pillow. Several seconds went by, but her heart rate refused to slow. She flipped over to her other hip, curled into a ball, stuck a leg out of the covers, and wiggled her bare toes. Her heart continued to boom.

Surrendering, she sat up to glare at the little lighted dial on the phone. As much as she wanted to be nonchalant about her upcoming date, such carelessness was not an option. Her heart was frolicking like an expectant puppy. She couldn't even remember the last time this had happened . . . because it never had. In the distance a faint voice was shouting, *Bring it on, Cupid!*

Oh wait, that was her own voice, albeit internal. How could anyone sleep with all that shouting?

Covers kicked off, feet stuck into her fluffy slippers, Barbie gave the Sand Man the slip and headed for the kitchen. Who needed a treadmill, the way her heart was aerobicizing? Who needed beauty sleep, if Darin Russell had looks enough for both of them?

Plunking her backside atop the counter, propping her feet on the stool, and with the leftover plate of Oreos in her hand, she sighed and opened her mouth wide.

"What the hell. Might as well make it an even dozen."

Chapter Eleven

Barbie was ready. She had even left a message on Angie's answering machine about where she would be, saying that she was on a blind date that had come up suddenly. Which was true. She'd left instructions for Angie to call her cell phone at nine thirty—a trick as old as time, and particularly handy if the date turned out to be subpar. Called the "oops, gotta go" routine, it was a staple Angie had mentioned long ago. On the off chance Barbie didn't require the interruption, it wouldn't hurt anything to take the brief call. It'd show she had friends.

Of course, the "Gypsy place" would pique Angie's interest even as it had piqued Barbie's. Definitely it had a non-gourmet ring to it. A non–Barbie Bradley ring to it. Would there be violins? Accordions? Belly dancers with clanky coin belts and scarves between their teeth? Would she be eating mysterious food with her fingers? She would find out any minute.

Peering out the window of the cab as it pulled up at the curb of a restaurant bordering, yet not actually in the seedier part of town, Barbie experienced a stomach flutter. Yep, she was nervous, all right. First-date anxiousness. She would be seeing Graveyard Guy up close and personal. What if he didn't live up to her fantasies? Or vice versa.

Fantasies of him? Yeah. She'd had plenty of 'em since yesterday. All about being carried around in strong male arms. About Darin Russell's physique matching the timbre of his sensational voice. About other things too personal to revisit in a taxi.

Eyes wide open, she stared outside. The restaurant was like a cave with lots of windows, all of them darkly tinted and partially curtained. Candlelight glowed from within, flickering invitingly, making the glass seem to expand. Garlands of evergreen branches were strung from several quaint exterior lanterns. A huge scripted sign, hand carved by the look of it, spelled out DEN OF INIQUITY.

Geez. Biting her lower lip, her carefully applied makeup threatening to melt from her oncoming blush, Barbie sat on the cab's worn seat a while longer supposing she should go home, change her phone number, and call for takeout. She *should* do all that. Pronto.

Then again, she'd never know anything more about Darin Russell, party-pooping graveyard keeper. It would mean admitting she was too chicken to actually go on a blind date. Bradleys were not known for freaking out. No siree. Bradleys had extra strong backbones and tons of courage most of the time. Her dad was a judge, for heaven's sake!

The cab driver was eyeing her in the rearview mirror when Barbie looked up. His look said, *Time to* BLANK *or get off the* BLANK.

She dug into her purse and offered the cab driver a twenty-dollar bill. He promptly shook his spiky-haired head, declining her fare. "Been paid by the gentleman," he said, as if that were the way cab drivers usually spoke: nice, polite, and explanatory. He had a slight British accent.

The cabbie waited in his seat as she climbed out of his car, not exiting to open her door, then drove off. This left Barbie on the sidewalk, money still in her hand.

"The gentleman?" she echoed, fingering the bill. "The *gentleman* paid?"

The cab gone, a chill wafted up Barbie's bare legs all the way under her barely there skirt. She shivered and straightened on her heels. With one tug at her ice blue silk jacket (another extravagant purchase, like the outfit last night, and just as worth it) and another slight tug at her form-fitting black skirt (slightly tighter for all the cookie-gulping), she inhaled deeply, able to focus more closely on her exotic surroundings.

Relief flooded in. Plenty of people were milling about, some of them rushing here and there on the sidewalk, some waiting to go inside the restaurant. Many couples of all sizes, shapes, and ages stood by the door. Relatively normal-looking people in nice clothes. This seemed to Barbie a good thing, and satisfied Requirement One for a blind date quite nicely: crowds.

She tucked the twenty into her sequined bag and snapped it shut, mentally dissecting the taxi incident. If Darin had paid for the cab, sent it to wait near her apartment, he knew where she lived. Since she'd had only a single conversation with him by phone without any mention of her address, he had to have found another means of information. Which inspired the question, *Was this creepy or acceptable?*

Reminder in need of attention: I haven't yet purchased that Texas-sized security bolt.

Assuring herself of the presence of her cell phone by squeezing her bag, Barbie brushed off her lingering anxiety and muttered a personal challenge. "Remember, Bradley, this isn't marriage, it's a date. In a public place. You're being adventurous, like you promised at New Year's. You're Adventure Barbie, and that's all there is to it."

Suddenly she felt better, and curiously upbeat. With an unconscious calming gesture, she smoothed her skirt a second time and patted her hair. "Let's get on with it."

She took a bold first step, head up, shoulders back . . . then hesitated, nearly tripping on her own foot. Some of the people in the doorway had moved aside. A man appeared beneath the garlands and the carved sign, as yet hazy in the shadows of the doorway. The man said, "Barbie, I presume?"

Courage fled—*pfft*, right out the window. Barbie's knees wobbled like a big chicken's might if confronted with a Zacky Farms truck. Shivers piggybacked up and down her bare legs. Talk about an awkward moment. She was experiencing hormonal whiplash!

She had to say something, had to respond. Etiquette demanded it. First, though, she leaned slightly on one hip to better show off her not-skinny knees, and swallowed to level her voice.

"Darin?" Her voice sounded fine. She squinted, trying to see past the shadows.

"In the flesh," the man replied.

There he was, tucked beneath the overhang: Graveyard Guy. And good lord, he was gorgeous.

No, he wasn't just gorgeous. He was closer to extraordinary. Super extraordinary. He hadn't been kidding when he said he had looks enough for the both of them. Barbie's lips moved before her brain could filter the oath. "Shit."

Darin Russell was a frigging dream come true. He was as tall as she'd imagined—at least six-two—with a lithe body, broad shoulders, and legs that didn't end. Darin Russell oozed sex. He wore his hair long, about an inch or so longer than hers, so that it covered his collar. Dark, straight, and sleek. Dark as in almost black. Sleek as in . . . damn him! That shiny black mass swung, seemingly in slow motion, stirred by a breeze. Barbie's friend Angie might have fallen off her chair and thanked the gods of beauty had she been there, for before Barbie stood a man with a mane, a regal stallion of a man who looked a little like a throwback to some old-world haunt. A Scottish castle, maybe. He should have been wearing a kilt.

Correction. Angie *would* have fainted dead away. Barbie herself was close to doing the same thing.

"Your ride okay?" Darin asked, waiting beneath the roof overhang, allowing Barbie a few more seconds to gawk.

Barbie nodded, not quite ready for speech. Her mental inventory was ringing up a preposterous number of visual pluses. His chiseled features were aristocratic. The high cheekbones, whittled chin, tanned skin, and exquisitely shapely patrician nose were painfully beautiful. His dark suit jacket, no doubt terribly expensive, hung perfectly on his frame, and was buttoned over a soft white shirt.

Was there more to admire? Maybe so, but she had to stop there; he was two feet away with his dark, perfect eyebrows arched. Barbie wanted to run right home and pluck hers.

"Barbie?" he repeated with a grin.

She smiled as she met Darin's eyes, which were either hazel or dark green. It was hard to tell the exact color in the dark, especially with all the noises in her ears. *Hubba-hubba* would have been the verbal translation of those noises. Or maybe, *My place or yours?*

Darin wore a grin that was packed with charm. His eyes were bright. Did he know the effect he had on women? He seemed very much at ease. Barbie herself felt tongue-tied.

"Darin? As in not-Bobby?" she said, sounding, she hoped, pretty much in control of her lust.

When he nodded, her confidence rose to a manageable level . . . then immediately melted. Darin's grin had become a full-fledged smile, changing his face from charming to disarming. There were perfect white teeth between sculpted lips, lips that had brushed hers the night before. Lips that had whispered into her ear and through the phone. And there actually were small laugh lines around his long-lashed eyes!

Oh boy. Try as she might, Barbie just couldn't stop her male-beauty inventory. She couldn't stop picturing this guy in the Highlands, in his castle, with very few clothes on. Lord Darin Whatever, with Barbie herself as mistress of his keep.

The air around her went warm and fuzzy. Her insides heated up. She needed something to suck on, quick. Oh, geez, she told herself. Like an ice cube!

Chimes rang inside of her head. What seemed like hours of walking to reach Darin must have been seconds, really. At a loss regarding what else to do, Barbie took a death grip on her purse. What she really wanted was to reach out and touch this stallion. This Braveheart! This heartthrob! She felt quite giddy, forgetting how to breathe as he drew her to him by merely nodding his glorious head. Lustrous black hair fell around his face. Her knees closed with an involuntary movement. *Snap.* She was sure her face reddened, sure he had noticed. His eyes were dancing merrily.

"Lovely," he said in that . . . that *voice*.

"You, too," Barbie heard herself say. So true.

Darin's terrific smile seemed to shine for no one but her. She glanced around to make certain. Yep. For her. It seemed as if a big light had appeared from the sky to descend over the area, highlighting only the two of them. The other people surrounding the restaurant faded away. There were now only two people, Barbie and Darin. One named after the doll, one after the singer. Man and woman. Male and female.

Was it hot here, or what?

Of course, the searchlight wasn't real. The light was behind them, coming from the moon, big and bright and dripping silver on the sidewalk. She and Darin were in actuality standing beneath the giant roof overhang of a Gypsy restaurant, blocking a busy doorway, concluding a first introduction. It would do her good to remember that.

Barbie gave her head a little toss. She licked her lips to make sure there was no goofy expression on her face. Chaperone? Hell, she was going to need a bodyguard.

Better yet, considering Braveheart here, a chastity belt.

Chapter Twelve

"Not a disappointment?" Darin asked as she approached him.

"Not completely," Barbie returned.

Her companion's expressive eyebrows arched in question.

"You're much too perfect to be looking for dates," Barbie said. "What's the catch?"

"I think I'll tell you about the catch later. Right now, I'd rather put my best foot forward, if you don't mind."

"I don't mind at all." Barbie gave Darin another curious once-over. Finding this guy's flaw, assuming there was one, took on a certain rabid importance. There had to be *something* she could pick on or be critical of. There just had to be. If not, if his virtues kept piling up, it would be difficult to keep from feeling inferior.

"Thanks for the ride," she remarked, hoping to pry loose some information on how he'd gotten her address.

He simply smiled that disarming smile. "It's the least I could do. You did agree to meet a complete stranger. And I did the asking."

"Yes, well," Barbie admitted, "I might have to take back what I said about your lack of civility. Good thing I'm not proud."

"Are you shivering?"

She nodded. "Blood-sugar drop."

More like panty drop, Barbie admitted to herself. Or the anticipation of one. Of course, she wasn't going to have that. Not tonight. Remember that resolve!

"Food will cure you," Darin suggested. "Food in abundance."

The next thing she knew, Barbie was curled up against him. God, where was her self-control? How had she gotten there, hugging him? Some kind of brain stall? Her hips were pressed lightly, though not too suggestively, against his. Her dreams had come to life in the doorway of . . . the Den of Iniquity. How apropos.

Barbie tipped her chin downward to make absolutely certain Darin wasn't wearing a kilt. Nope, no kilt. But that meant . . . Oh, God. Yes, this was reality. It was not a dream.

Darin's lips, when she glanced back up, were barely inches from hers. Barely. And they were sort of hovering, turned up at the edges. What was he smiling about, exactly?

"This *is* a restaurant, isn't it?" she asked.

"What else could it be?"

"I don't know," she replied. "A bordello?"

Darin chuckled and backed up to gesture her inside. "Are you hungry?"

"Famished."

However, Barbie noted, those weren't hunger sounds in her stomach she was hearing now; they were wailing sirens . . . in her head. On top of all the bell-ringing and chiming, this guy was tripping all her warning signals. Too perfect, her mind was crying. Too frigging perfect. There had to be a hitch. Like, he was an actor in town visiting and having the time of his life bursting hearts right and left. A male model doing the same. A government experiment in the latest Bond-type spy guy, doing his training here.

Was he faster than a speeding bullet? Able to leap tall

buildings in a single bound? Or possibly he was a homicidal maniac with a million-dollar smile.

"Come inside," Darin said.

"Lead the way."

Darin shook his head, tossing that mane of glorious black hair with a stallionlike gesture, and said simply, "Shall we go in together?"

The man, in this day and age, was a gentleman.

Side by side they turned to enter the restaurant. Together, like young sweethearts moving in time to the sound of the drums originating somewhere deep inside of Barbie's body. And what did the drums say? *Barbie Bradley, you might actually, really, truly have a fairy godmother after all.*

Yay.

Inside was a blur. How could Barbie possibly glean any details, when Darin's fingers had closed over hers, electrifying her nerves? She absently took in dark corners, randomly placed lights with stained-glass shades, candles aglow on tablecloths of tapestry and lace, tables that were all occupied, except for one. Without a host or maître d', Darin ushered her to that unoccupied corner deep inside the place, far from the door, and pulled out her chair. He waited for her to sit, then pushed it in. Gentleman to the max.

Long-stemmed crystal glasses sparkled on the lace tablecloth like stars fallen to earth. Each table had its own light, all of them looking like little islands of illumination on a darkened sea.

The ceiling was low and dark stained, truly cavelike, providing a warm, muted canopy to a place as romantic as all get-out. Soft violin music drifted from somewhere unseen. Before Barbie could whisper her approval, a server appeared. Male, about thirty-five. He filled her glass with a liquid so deep red it looked to be made of strained rubies. Then he filled Darin's glass as Darin settled himself opposite her.

A length of ivory lace stretched between them, at least two feet, studded with gold flatware. Barbie was grateful for the distance. Breathing room. She felt the need for some air, and also appreciated the direct approach to further scrutiny of the Russell charms. As it was, the dimness, the candle-light, the violins, and the sparkling crystal, coupled with the hot hunk across from her . . . all pointed with the subtlety of a gigantic neon arrow in the direction—sometime soon, and at the very least, sex.

She'd never had a one-night stand. Not for a lack of guys trying. She'd never met a man she'd wanted to throw cau-tion aside for. Could this Adonis across from her be the one to change all that? All her senses screamed yes.

Barbie waited until she felt confident enough to look Darin in the eyes without hearing distant strains of the "Hallelujah Chorus" before raising her glass. Darin raised his. He placed his lips on the rim of the glass. Barbie did the same, envying Darin's glass the touch of that remarkable mouth.

The wine not only looked dazzling, it smelled wonder-fully exotic. As Darin took a sip, Barbie did also, continuing to eye him over the rim. Liquid rubies . . . yes, she noted happily, her lips stinging from their first encounter with liq-uid opulence. And Darin hadn't drooled or anything. No flaw there. Darn.

"You like the wine?" he asked, green eyes hypnotic.

"I'm not exactly a connoisseur," Barbie confessed. "It's nice. Smells sweet, like nectar."

Darin smiled. He really was trying to please her, Barbie decided, quite possibly making up for the sack-of-potatoes business of the night before. She wondered what he'd do if he knew she'd swap every single bottle of ancient wine in the restaurant for one real peek at his pecs, which she al-ready knew were spectacular.

Smiling to herself, Barbie watched Darin take a second

sip of wine before she did the same. This time, her taste was a tad larger. The lip sting became a buzz that tickled her tongue and heated her throat.

"It's hot," she remarked with an astonished gasp.

"The burn will diminish in a minute. It's a rare old wine."

Barbie was having a minor meltdown. Everything the liquid touched burned, and there wasn't any water in sight.

As if wanting to get in on the meltdown, her shoulders became warm, then her upper back. Barbie's arms heated, elbow to fingertips. Her cheeks again flushed hot, and most likely a shade of bubble gum pink. Who needed headstands, anyway?

"Truly like drinking fire," she declared, beaming at Darin, wanting to fan herself with her napkin.

He rewarded her with a conspiratorial smile. "A special wine for a special night."

Gad. Darin's smile sent the spreading heat rapidly downward, toward *there*, the spot he'd reached just by talking to her on the phone. Barbie moved in her chair, repositioning to stop that particular feeling, determined to keep herself in control.

"How old is the wine?" she asked. The words *brilliant conversationalist* came to mind in relation to her lack of skills in a time of need.

"A hundred years," Darin replied.

"Really?" Barbie swirled the dark red liquid in her glass before taking a third sip. Her teeth were now numb. She coughed and let out a spurt of laughter before admitting, "I like it! I *really* like it."

Darin chuckled. "Good. I've ordered a light supper. Of course, for this place, light means a feast."

"A feast is no problem," Barbie said. Or it wouldn't have been, except for all those calories consumed the night before.

She looked up to find Darin staring. Squirming beneath his scrutiny she said, "*I'm* not on the menu, am I?" Man!

Had those words come out of her mouth? Barbie touched her fingertips to her lips and applied a little pressure. Both of Darin's eyebrows arched in question.

"You're staring," Barbie explained, marveling over how she could speak when she couldn't feel her tongue and realizing Darin was likely taking a silent inventory of his own. A good-sized drink of wine was the only way to go. She needed to show him she was no lightweight, and that she wasn't concerned about what he might be thinking.

Rats! Mistake about the large ingestion of wine. Her fourth sip—a gulp, really—went right to her calves. Her knees appeared to be stuck together.

Giving up on the leg position, Barbie was startled to find Darin sitting beside her when she again glanced up. Right beside her. Truly faster than a speeding bullet. Maybe he had slipped through a ripple in the space-time continuum?

He offered her a bite of something he held in his fingers. She hadn't even noticed that some of the food had arrived! Not knowing what else to do, she took the offered food between her teeth, nibbled, swallowed. Yum. Nice, chewy, phyllo-covered thing. Artichoke? Spinach? How was she to decide when her heart was hammering? When her legs were glued together? When the handsomest man she had ever seen was feeding her finger food with his own fingers—and she had an urge to lick those fingers clean?

Their eyes locked for a heartbeat or two. Heat singed the air. Darin slid her glass toward her.

"Not hoping to get me drunk, are you?" she asked.

"The thought crossed my mind," Darin confessed, reaching up to tuck a wayward strand of hair behind her ear. "Although I'm afraid I prefer my women conscious enough to participate fully in whatever we're doing."

"Ah. Then I'd better not have any more of this," Barbie said, glancing toward the glass.

"You do like it?"

"Very much. Maybe even better in a snowy climate."

Another grin crossed Darin's extraordinary face—a reward of sorts. He was quick to smile, quick to laugh, and his green eyes flickered becomingly. Fine as Darin Russell was, he didn't really seem vain. No glancing at himself in the shiny metal tray. No ticks of any kind that Barbie could see. His posture seemed loose, relaxed. His smile was easy.

Barbie found herself envious, while still aware of those clanging sounds inside of her skull. She had to be careful. Not used to wine or dedicated male attention, enough of her body buzzed to make her want to leap into some male-female lip exploration. In public. It was, she decided, the wine working its magic. And hormones. She failed again to uncross her knees.

Possibly it was too late to worry about the wine. She was already alcohol silly. A real lightweight. And Darin was so darned close. So damned fine.

"Do you think—?" she began breathlessly.

"I think as much as I can," Darin remarked, popping a spinach wrap into his mouth, running his lips across his fingertips rather . . . what? Seductively?

Barbie tore her focus from his fingers and sighed in exasperation. She was feeling feverish, giddy even.

"Sorry. Speak your mind." Darin's hand moved toward one of her exposed and malfunctioning knees, apparently spontaneously. But it stopped midway without touching down. Even so, an earthquake rocked Barbie. Seven on the Richter scale.

"Do you think you might sit over there for a while yet? At least until we have dinner?" she requested, staring at the hand hovering above her kneecap.

"Am I bothering you?" He withdrew his hand, combed his fingers through his hair.

"The teeniest bit."

Without registering disappointment, Darin did as she asked. Back in his original position, he stretched out his long legs for several seconds, then tucked them beneath the table. Part of Barbie felt relieved by this separation. The mental part. Everything else mourned the distance.

It was the dastardly Bradley blood causing all this hormonal trouble, Barbie decided. There were plenty of black sheep in the family history. Probably pirates in there somewhere. Yo ho. But even allowing for those skeletons, it wasn't usual for her to lack in conversation. It wasn't usual for her to get into a tizzy over a man. Honestly, for all her current misguided thoughts, she wasn't easy. She was a schoolteacher, the third child of a relatively normal family, the product of late-blooming Baby-Boomer parents, Brenda and Sam. She was a good girl. *Bleh.*

Where was Adventure Barbie? Surely Adventure Barbie could have a glass of wine and still maintain the use of her toes? Surely Adventure Barbie could down this glass of wine, enjoy another, and be dancing on tabletops by the end of the night. Having . . . you know, *fun.*

Then again, this wasn't really about Barbie Bradley, in whatever imaginary Mattel incarnation. This was about Darin Russell and why he had chosen her. Why this hunky guy was pursuing her. It was time to talk about this and to confess to Darin, who might have preconceived misconceptions, that she really was much more intelligent than her name and recent behavior implied. She really was only temporarily silent due to some sort of ill-timed mental cramp.

About to start the explanations, lips parted to speak, Barbie paused. A strange muffled sound arose from under the table: music, sounding a little like a Bach concerto.

Chapter Thirteen

Unable to stop grinning, despite his very real and growing problems, Darin watched his date. She had green eyes, the color of new leaves. She had full lips painted a flattering shade of pink, a small tapered nose, wispy bangs highlighted with auburn edging her eyebrows, and an inquiring expression singular to people of imagination and openness.

He liked everything about Barbie Bradley. For real. Even though her lap was making music. Er, no, it was her purse.

"Oh," she said, apologizing as she produced the bag. "My phone. Truly sorry. Might be important."

Barbie's body, encased in a little black skirt and blue jacket, was long and slender. He'd known all along what her knees were like—graceful, shapely, and now regrettably hidden under the table.

Barbie Bradley, all in all, was exactly as he had anticipated. Not beautiful in the classical sense, but extremely attractive. Cute. Energetic. Everything in the right place, in the right proportions. Barbie Bradley, out of that imaginary bathtub and bubbles, was every bit as tempting. Add to the list that she was slightly quirky and fairly brave, and Darin Russell was certain he had found his ideal match.

Unable to help himself, Darin lowered his gaze a bit,

seeking white lace, drawn to the spot he'd last seen it. This time the lace was black, visible beneath the low-cut neckline of Barbie's blue jacket. A fashionable black. Innocent, in a wickedly feminine way. It became a toss-up where to look: green eyes or black lace?

Better the eyes, Darin decided. Less intimidating. Less suggestive. Slightly less sexual. Well, not really. No less sexual at all, as a matter of fact.

He tried not to stare. Tonight, the objective was to encourage Barbie to loosen up and to get to know him as a man, not to see her hit the door running. The objective was particularly difficult, since he was already feeling the effects of the moon, even with the roof over his head.

He was out of direct moonlight, sure, which meant he could hold off the changes for a bit, but he sensed he didn't have much time left. With Barbie so much like moonlight in human form, and with the moon pressing in . . . Well, he was stuck between a rock and a hard place, as the saying goes.

He fought a frown. There was much to say, to know, and for Barbie to fear if she accepted him. He was no Prince Charming by anyone's imagination, more the Big Bad Wolf. Barbie would certainly find this out. How would she react? He had no way of knowing. The spotlight was entirely on him. He couldn't slip up, not until he'd won her heart. Not too much wine or food, no nuzzling the long, beautiful neck.

Definitely no nuzzling.

Yes, it was of paramount importance, he reminded himself, that he make sure she didn't touch him. He couldn't hold on if she did.

He was aware of the exact position of the moon in the sky outside. That silver seducer, in all her glory, waited for him. In the same way, he was aware of the exact position of Barbie's body—those long legs beneath the table, her fingers

on the stem of her glass. The combined desires of Darin
and his beast were escalating.

Not yet!

He had to control this. Already the room was pulsing,
his breath quickening. Though his resistance was fierce, the
moon would win eventually. She always did. It was at heart a
game to see how far he could go, but if he were to feel that
moonlight on his skin or even experience too much emotion
all at once, he would turn. This drove the point home: touching Barbie again, or having her touch him invitingly, was
something he could not afford.

With this firmly in mind, Darin kept his attention on
Barbie's face—her lively, expressive face, which was now
tinted nearly as pink as her lips with wine and embarrassment. She had set up a rescue call. Had she realized on some
subconscious level that she might need help? Did she think
she might need saving? From him?

He couldn't worry about it. Nor could he laugh at her
fear. His own challenge was to make it through dinner and
then see Barbie to her door. In this he could not falter.
Willpower was being strained to its limits. But he could manage, he told himself. He *could*.

Only, if he did manage, and if the date went as he hoped,
what then? Would Barbie understand the need for his distance? Would she think him cool and uncaring if he deposited
her on her doorstep without any physical touch? Would Barbie allow things to unfold so slowly?

Yes, if she was the woman he assumed she was. If she was
the woman he hoped she was. Someone to talk to, tell everything to, share the whole story with. Someone he could be
with 24-7. God, he longed for that.

"Sorry," she said again.

"No problem," he replied.

But there *was* a problem, of course. A very real, growing

problem. His legs had begun to twitch beneath the table. His shoulders ached. It had been insanity to meet Barbie tonight, pure and simple. But he'd had to. She had asked to meet tonight, instead of the safer time he'd suggested. How could he have turned her down, when he had been so adamant about pursuing?

Of all the luck, or lack of it! Wolfy only visited three nights a month, and this had to be one of them. Three per month, and here he was, across the table from his one chance at happiness. If he didn't make it through dinner, he'd never get another shot.

His eyes slipped, independent of his will, back to the black lace above her breasts. So tempting. All that silk and lace wrapped such a pretty package. What he wouldn't give to be able to feel that lace between his teeth, and the flesh beneath.

Focus. Think of what you'll tell her when the time comes to explain all this. Plan it out. That will sober you quickly enough. Better be prepared in case you slip up.

Explanations? Reverting to his rehearsed spiel, he'd say that unlike in the horror movies, where the beast takes over the host's mind and body completely—where differing personalities vie for dominance, one of them criminal—the changes in him were a bit more subtle. Although his behavior became more animalistic, and his body a furry mess, Darin the man remained present and participating. It was no fantasy. Nor was it a bad dream. Yes, truth was sometimes stranger than fiction.

Barbie wouldn't have to be afraid of what he really was, once she knew about him, she just had to be accepting. Would she have the right stuff to comprehend this? Accept this? Because if she ever accepted Darin the man, she also took the wolf. A surprise bonus. The "catch" she was looking for but would never expect. Who in their right mind would?

Dammit, his legs were shaking. Though he'd carefully folded them at the ankles and willed them to be still, they kept right on. Bloody damn, and the f-word five times over!

So, all right. The wolf wasn't so easily fooled by this dark restaurant. The wolf was impatient and hungry for his turn. Weird, yet understandable—Wolfy only had three nights to Darin's twenty-plus. Nevertheless, Darin pleaded silently to the inner beast, they could not blow this. The man needed this woman. The man needed her long term. More time would be necessary to win her.

It wasn't as if he was being melodramatic, either. Darin Russell needed a girl who joked with her pals, kicked off her shoes to see where they'd land, and spoke her mind. A girl who would try anything set before her in this restaurant because she was curious, and because she loved life. Darin Russell wanted a girl who left crazy messages on her answering machine, wouldn't care if she broke a heel or misplaced her wallet, and didn't really give a fig about graveyards. Darin Russell wanted a girl who, though she didn't drink much, enjoyed wine. He wanted Barbie Bradley, this girl who, though uncomfortable under his scrutiny, was dishing the scrutiny right back. No flapping eyelashes. No demure looks. No especially provocative clothes, but with assets a burlap bag couldn't have hidden.

The beast wanted all those things, too, but the beast couldn't verbalize its needs. The beast relied purely on the physical.

Darin slid on his seat and gritted his teeth. Old Wolfy was gaining power with the mere thought of Barbie's assets. Beads of moisture dampened the hair on his neck—a second bad sign. The first had been the sudden twitch, and the ache. The third sign was following: his heart had begun to hammer. The beast was urging him to action. The moon was doing her voodoo, after all.

It had been too soon for this date. He had known it, but had been helpless. His arms were now visibly shaking. He clasped his hands together. His skin went hot beneath his clothes, hot to the touch, because the wolf's shape was larger, bulkier and at this minute was pressing against the man's insides. His organs were in turmoil, his stomach churning, bones shifting—bones that seemed to become elastic, or whatever the hell they became to allow the beast its form.

The curse had come knocking. Now. In Barbie's presence.

She smiled at him across the table, her cell phone against her right ear, and the beast inside wanted Darin to close the distance. As Barbie's lips moved—lips that were no doubt warm, tender, and tasty—Darin felt his beast hurl itself through his bloodstream, swimming upward, trying to surface with claws extended. His mouth felt dry and strange, as if his jaw had come unhinged. Soon his face would lengthen. He couldn't allow that, not at a restaurant, in public . . . in front of *her*.

"Good," Barbie said into the phone.

Not good! He'd torn a hole in the tablecloth with unwieldy claws! His shoulder muscles rippled beneath his clothes.

"Okay," Barbie said into her little metal phone.

Not okay, Darin thought as he closed his eyes. So . . . not . . . okay.

Chapter Fourteen

"Time to go, or time to know?" Angie whispered into the phone, as though Barbie's date might be able to hear.

"I'm sort of busy right now," Barbie replied.

"Busy good, or busy bad?"

"I'm not sure," she answered cheerily.

Darin's eyes met hers. His face was highlighted by the flickering candle and truly a sight to behold. All those beautiful angles and shadows made Barbie's heart rattle.

"Good," she decided.

"I'll ring again in a half hour." Angie disconnected.

"That was embarrassing," Barbie confessed to Darin, sliding the phone back into her bag.

Though her date shrugged, his focus remained intent. His features seemed sharper all of a sudden. Was he annoyed?

"Merely a precaution, and well within your rights," he said agreeably.

Hmmm. Being agreeable wasn't a fault, Barbie reflected. Other men might have been annoyed, had they caught the purpose of Angie's call, but not this one. Or maybe he was the smallest bit upset? He was looking at her differently. Seductively, inquisitively—and also a bit darkly. Something new swam in his eyes, an altogether unidentified emotion.

Picking up her glass, Barbie swallowed more wine. She set the glass down. Pause. Glass back up. Another sip. And another. Take the edge off, she reasoned. This would make her more comfortable.

Now let's see, where did I leave off in this conversation?

"Back to why you were in the graveyard last night," she said. Surprisingly, her words slurred. Small talk. Lots of it. That's what she needed. No slurrage. But, cripes, her right elbow wasn't working properly now. Is this what strained rubies could do?

"I spoke the truth last night," Darin replied, his speech slow, precise, almost as though he too was having a hard time formulating words. Had he also had a few sips too many? "I was . . . making sure those party folks didn't do any harm to the place."

"Really?" she asked. Darin's voice had deepened a little more and sounded gruff. Barbie took another sip of wine. "You work there? No joke?" She hadn't been sure if she believed him.

"It's one of the things I do," he explained. "The other is a part-time gig with the police department—in a consulting capacity."

"What kind of consulting?" she asked.

This was getting more interesting by the minute. Barbie took another drink of wine, which was difficult, since she had to lean forward to get the glass to her mouth.

Darin removed his hands from the top of the table. His voice emerged as a whisper. "I help them deal with people with unusual physical and mental problems."

"Like those frat boys in the cemetery?"

Another sip of wine seemed necessary in order to dim the edges of Darin's appeal, even though his glorious image seemed to be growing darker still and starker in beauty in the feeble light of the restaurant. He was so very handsome.

Each time she looked at him, Barbie could swear she found something different to praise. She drank carefully, trying not to spill.

"Last night I was merely keeping an eye on things," Darin said, coughing, tossing his head as if his shoulder was sore. "Making sure no one got hurt."

"So you thought I might need saving."

"You were headed that way."

"Were you planning to single-handedly clear everyone out?" Barbie enquired.

"Only you."

"Because you liked my voice."

"You have a beautiful voice. Low. Spirited. Honest."

Darin's whisper could hardly be heard. His face had taken on a whitish glow. Maybe, Barbie reasoned, he couldn't hold his wine? Or maybe he was allergic to spinach or violins?

"Thank you for the compliment," she said, her skipping heart requiring that she imbibe more wine. She spilled, and the beautiful lace tablecloth stained as the liquid dripped down the rim of her glass. But Inquisitive Barbie would not be daunted. "Why would you single out a person because of her voice? I mean, you don't find that unusual?"

"In the dark, that was what I noticed about you first."

"But you can see in the dark." She'd remembered this little item, and she gave herself points for it. "That," Barbie continued, "brings us back to random pick ups strung on a thread of surprise, and the in-the-right-place-at-the-right-time theory for dating. Maybe you often practice this sort of thing?"

Man, that was a mouthful, and annoying if it was true. Maybe it was that flaw she searched for in Darin Russell. Never mind the fact that she was no longer looking for flaws too studiously.

His face seemed to be blurring slightly. Blinking, Barbie

reached for her glass again and asked, "Would you have gone back for Angie if we hadn't met up?" She fired off this question before realizing that Darin hadn't answered the last one. "Why do you need a random find, anyway? Look at you, so near to perfection." She leaned closer to the table, blinked a few more times in succession to clear the blurring. "Sorry if that embarrassed you."

"I'm glad you approve of my looks. However, what do you mean by *near* to perfection?"

"Nobody's completely perfect, are they?"

"I guess not. Just so you know, though, my answer to your question is that I didn't think about your being a 'random find.' I liked what I heard and wanted to meet you, that's all." Back was that strange light in Darin's eyes, the one that took them from green to gold to shadowy. His lips upturned as he leaned back from the table, away from the candle. "Something in your voice suggested you'd be right for me. I went with the notion."

"Psychic, eh? For real?"

That hadn't come out anything like what Barbie meant. Had she used a cynical lilt? Had she babbled? She put a hand to her head to feel for brain leakage and offered her date an apologetic smile.

She was saved by the server, who appeared tableside. With his puffy white sleeves restrained by black garters, presumably so the fabric wouldn't drop into the sauce, he set down a large platter, then silently withdrew. Whatever was on that dish smelled heavenly: onions, green peppers, and garlic wrapped around a mound of brown.

As hungry as she was, Barbie didn't take her eyes off her date. You never knew where Darin would end up if you lost sight of him. Her heart couldn't take any more closeness at the moment. Any more random touching and she was a goner.

"You know," she said thoughtfully, with another sip of wine, "although I've been drinking this stuff, my glass isn't empty."

"A sign of very good service, don't you think?" Darin asked.

Did he have laryngitis? His voice was becoming more and more strained. Maybe he was a vampire, and the garlic from the appetizers was getting to him! Alas, more likely the difficulty in her hearing had to do with the wine. *Frigging lightweight.*

She gripped the crystal stem of her glass tightly. "Yes, but if someone keeps filling my glass on the sly, how do I know how much wine I've had? I think the room might be tilting."

Why hadn't she noticed anyone refilling her glass? Because Darin Russell was a Barbie magnet, that's why. Screw Blaine. Heck with Ken.

"Time to try some of this dish—to dilute the effects of the alcohol," Darin suggested. "By the looks of it, I'd say the chef has outdone himself for you."

The server returned from out of the blue to dole out some of the delightful-smelling concoction. Barbie waited until Darin's plate was also filled, then she sniffed at the steam rising from hers. She glanced up, saw that Darin's gaze was zeroing in on her.

"What?" she asked.

"You sniffed at it."

"Oops. Sniffing is not quite proper etiquette, is it? It's just that whatever this is smells delicious."

As Barbie dipped her fork into the meal, she barely noticed that she didn't have to eat with her fingers. She barely noticed that the meat looked like lamb, one of her favorites, because Darin had put his face close to his plate and was copying her action. The moment seemed somehow removed from time.

The soft Gypsy music in the background, the scent of the lamb, the sparkling everything, and that glorious hair of Darin's falling around his face as he leaned over his plate to sniff in a decidedly animalistic fashion—it all was, Barbie found, faintly disquieting. Also, incredibly fascinating.

She set down her fork, no longer hungry. She couldn't have chewed if she'd wanted, not with Darin there. What was it about him that she couldn't put a finger on? What lay beyond her reach? She could hardly breathe with Darin's eyes on her, burning each inch of her that they took in. His attention made the wine seem harmless in comparison, and the savory lamb forgettable.

"What?" she said again, finding that Darin was no longer grinning. He wore a new expression, an almost pained one. This particular rearrangement of his features produced a pang in Barbie's panties, a pang that was a distinct precursor to a state described glibly by her college roommates as being horny. Her date stared at her with those luminous green eyes beneath that dark mass of hair, and she wanted to . . .

Yep. Horny, all right. Already her hands were advancing toward him on the tablecloth, moving independently of her will.

Stop! Stop, I say!

Her fingers detoured, paying heed. Sort of. They climbed up the stem of her wine glass instead, closed around it, and began rubbing up and down, slowly, suggestively, shockingly. She couldn't stop herself. Seduction Barbie had entered the room.

A nebulous giddiness came on, as though someone had dropped silly pills into the wine. Barbie felt like laughing. She really did feel like dancing on the tabletops. All of sudden she didn't care why Darin had asked her out to dinner, only that he had, and that they were connecting in some extremely hot and sensual way that conversation played no part in. Theirs was a connection that even his supernaturally great looks had little to do with. It was something more elemental.

Strong fingers closed over her wrist. The rapidly beating thing in Barbie's chest fluttered. Darin had hold of her! Darin's heat coursed through her, over her, hotter than lava.

Wait! Could anything be hotter than lava? Yes! And hotter than the hundred-year-old alcohol, too. Darin's fingers on her wrist were like nothing she had ever encountered. It occurred to her that if he didn't remove those fingers in the next two seconds, she'd shout, *To hell with dancing on the tabletops*, and demand from Darin a more intimate performance. Something involving the exchange of bodily fluids. While the violins strummed on.

"Perhaps some water?" Darin suggested, eyes locked on hers.

A swim? A shower? Kinky, Barbie thought, swallowing hard.

"I want . . ." Slurring big-time, she pressed her lips together. Okay, the lip-closing wasn't entirely due to the slurrage, but because Darin's fingernails, long and sharp by the feel of them, were raking her skin.

Barbie shot to her feet, stared at her wrist. Talk about suggestive! Talk about erotic! No, she didn't want to talk about this at all. She wanted action. She tipped forward, caught herself with a hand on the table. Holy crap! She was drunk as a skunk!

"Are you all right?" Darin asked nicely enough, but he looked hungry. Not the food kind of hungry, either. There were dark flecks in his eyes. There were amber rings around those dark flecks. His pupils were huge. They were animal eyes, similar to a lion's or a tiger's, and they were following her movements as though she might be dessert.

"You'll be all right," he promised.

"I'm n-not so sure," Barbie stuttered.

What an understatement. She was sure she would *not* be all right. She was completely unstable. She'd ingested a gallon of wine and had eaten nothing. Darin was a god in human form, had kaleidoscopic eyes reminiscent of a four-legged predator, and had fire in his fingers—fingers in serious need of a manicure. Was she nuts to want those hands on her? All over her? This equaled "not all right" if the rules she'd been given governing female dating were worth the paper they hadn't actually been written on.

"Right there with you," Barbie thought she heard Darin mutter, though she couldn't be certain. The music had grown louder, probably in direct correlation to her wine intake. Darin's arm trembled as he eased it around her shoulders to steady her.

Maybe, Barbie thought, maybe—hopefully—he'd just had too much to drink, hence the intensity of his concentration. Maybe . . . she wasn't ready for this.

She teetered when drawn closer to his fiery aura. The room revolved. Darin's face seemed to change shape in and out of the shadows, sort of like Elastic Man's.

Ridiculous! Barbie closed her eyes, then reopened them. His face was there in all its godlike beauty. Two eyes, a nose, a mouth.

"I think perhaps the wine might have been a bit much. I'm sorry," he apologized, saying the exact thing Barbie had been about to say. Only, Darin's voice made the words beautiful. They were like low vibrations drifting over the bare skin of her neck. Like silk being dragged very slowly and sensuously over naked body parts. His voice was stirring up thoughts that reeked of sex and innuendo. Spasms of longing pierced Barbie to the bone.

"I'm still fully par . . . par . . . partiffficating," she insisted, realizing only then that the plates on the table wouldn't stay still. *Whoop, whoop, whoop.* Head spin. Stomach whirl.

Darin's arm tightened more protectively around her, and a twinge hit Barbie, a realization as powerful as the longing she felt. There was no flaw in this guy. Not a single one. She was tipsy and he was going to protect her. She had poured the wine down her own throat, and he was going to take the blame. Truly, she was staring at perfection in human form, both inside and out. Or trying to stare at it, if only he would stand still. If only the room would stop spinning.

"Shame," Darin said for the second time in two days, holding her so close that she couldn't look up to see his lips move.

Had he just suggested "doing it" under the table? Of course not! Pure Barbie imagination. Though he might just as well have suggested it, for all the rippling and buzzing going on between her thighs.

"W-what's a shame?" Barbie stammered, tongue twisting in her mouth with a desire to lick his soft white shirt. She stared wide-eyed at the mutinous wine glass.

"A shame . . . that you can't sample more of this food. We'll box it up, shall we?" Darin said.

He had meant to say something else, Barbie knew. That unsaid thing lingered in the air, mingling with the already-present heat. Darin had something on his mind. But what? They were so close, not even breathing space between their bodies.

"You're sending me home?" she asked disbelievingly.

"I'm taking you home."

"Calling the date off?"

"Keeping it on track."

"You can't do that!"

"I have to protect you."

"Beast," Barbie said.

"If you only knew," Darin whispered.

The room twirled again as Barbie turned her head. Her chin bumped Darin's chest, all six foot two of him and smelling better than the lamb. Barbie lifted her gaze, slowly, and though the room temporarily ceased to dance, Darin's eyes sure did. Those eyes looked right through her, down deep inside of her, haunting, calling, challenging.

You with me, Barbie? he said.

But his lips hadn't moved.

You enjoyed the feelings of wildness in the cemetery, the voice inside of her head prodded.

Nonsense, Barbie told herself. She was sloshed, that's all. There was no voice inside of her head. Darin couldn't get in there. He was too darned big.

The abandon. The scent of damp grass in the night, the voice suggested.

Okay. Okay. His suggestions were correct. As incongruous as it might seem for a high school teacher with a normal life, she had enjoyed all those things. She suddenly craved adventure, just as she craved the safety of Darin Russell's arms.

Well, not safety, exactly, she amended. There was danger in Darin's embrace, as well as the hint of comfort. There was danger in investigating a magnetism like this between strangers who hadn't even exchanged two hundred words, total.

"It's a question of addition," she said aloud, without realizing it.

"Adding up to what, Barbie?"

"Four letters."

"What do those letters spell?"

"Lust."

Of course, she wasn't so tipsy that she didn't recognize the word and the ramifications of her admission.

"Full-on lust," she repeated. "Pure animal magnetism. *Woof*."

Behind Darin's expression lay a sense of urgency that caused the air in the room to electrify. The music became a distant hum. The tables melted away.

"Come, my lovely Barbie doll," he urged, his mouth brushing along her hairline in a way that made Barbie's hips undulate. "The food will be waiting by the time we get outside."

"Food?" Lordy, Barbie wanted to *be* the food. She had made a joke about it earlier, and now might get her wish. They were going outside. They were leaving the crowd, going someplace private.

Taboo!

She was weakening!

She was drunk!

Darin was still staring. Could he read her mind, her thoughts? *Really* read them? Wasn't that a flaw? Extrasensory perception was a drawback, right? A huge advantage for him? Could this be fair?

"Then what?" Barbie asked, barely managing the question, since her nipples were straining against Darin's jacket in a way that made her gasp through partially parted lips: "What will we do when we get outside?"

"I thought we might start by breaking some rules," Darin said.

Rule breakage! Although her legs were weak, Barbie nonetheless wanted to shout, *Bring it on!* Not Rebel Barbie. Not Seduction Barbie or Adventure Barbie, either. This was Ms. Barbie Bradley, teacher. This was what her very soul wanted. It all seemed so shocking. So promising. Yes. She longed for this. She wanted to be his dessert.

Turning precariously, Barbie wobbled a first step. Darin had a firm hold of her elbow. Willing herself to keep it together—and to maintain some distance between herself and this man, even if measured in millimeters, at least until they were free of the restaurant—Barbie made for the door.

Yes, she had to retain some dignity here, even if she was about to become part of her date's meal. Even if the Barbie Bradley she had always known and liked was, just this once, taking a vacation from mental acuity.

Good thing Angie isn't here, she thought as she passed between the other tables. Good thing no one knew about this potential moral slippage. Good thing she was slightly sloshed.

And just for the record, *Yo-frigging-ho*.

Chapter Fifteen

Darin, Graveyard Guy, police department consultant . . . had a Porsche. A black Porsche tricked out with darkly tinted windows and a Blaupunkt stereo system, though there was no sound at the moment. The Porsche's dashboard appeared to have every single gadget known to man, all of them shining in various hues of bright. The car's interior was tan, pliant leather—with a surprising couple of slasher-style rips on the passenger seat. Barbie was not too sloshed to notice this.

"What happened to the up . . . up . . . upholstery?" she asked, head lolling back as the Gypsy valet shut her door behind her and Darin slid into the car.

He'd had to have had a lot of dinners at that restaurant. His Porsche had been kept in a special garage in the back alley. A porte cochere led from the restaurant to the garage so that he wouldn't get wet if it rained. Those were definite perks.

Also, Barbie noticed, moving her right foot around, there were no S-and-M shackles obvious in the Porsche. Noting this, she relaxed a bit more as Darin eased the car into gear and maneuvered it onto the street. The vehicle purred like a tiger as he stepped on the gas.

"The rips?" Barbie repeated, unable to hold her head upright while driving at Mach 2 and having ingested a bottle of wine.

"Dog," Darin said, both hands curled tightly around the steering wheel.

"Shame," Barbie said. This earned her an affectionate if fleeting smile from the hunk. Not merely pleased, but truly affectionate.

The drive took no time. Although Barbie had a bit of trouble emerging from the sporty, low-built car in her tight skirt without flashing Darin royally, she managed. Still woozy and teetering slightly, she flinched when he again took hold of her arm.

Zing! Another lightning bolt of lust struck her nether regions, and from nothing more than his helpful hold, as if elbows now were directly connected to the body parts below. So, Barbie wondered, approaching her apartment building, what would happen if Darin wanted a good-night kiss? If a touch to an upper extremity was this good, what might happen when their lips met? Who knew how the gods of attraction might react? How did you one-up a *zing*?

Or, what if he didn't try for a kiss? Well, she would fix that. Hormones were in motion. There was no stopping hormones.

Darin's lusciously musky scent filled her nostrils as they entered her apartment building hallway. If he smelled this good, Barbie just knew he'd taste even better.

They were beside her front door in no time, Darin's exotic eyes shining like night-lights focused on her. *Zing!* And right on the tail end of the zing, as if surfing the afterburn, came a sudden and unwelcome remembrance of Rule One.

Rule One on the list of rules governing dating behavior stated firmly that first dates should be left at the door. *Outside* of it. As Barbie now recalled with a wince, this rule had three exclamation points after it in every book she'd ever seen. The information this rule was trying to get across? Don't be easy. Translation, don't act like a slut, even if you are or have ever desired to be one. Practice discipline.

But this rule, Barbie thought, grasping for straws of exemption, had obviously never encountered female hormones on the rampage. This rule, Barbie decided, did not take into consideration the fact that things had changed in the last several decades. But darn it all if Rule One didn't conjure up the fact that there must be a Rule Two.

Rule Two. Rule Two. Geez, what was Rule Two? How could she think, when Darin was looking at her that way? As if he'd devour her when she said the word, and maybe even if she didn't. Could it be the damned rules worked best in dousing the flames of sexual desire through the mere act of trying to remember them?

Nibble away! her hormones were shouting. *Go to it, Darin! Nibble away!*

Rule Two . . . Oh, just make one up! Rule Two (creative, if not actual): if your date is a true gentleman, he will leave you with the doggie bag.

There. Not so serious. Not involving hormone and testosterone levels, either. She'd sidestepped a land mine. Darin had suggested breaking some rules, so let them get to that. Rule breakage, mouth to mouth. Or, oh God, Barbie thought now, unable to keep her thoughts from evolving, maybe his plan to break rules meant that *he* would take the doggie bag? The rat!

Then again, maybe Darin's promise of rule breakage actually meant what she'd first thought it might mean. Rule breakage as in sharing other things. Sheets, for instance.

With a hand to the wall for support, Barbie faltered. She'd gotten mentally to sheets, and she didn't know this guy at all. She needed more information. For example, did he have parents in the area? Siblings? Did he have an apartment, or live—again, *euw*—in Forest Lawn graveyard somewhere? Was his dog, the one that had ripped his leather seats, a Yorkie or a German Shepherd?

The thought of Darin with a Yorkie made her laugh out loud. This, in turn, got her another puzzled look and a brief grin from her chiseled-featured fantasy date. *Zing!* Another lightning strike, straight as an arrow, caused panty moistness and obliteration of the rule-book pages now flipping through Barbie's head.

"You okay?" Darin asked.

"Sure. You?" Barbie replied. Okay, if she hadn't ever jumped into bed with a stranger, there was always a first time, right? No one could be in charge of their needs all the time, could they? She wanted this, didn't she?

"Barbie?" Darin said, his voice wreaking havoc with her equilibrium. "Keys?"

Barbie handed him her purse, reminding herself that beauty wasn't everything. Some people thought snakes were beautiful, but look what damage a fang could do. Darin was downright beautiful, all right. And though his face seemed to swim in and out of focus, she was almost completely sure there were no fangs.

As for her own darned self, everything seemed to be swimming and shaking, even Darin's hand as he held up her key. He missed the lock a couple of times before finding the slot, leaving Barbie to hope he'd be better at sticking things into small spaces later.

Weeks later.

Her door opened. Darin waited for her to cross the threshold. *Trip* across the threshold, actually. He waited in the hallway until she grinned at him over her shoulder. Apparently assuming it was a come-hither invitation, he followed her inside.

So it *had* been a come-hither invitation. What of it?

Fine. She had obliterated Rule One. So? There was little possibility the guy was a vampire or anything. It was no big deal to have him in her apartment. Not necessarily.

A tinkling sound came from behind. Darin had dropped her keys onto the table by the door, as she herself always did. He went into the kitchen and placed the doggie bag in the refrigerator, following her new Rule Two to the letter.

Circling back from the kitchen, Darin stopped Barbie when she went for the light switch. Catching her hand in his, he pulled her gently to him. Not too close, not too many touching parts. No great cause for concern yet.

Hardly any light penetrated her closed window blinds, merely enough to see that they had plenty of clothes still between them. All sheets remained in the bedroom. She was safe.

"The place has a fragrance," Darin whispered, his mouth close to hers, his demeanor slightly antsy, it seemed to Barbie. Tense. "A strangely sweet fragrance."

"Oreo," Barbie said.

"What?"

"Chocolate, sugar, cocoa."

"The smell is strong."

"The people who make Oreo cookies know how to hook everyone. Everyone with a chocolate fetish, anyway. Those little round things are quite intoxicating once you get a sniff and a taste. Don't tell me you've never had one?"

Darin's mass of dark hair fell across his face when he shook his head, but not before it had feathered downward over Barbie's cheek. She was sure she would pass right out of this world if he continued with that.

"Are you going to kiss me?" she asked hopefully, lips already at the starting line, her motor revving.

"No kiss," Darin replied.

Her engine sputtered. "Why not?"

"Rushing things a bit, don't you think?"

"Right," Barbie agreed reluctantly. "We have to get to know each other better before kissing." But why was that, exactly? she silently wanted to know.

Her date put a few more inches between them. Barbie didn't need to touch him to feel the now-familiar sizzle radiating through and around their bodies. It felt like the summer sun on wet pavement.

"We'll have plenty of time for getting to know each other better," Darin said.

"Yes, and after Rules One through Ten are broken, then what?" she murmured.

"Rules?" Darin queried.

"Some people live by them."

"Ah." Darin nodded. "In that case, after Ten we'll progress to Eleven."

Barbie felt her date's body twitch and took this for a sign of shared sexual tension. She cuddled up closer to the studly male, her mouth raised as if to find his. No more time-wasting, she was thinking. She wanted to find out what the kiss would be like. She wanted to find out what it would be like *now*, to see if there would even be a future.

Darin obliged. Lips to lips. Mouth to mouth. Followed immediately by fireworks that blasted away at the inside of the apartment. The darkness behind Barbie's closed eyelids vanished. This small meeting of their bodies had all the subtlety of an atomic blast. They both groaned at the same time.

Darin's mouth was lush, expert. No huge surprise there. The kiss was rich, mind-numbing, state altering, and better than chocolate. His kiss was adroit, sublime, like a flash of insight—a green flash, outlined in auburn and studded with stars. Hundreds of stars. Millions of stars. So many stars that

Barbie was pretty sure they must have gotten to Rule Eleven already.

Soaring through these sensations, fueled by the wine she had ingested, Barbie was helpless to resist the ministrations of Darin's lips. She didn't even pretend to be offended by the deep, drowning feeling that overcame her in his arms. She didn't try to pull away. Dessert had been served. She was enjoying being devoured.

Her mouth moved with his, countered his, accepted his, even as she wondered fleetingly what kind of a man would never have tried an Oreo. Her body shuddered continually. More moistness gathered between her thighs. Chills crashed over her with the intensity of a tsunami, except that this tsunami wasn't water, but wind. She not only saw stars, she felt the wind on her face and in her hair. She smelled the greenery of the cemetery, tasted it in her mouth, and felt the abandon of running shoeless, damp grass beneath her feet.

Weird. Exquisite. Absolutely wonderful.

So wonderful, in fact, that Barbie was sure part of her was separating at the seams. Concentration seemed a thing of the past. She wanted to shout as Darin's fingers moved up through the hair at the nape of her neck. *Zing! Clang! Omigosh!* Yet those sounds and inner cries no longer did justice to the moment. Darin's closeness called to attention every inch of Barbie's body, every single cell. His touch electrified all.

Their essences clashed. Steam billowed. Absurd, but true, Barbie realized in a second of perfect clarity: this was the first real kiss she'd ever had.

The realization fled. Darin's embrace tightened. The kiss she and Darin shared intensified. Yes, even perfection had room for improvement, it seemed, as Rules Eleven though Fourteen passed before Barbie's closed eyes—the ones about clothes in heaps on the floor, naked limbs entangled, and taking this guy home to meet her parents. Then there were the ones regarding breakfast in bed on Sundays, dual soaks in the tub, with bubbles, and long walks, hand in hand, through the . . . graveyard?

This was her final thought before Darin took his mouth back in a separation so untimely that Barbie uttered a whimper of protest. However, her date did not flee. Oh, no. His arms slipped beneath her and, reminiscent of a hero in a nineteenth-century novel, he lifted her high off the ground, off her feet. Not like a sack of potatoes this time, yet definitely uncivilized. A whole lot of insinuation was packed into this move, punctuated by the sound of her shoes hitting the hardwood floor.

"No sack-of-potatoes thing?" Barbie asked breathlessly, eyes locked to Darin's in the semidark, her arms closing around his perfectly defined shoulders. Shoulders that were actually *rippling*.

"I've never thought of doing to a sack of potatoes what I'm thinking of doing to you," Darin replied.

Heartthrob! Stud King!

"What are you thinking of doing with me?" It was a silly question, Barbie realized, though the answer was of the utmost importance.

"Bending all those rules in half," Darin growled.

"How?"

"By taking you to bed."

"My bed?"

"Assuming you have one."

Barbie could hardly draw breath. "Then what?"

"Then I'll tuck you—"

"What?"

"Then I'll tuck you in."

"With a *T*?" Barbie laughed, giddiness morphing into euphoria. Surely what Darin meant was that the tucking would come after all the rule bending. After they did the thing that *rhymed* with tucking. She had no doubts that Darin, so adept at kissing, would know a thing or two about the finer art of . . . tucking.

"Not tonight," Darin whispered as though he could read her mind.

"Not . . . ?"

"Tonight."

"I have no idea what you mean, Darin."

"I think you do."

"No . . . untucking?" she asked quietly.

"No taking this all the way."

All the way? Had he said "all the way"? Barbie hadn't heard that particular phrase since the old seventies TV shows. She hadn't actually known what it meant until college, but now that the major question facing them was in the open, Barbie wondered why. Why no untucking or tucking? Why wouldn't they go all the way?

"Do not rebel, my lovely Barbie," Darin urged with the singsong of a Shakespearean sonnet. "It's for your own good that I'm making this stand."

What? He was making a stand? Without asking her? Wasn't the woman supposed to decide whether or not to halt a perfectly good mauling? What right did the man have to do so, chivalrous intentions or not?

"But you want to, don't you?" Barbie said.

"You have no idea how much." Darin shook his head. "There is no rush. This feeling won't go away. It's just that now is not the best time to—"

He carried Barbie to the bedroom, leaving his unfinished sentence in the hall. He had no difficulty finding his way, as there were only four rooms in the entire apartment. So there they were, in near-complete darkness, in her apartment, in her boudoir. On date one. This should have been scary. Instead, the night felt to Barbie like a howling success. Graveyard Guy had swept her off her feet—again.

Uncivilized? Hooray for uncivilized.

For reasons best left unexplored at the moment, she simply couldn't resist this guy. One kiss wasn't enough. Tucking wouldn't be enough. After glasses and glasses of wine, she'd had some sort of breakthrough.

"If you're leaving, why are you carrying me?" she asked. "More particularly, why are you carrying me into my bedroom?"

"I didn't say I was leaving," he replied.

What might have been a clap of thunder was in actuality the turnover of Barbie's heart in her throat. Then again, it could have been the building collapsing. She wasn't sure.

"You're not leaving?" Was that her voice, up an octave?

"Not yet."

"But we aren't going to—"

"Plenty of other things to do, if one has time and imagination."

Other things? A peal of thunder crashed down low in Barbie's body, somewhere near her baby blue lace thong.

"Unless you object," Darin said.

Object? Was he kidding? "Well, I . . ." *Come on girl, finish a darned thought.* They were closing in on the mattress.

"I won't hurt you, Barbie," Darin whispered to her. "Ever."

The fact that a lot of guys with women in their snares had no doubt uttered this very same sentiment while trying to get into lacy panties was not lost on Barbie. But *ever* was the word he had used. This man had used the E-word.

He carefully laid Barbie down on her pink satin comforter so that her head rested on familiar, lavender-scented pillows. Distant illumination from a tiny night-light in the hall cast a faint shadow over the bedroom rug. The dial on

Barbie's retro pink princess phone radiated with a mild fluorescent glow. Otherwise, the room lay in total darkness.

Darin's hands squished the pillows on either side of Barbie's head. He was standing, leaning over her. His breath, as he sighed, reached her cheek.

"Bedroom," Barbie said, wondering if he would kiss her again, this man, this Braveheart, this stallion who didn't really seem so out of place here in the dark. All that maleness in her ten-by-twelve-foot pink boudoir. All his energy contained.

"Yes. Bedroom," Darin said.

No kiss came. What seemed like eons passed before Barbie again encountered his touch, and then it was his fingers, not his mouth. They skimmed the front of her body, truly like a Braille reading, hesitating on the buttons of her blue silk jacket.

Fearing to move, Barbie held her breath. As she pondered what "not going all the way" might mean, in light of him having his hands on her buttons, she heard in the distance the muffled strains of her cell phone.

Darin started to unbutton her jacket. They were very small buttons. Bach was chortling out a tune in the living room. Old Bachster was ruining the moment. *Bad timing, Angie! Damn the rescue call!*

Darin was at button number two, over her breasts, but who was counting?

Barbie turned her head from side to side on the pillows. Unable to see Darin, she could only feel what he was doing, and she thought she might go mad with it all.

Darin had reached button three.

The moment was over-the-top erotic. She had wanted this all along. She had forsaken the rules and willed Darin into this. Now, her lungs burned from withheld breath. Her breasts strained toward his hands. Her mind reeled from wine, excitement, and a lack of necessary oxygen.

And Darin was at button four. Out of six.

But that darned Bach was a persistent so-and-so. This was so not a Bach moment. Not an Angie moment. So *not*.

Button five. Button six. Darin had mastered the jacket. He slowly separated the silk from her skin, pressing the fabric open. The air in the room felt cool on her chest in comparison to Darin's volcanic heat. Oh sweet heavens! There was nothing left for him to deal with now, at least on her torso, except the thinnest of camisoles, the faintest of barriers. What would he do? What would he touch?

Tomorrow, Barbie vowed, her mind swirling, chest heaving, as she waited for what was to come. Tomorrow, she'd change that damned cell phone ringtone to something more appropriate. Something in honor of Darin.

"Disco Inferno."

Chapter Sixteen

Burn, baby, burn! She was a Barbie doll going up in flames. The flames of anticipation. Was that plastic she smelled?

Whatever Darin was doing, it should have been illegal. His hands were gliding down the front of her lace-trimmed black cami, exploring, mapping, touching. Lightly, barely, almost, not quite. There was nothing about this in the rules.

Barbie's feeling was one of frivolity. Otherwordliness. Powerlessness. Pleasure slipped in and out of focus as she labored to think. Was she enjoying this? Yes, absolutely. *Should* she be enjoying this?

Darin slipped her arms from the jacket. Deftly. Carefully. His lips, so warm and utterly fascinating, rested not on her mouth but on her right wrist. Like a moth across a watery surface, his long hair flitted over the naked flesh of her forearm. The tickle of his hair followed the slow upward drag of his lips.

Zing! Crash! Bam!

The glow inside of Barbie was raging fast and furious now, spurred on by the movement of Darin's mouth, her hyperactive nerve endings, and plain old curiosity. It was probably a good thing her mind had taken a holiday. She thought she might be glowing.

Darin's magnificent mouth brushed across her right biceps, never actually landing. Barbie undulated all over. Oh, she knew her anatomy and physiology all right, enough to know with certainty that he was a long distance from where "all the way" began and ended. Yet each touch in the dark reminded her of what all the way might feel like. The sheer ecstasy of a good tucking was, seemingly, a universe unto itself.

Who was breathing so loudly? Her? Darin? Why did her chest rise and fall with effort now, as though the Angel of First Date Tucking might be sitting on it?

Lips! On her shoulder! Soft. Caressing. Moving on, Darin took a detour with a sensual, slow, drawn-out trail of his mouth, alternating with little kisses across her collarbone to where her satiny camisole strap lay loosely against her skin.

A brief kiss to the strap, then the tip of Darin's tongue drew a circular pattern at the crown of her shoulder, almost like a plane coming in for a landing. He took some skin between his lips and sucked lightly, then he bit down gently with his teeth. He repeated this process on a downward angle. Lips, teeth, tongue, suck.

"God," Barbie groaned, reaching for him. This was absolutely too much to bear. Could she have interpreted Darin incorrectly? Could all the way have meant marriage instead of sex? Because this was sex. Really good sex. They were starting it, or her initials weren't *BB*.

He caught her hands before they touched him, raking her again with his nails as he held them both in one of his, against the bed. Being ravished without being able to participate was the pits.

"You are *gooood*," Barbie sputtered.

"Yes, well, your four glasses of wine helped," Darin teased, his voice as dark as chocolate chunk.

"You were counting?" Barbie asked.

"Nope."

"I'm drunk now? I could be dreaming in a drunken stupor?"

"I prefer to think you're under my spell."

"Love spells are not acceptable on first dates. Definitely no love spells," she muttered.

"What about more kissing?"

"Will tongues be involved?"

"Is there any other kind?"

He had her there. Barbie was pretty sure there was no other kind. No other kind that she wanted with him, at least. In for a penny, in for a pound.

"Kissing leads to other things," she noted breathlessly.

"Yes. Maybe even second dates," Darin agreed.

"Sometimes not," Barbie pointed out.

"I don't think that'll be the case here, do you?" This was said with his hair tickling her neck.

"No?" she replied faintly, her body pulsing on the comforter, chills zooming in all directions, most of them heading south.

Darin's mouth came to rest on her collarbone. Though Barbie couldn't see his face, she imagined those dangerous eyes looking at her. Those double-ringed, two-colored, animalistic eyes. She wanted to purr in response.

"You like this?" Darin's voice was barely recognizable, raw with what must have been submerged passion. Or maybe it was just muffled with a mouthful of her quivering self? He must have tilted his head; more of his hair teased her cheek.

"I . . . Tongues. No. First date." She barely got that out, lost as she was in pleasure.

Darin's face came close to hers. After several seconds of hesitation, he laid a kiss on her chin, followed by a kiss to her nose. Then he hovered, Barbie knew, above her parted lips. Even in nearly total darkness, without the use of sight or her hands, she felt his predatory looming.

"No love spells. No tongues? What do you allow?" Darin asked, his mouth resting on hers for a couple of seconds. But then he backed off. The bed vibrated—swear to God, like one of the beds in those old movies, in old motels where you put in a quarter and rode the wild sheets.

Was her body making all this commotion? Barbie wondered. Was his? She couldn't seem to stay still. She could hear his labored breathing.

"Talk . . . to me," Darin requested. "Please."

Talk? She could do that.

"I allow dinner, movies, shopping," she said, twisting her hands still held in his easy grip, needing to wrap her arms around his shoulders, do some feeling around of her own. But, no. Darin held her back.

"I like guys who aren't afraid to shop," she added, all in one long stream of air.

Darin cleared his throat and maintained a bit of distance. "Have you ever found any guys who like to shop?"

"Do you see a wedding ring on my finger? Because that would be a guy worth keeping."

Shoot. Nothing like a little mention of the M-word to spoil the mood, Barbie thought right after.

Darin said, "That's a test you give guys who want to date you? Dinner, a movie, and shopping?"

"Sure. Shows who has relationship potential."

"We had dinner," Darin said.

"I beg to differ. We ate pretty much nothing. You plied me with wine."

Barbie made a direct prayer to the sex gods. Would Darin for Pete's sake nibble her some more, please? Turned out those gods must have been busy elsewhere. No nibbles came.

A few heartbeats of silence passed, and then the tickle and tease of Darin's hair returned to drag silkily downward, pausing, Barbie felt, just above her nipples.

He planted a kiss dead center on her sternum, equidistant from both breasts, and it might as well have been her G-spot. Skin exploding with heat and surprise, Barbie sprang from the pillows uttering a yip. Her entire body was quivering.

"Do you mean to say that tonight doesn't even count as a first date, since we didn't get to finish dinner?" Darin asked, allowing her to slowly settle back to the pillows.

Barbie nodded halfheartedly. A seismic pulse shot down through her thighs as she tried hard to restrain herself from flopping all over the bed in anticipation of his next move. A funny feeling had risen deep inside—a new feeling, not really so funny at all, more like a submerged promise. A bigger something was about to happen. She rode out the rising new sensation with her eyes closed.

"It's no first date," he clarified, "even though I was gentlemanly enough to bring you home, to forego taking advantage of you in your rather sozzled state? No credit for that?"

Unsure how to answer, since he was in her bedroom with his hair and hands all over her, and given the fact that she was quivering with expectation, Barbie withheld comment. None of this really mattered, after all. In this particular game there could be no loser. If this were to be a one-night stand, so be it. Patterns like lifelong periods without sex or Gypsies were eventually meant to be broken. Virgins weren't supposed to remain virgins. Right?

"Well," Darin said, voice deep, serious, and deliriously sexy, "we'll have to fix everything with the next date, won't we?"

Barbie squeezed her eyes tighter, said, "There will be another one?"

"Is there any doubt?"

Fortified, she changed tack. "Second dates involve movies." Man. She was pushing things a bit, but she decided to play on, see what happened. Give herself time to get her breath back.

"What about tongues?" Darin asked.

"I'm not sure about French kisses on a second date," she admitted.

His voice was firm. "Your only option for tongues, sweet Barbie, is the first or second. You decide."

"Okay. Second. Maybe." Hadn't they done tongues already? If not, God almighty, what else could he do with his?

A possible answer to this question brought her upright, gasping. A thrumming had started in that deep place inside, unignorable.

"Do you always postpone the inevitable?" Darin asked.

"I've never been confronted with an inevitable quite like this," Barbie replied. It was true, too. No man had ever made her feel this way, all lusty and discombobulated. Certainly not Liar Bill, with whom she'd allowed no tongues or anything else. But then, Bill's tongue had been forked. A man had to earn tongue time, and then know what to do with it.

Also, no other man had set foot inside her apartment, let alone her bedroom. Her *bedroom*, as in her sanctuary, the room with her bed in it, had always been a place reserved for "the one."

After tonight, she'd never be able to say that again. After all, it was her body, her bedroom, her dream date, and her decision whether or not to abide by the silly set of rules she'd had heaped upon her by her parents. Guilt and rule books be damned—French kissing was very nice indeed. Sex, she was fairly certain, would be even nicer.

She wondered if her mom, Brenda Bradley, had abided by these same dating guidelines. Maybe even after one milkshake too many at the soda fountain, her mother had indeed left her father at the front door. Then again, they were Boomers. There was no explaining this cultural phenomenon. And though Barbie knew her mother had the temperament for fending off suitors, she doubted very much that her father would have put up with such antics for long. He was a so-called man's man whose idea of a hero was James Bond. Adventure Barbie had to have gotten those genes from somewhere, even if only in minuscule amounts. Most likely they were from good old Dad.

When you came right down to it, the whole idea of dating rules was to protect a woman's virtue. A woman who wanted her virtue protected, that is. She'd taken heed of the fact that there had been no Easy Barbies on the toy store shelves. Nor were there Unvirtuous Barbies.

Come to think of it, Mattel didn't have a Wedding Barbie, either. Not one. It had always been *Dream* Wedding Barbie. The white gowns, bridal veils, and tiaras had all been *dreamed* by Snoozing Barbie. By Bridesmaid Barbie. No, there was no wedded bliss for Barbie and Ken, because everyone, especially little girls who knew no better until puberty, and sometimes not even then, figured the fun was in the chase.

Or maybe it was because neither toy Barbie nor toy Ken actually had the sexual parts, aka genitalia, with which to fulfill a wedding-night consummation.

Well, boy, *this* Barbie sure had the right parts. All those parts were humming and shimmying with thoughts of Darin. They were wondering what a really good orgasm might feel like, and assuming Darin could help them find out.

Yet . . .

Now that Darin's incredible hands and mesmerizing lips were again motionless, some of her mother's comments, the old thoughts and values, fought for elbow room. Most notably, *The fun is in the chase.* The chase. As in close, but no cigar. As in fool around, but don't *be* a fool if you want a man to stay interested.

Barbie's eyes fluttered open. Cripes! Could this be true? If it were, was she making a mistake? Would Darin turn out to have staying power? Would he be an exception to the old saying? If she rolled with this, gave in to what she was feeling inside, would he spend the night *after*? Would he call her tomorrow to say how good it was for him? To ask her which jeweler she preferred? Surely *all* the fun wasn't in the chase.

Her brain suddenly hurt. The roiling internal sensations of lust dimmed, still unexplored and untapped. Barbie wanted to scream, shout, whimper. The lull between Darin's touches was akin to sabotage. Trying to stop thoughts of virtue and strategy once they'd zigzagged into the mind took a concentration she didn't possess at the moment. It could be that she had never possessed such concentration.

The spigot, once open, opened farther. Questions arose. *How much money does a graveyard-keeper make? How can he afford that Porsche? What about being a part-time consultant for the Miami PD? Is that job dangerous? Does Darin have his own apartment? Does he ever wear jeans with a hole in one knee? Does a graveyard keeper have to spend a lot of time with dead people?*

All this mental jumble was a prime example of Barbie Bradley, overintellectualizer. Barbie Bradley, twenty-something and never been pursued properly. Barbie Bradley, with nary an orgasm in sight, since *tucking* actually started with a *T*. Thoughts. Thoughts. Bridesmaid Barbie. Bridesmaid Barbie. It was enough to make a girl insane!

And damn, she'd lost track of Darin again. Was he waiting for the go-ahead? The green light? Permission to go in for the kill?

Heck, she wanted those unmentionable things he might do with her, *to* her. The bed was still shaking. Her body was atwitter with hopefulness. She liked the licking stuff—his tongue on her bare skin, his mouth dragging over her teasingly. She liked it a lot. And while this would be a problem for a girl with rules governing her behavior, girls who listened to their mothers . . . Her own mother would say that there could be only one acceptable word for girls who took a licking and kept on ticking: *engaged*. Thank heavens her mother wasn't there!

The mattress squeaked beneath Darin's weight as he sat heavily on the edge of the bed. His hand, on hers, had started to shake big-time. He was shaking all over, as a matter of fact. He was shakier than she was. All revved up and ready to go?

His voice sounded weaker than before, as if he had to force it out. "Barbie, I have to tell you something," he said.

"You'll take me to a movie?" she guessed hopefully, not wanting any bad news, afraid there might be some.

"Yes, a movie. There's something else."

"Shopping?"

"I . . ." Darin trailed off, then picked up again. "Shopping, too."

"Really?" Barbie pushed up on her elbows, slightly dazed, feeling the possible return of her internal buzzing.

"I need to tell you . . ." Darin stopped again, throat filled with an audible rawness, as if something was stuck there.

"Tell me what?" Barbie's scalp prickled in anticipation. Would he tell her he had no condom? Would he ask if she was on the Pill? Would he tell her he was actually engaged to somebody else? Or—oh crap—that he is genitalless, like Ken?

Darin's finger rested on her lip to keep her from speaking, then immediately retreated. He said, "First I'd like to know why you think shopping allows you to know another person better."

Nothing about contraception. Nothing about Ken. Hooray!

"Barbie?" Darin whispered.

"It's a girl thing, Darin."

"I'd like to know."

"It has to do with a person's ability to give and take, more than the actual act. If a man agrees to do something so against his natural compulsions for the sake of the woman he's dating, it's a compromise. A man who will compromise has relationship potential."

"Tough test," Darin said.

"Yes. I'm sorry."

"I prefer my way."

Barbie drew her legs a little closer by bending her knees. "Tongues and lips on skin is fast, a jump-right-in-there method of testing, I suppose," she admitted. "Though, don't you think that dinner, movies, and shopping are less complicated ways to get to know someone? Lots of opportunities to talk."

The more Barbie thought about it, the more she realized that talking would be listed right up front in the rule book as a never-do if one is about to—or hoping to—have sex with a guy. And she *wanted* sex with this guy. What complicated matters were those two little bothersome words: *Bridesmaid Barbie.*

Fickle, that's what she was. Totally and utterly fickle. She should shut up. She should make a decision. She should rise up and kiss Darin, rip his jacket off and see what lay beneath those togs, if sex were truly a goal. If she had her hands free . . . would she actually go through with it?

There was a 50 percent chance there would be another date, no matter what they did or didn't do. There was a chance there might be a relationship après the deed of tucking. The odds were fifty-fifty that he'd call back tomorrow.

And fifty-fifty not.

Her dilemma. Did Darin get it?

The bed squeaked as she fell backward, but she bounced right back up again. Wait just a darned minute! Hadn't *he* started all the talking? Hadn't *he* asked *her* to talk to him? Why would he do that if they both knew talking tended to ruin a perfectly good sexual moment? Maybe he truly wasn't planning on having one?

She said tentatively, "So, tell me how you decide if you want to see a person again." *And please want to see me.*

"Tactile sensations," Darin whispered, sounding as if his voice were coming from inside a long tunnel. "Taste. Smell. Feel."

"Yes, but that's too quick, Darin. Scratch-and-sniff comes after dinner, movies, and shopping."

She said this teasingly. When Darin took a long moment of silence, she wanted to strangle herself for being so honest. Men had their ways of testing the lay of the land—so to speak—and women had theirs. Somewhere in the middle, hopefully, if the stars were aligned, they met.

Those stars were aligned here, now. Darin dropped his face to hers and kissed her as though there were no tomorrow, with plenty of French and oodles of ardor. Barbie's emotions spun upward, somewhere between an urge to slap him and an urge to wrap her legs around his waist. Some variance. She was still fickle.

Decide, Barbie told herself. You must decide now which it is going to be.

"Close . . . your . . . eyes," Darin sort of barked.

Barbie obeyed, her heart thumping hard and fast. Something was vibrating upon the bed, something very specific this time. It was probably her, in reaction to Darin's closeness, something inside of her that needed attention. Which meant there was no need to flip a coin. Her decision was made. Her body had won. She'd go with the flow.

"Keep . . . your eyes closed, Barbie. Breathe."

Barbie took in some air. Darin kissed her again. Fully, Deeply. Wondrously. Turning up the heat.

Barbie shuddered on the bed in a dance of the senses. Her body pooled with chills, then instantly heated. Hot and steamy. The only thing better, Barbie decided, would be lying beneath that marvelous body of his . . . on date twenty-five.

Oops. She'd forgot. Sooner!

Darin sort of growled. Wasn't that cute? He was fighting to hold himself back. He really did want her!

His mouth was supple and had tasted so darned delicious. His spicy scent was an aphrodisiac. It would be worth the chance there might never be a second date, Barbie told herself, as her lover's sharp nails began to burn across her rib cage through her silk camisole.

"Oh God, oh God," she murmured, sure she would soon get to feel those ripped abs of his directly against hers. With luck, they would both be naked soon. His tactile theory had been a good one. She had folded. Her decision would stand.

Back arching off the mattress, hands fluttering with the urge to tear off Darin's clothes and get a start on everything she'd once eschewed, Barbie smiled.

Oh, and was she levitating?

Darin growled beneath his breath again, and she blew out a long, low sigh. This had to be a spell Darin had cast over her. She simply was not used to handing over her body. She didn't have any more protest left in her.

Darin paused again. He cleared his throat. Maybe to hide a moan?

"The best part is yet to come," he whispered over the snap, crackle, and pop of the sparks going off in Barbie's mind. Tiny hairs all over her body stood on end with the insinuation that anything could be better than his lips on her shoulder or anywhere else.

"I promise," Darin continued, oh so seriously, oh so sexily and earnestly, as Barbie imagined his lips trailing lightly down to find her silk-clad nipple, and the conniptions that would bring.

Best is yet to come? Was that a play on words? Barbie's insides were aching. She reached for him with sheer exuberance this time, her finally freed fingers opening and closing, her body leaning toward him. She wanted to feel Darin. To see him. To experience *everything*.

Her fingers grazed his cheek and chin in the softest of caresses, then veered toward the cord dangling from the Roman shade at the window beside her headboard. She wanted to see him in the moonlight. She heard Darin gasp and utter an oath. She smiled. Had her merest touch driven him as crazy as his touch had driven her?

The bedsprings squeaked again as she grasped the cord and tugged, wanting to let the moonlight in, eager to see the passion on Darin's face. As the shade curled up, she squeezed her eyes shut and struggled to recall his list of selective sensations.

Taste.

Smell.

Feel.

Her selection was made. *Oh yes, God! Let's tuck!*

Chapter Seventeen

The word alone—*tuck!*—set off a bomb in Barbie's gray matter. For a few seconds, as moonlight from the window flooded the bed, she remained perfectly quiet with her eyes squeezed shut. What would Darin's next step be? She felt nothing. Opened her eyes. Saw no one.

"Darin?"

No answer.

"Darin?"

Was that a sound in the distance?

A *door*?

Sitting up too fast, Barbie's head whirled with leftover wine-induced vertigo. Tossing her legs over the side of the bed anyway, she stood by holding the bedside table. She'd had much too much to drink.

"Darin? You there?"

No sound. Odd.

Barbie padded into the hallway, then to the living room, her head still running in spin cycle. But there was no Darin in the living room. No Darin in the bathroom, either. Did this mean there would be no tucking? Was this a big gyp? Where the heck had Darin gone?

The muffled sound of her phone, returning suddenly, shocked Barbie into a shout. Puzzled, wary, then slightly enlightened, she dove for the couch.

"Barbie?" Angie whispered from the other end. "What are you doing answering the phone?"

"What are you doing calling?"

Angie ditched her conspiratorial tone. "Ooh. Are we grumpy? This isn't good. I'm sure this isn't good. Where are you?"

"My apartment." Her voice was flat, petulant. The vertigo was returning. Riotous confusion.

"Alone?"

"It seems so, as of a minute ago."

"Good for you! Stand your ground on the no-sex thing. Or did the guy even have sex potential?"

Barbie fell silent, feeling a sob coming on.

"Who was he?" Angie asked with interest.

"Darin. Russell."

"You make any second date plans?"

"Thing is, I'm not sure."

Barbie got slowly to her feet and tiptoed toward the living-room window. She separated the blinds, peered out. No one out there on the sidewalk. No gypping tease of a guy anywhere in the neighborhood, though she couldn't see the portion of the street directly beneath her window.

"Not sure?" Angie said disbelievingly. "You either made plans or you didn't."

"He said he'd take me to a movie."

Another peek at the street outside. Another big zippo.

"A movie? Really? He agreed to that?" There was lots of interest in Angie's voice now.

"Plus shopping," Barbie added softly.

"Are you serious?"

"He used the E-word, Angie."

A small hesitation. Then an audible gasp. "The E-word? On the first date?"

Well, Barbie mused, it was actually their second meeting, but Angie's question was a valid one. Tonight was, after all, their first actual date. Carting her around a graveyard didn't count. Still, Darin had said he wouldn't harm her tonight or ever. He had stated very clearly that they would have another date. So, what had happened to him?

"He used the E-word? Then what?" Angie wanted to know.

"He left."

Good to do some editing here, Barbie decided. Nothing about deep kisses and longing for licking.

"Before he left, did the movie and shopping date have a day of the week attached?" Angie asked.

"Not really," Barbie replied. "Is that bad?" She knew the sudden lack of Darin was bad even without Angie's two cents. Darin had just up and left. Disappeared. Poof!

"Maybe bad, maybe not," Angie said. "The E-word is a good start, I think."

"There's something else, Angie." Here it comes, Barbie thought. Don't shriek. Don't start shouting, crying, or sounding overly concerned. "He didn't say good-bye when he left."

"Uh-oh."

"Geez, Angie! You used the tone!"

"Well, I suppose there were circumstances for this non-good-bye sayage?"

"Lips on my throat one minute, non-good-byes the next. I think I heard the door close behind him."

"He got to lips on your throat?" Angie sounded flabbergasted.

"Now's not the time, Ang. But yes, he did, so sue me."

"I'm not chastising, Barb, I'm jealous! Been a long time since I had lips on my throat. Now . . . as for why he left.

You didn't have anything weird on your throat—like misplaced food or drool or something?"

"Only a little lotion."

"Good stuff or cheap stuff?"

"Ten dollars a bottle." That would fit Angie's definition of good, surely.

Her friend took a few seconds to think. Then she cleared her throat. "You didn't by any chance, um, accost him with rules while his lips were on your throat?"

"Well . . ."

"Lordy! You didn't! Barb, listen. We need to talk about this."

"Might not be the time for a lecture, Ang," Barbie reminded her. "Some confusion over here."

"Okay. Okay. Don't get your panties in a knot. Well, my thought is that if the guy agreed to a movie, and if he used the E-word, I'd say you had a successful date, plain and simple."

Barbie sighed. "It doesn't feel successful. We'd only barely gotten to scratch-and-sniff."

"What?"

"Never mind."

"Did you say what I thought you said?"

"Probably," Barbie admitted with a wince.

Hesitation, then: "You didn't get to—"

"Nope." *Not quite.*

Angie sighed audibly. After a few moments, probably trying to sound cheerful, she added, "I say he'll call."

"The problem is that he might think he has *E* to do it in, Ang. *E* being *eternity.*"

Angie made sympathetic sounds. "Plenty of other fish in the sea in that case, my friend. It was only one date, after all."

"Damn right. Plenty of fish," Barbie agreed, though she had an inkling none of those fish would be like Darin.

"We are prime fisherwomen," Angie continued. "Adept at hook, line, and sinker."

Not so adept at wine ingestion, though, Barbie thought. Nor in reeling the fish into her bed. It looked like she'd definitely have to work on that.

"Don't worry, Barb," Angie cooed. "Take a bath, eat those leftover Oreos, and get some beauty sleep. Remember in those Harry Potter books when the witchy nurse at Hogwarts gave them all chocolate to ease their minds and—"

"Angie?" Barbie interrupted, her voice quavering. She squeezed her eyes tight.

"—the chocolate made them better? And—"

"Angie!"

"Yeah, Barb?"

"There aren't any leftover Oreos."

Silence. Dead. Thick. Murky. Followed by some heavy breathing on the other end of the line. Then, "Uh-oh. This isn't good, is it?"

Barbie shook her head as much as her vertigo would allow. "I think I'm going to—"

"No! Don't do anything. You hang on, Barb. I'll be over in a half hour. Can you wait half an hour? Hang on until then, okay? Take a shower. A hot shower. No, a cold shower. Definitely cold. Put on your poodle pajamas and drink some milk. Have some cheese. Cheese is almost as good as cookies. Turn on the TV. You're going to be all right. Do you hear me, Barbie? I'll be over as soon as I can!"

"Okay."

Well, Barbie sniffled to herself as she hung up the phone, she might not have Darin, but she did have the doggie bag. That was something, wasn't it? And help was on its way.

Chapter Eighteen

Too late!

Darin, panting on the sidewalk beneath Barbie's window, pressed his back against the warm brick wall. He was out of the moonlight and out of breath, but what did that matter now? Either way, Barbie was safe. Safe from him. Or was it the other way around?

Like the moon, full and lusty in the sky, Barbie Bradley wielded power over him. Being with her, even without direct moonlight on his skin, could definitely bring on the change when he didn't concentrate. Bits of the change, at least. Claws, for one. And a bit of fur on his arms. He'd been right about that. Barbie Bradley, it seemed, was a chip off the old moon.

Miss Bradley would also no doubt be pissed over his not-so-grand exit. Over the lame and (she would believe) inexcusable way he had up and left her. Hell, it *was* inexcusable. Totally. She'd have every right to be angry. He'd have been angry in her place.

Darin pushed his claws into the mortar between the bricks and felt the grinding of his jaws. He tugged at the collar of his shirt and eyed the closest window. No lights in there. Raising the very sharp claw of his index finger, he scratched a heart into the wood of the shutter. He added *BB* and *DR* to the center of the heart. Childish, yes. Destroying her property, admittedly. Still, Barbie might see it and believe it a sign that he cared.

He did care. He cared a lot. Yet for now, he could do nothing more than scratch this bit of graffiti. He was unstable. His insides were liquid, responding to the gravitational pull of the orb in the sky. His outsides had become a suit of rubber, expanding, contracting, never quite completing the shape of what he needed to become. He wouldn't allow it. Not yet. Not fully. It was exhausting trying to hold on when Wolfy was so strong.

One more glance at Barbie's window. One more moment of regret. He was sorry to leave her, sorrier than he had ever been about anything. He couldn't control the slippage, however. He'd tested himself and how far he could go in that apartment, but Barbie had touched him as he feared. Her touch had been . . .

Willpower could only take him so far.

One sharp tear of Barbie's flouncy bedspread with his wayward claws would have been the end. A nightmare. Worse yet, one mistaken nip to her neck or thigh—all in the name of love, of course. But Barbie wouldn't know his fear, and he had to leave her with some hope. As well, in spite of his sorry exit, he himself had to continue to cling to the hope that she would not forsake him for this first faux pas. In no way did he want to frighten Barbie. Not now. Not ever.

He had a few minutes left, he figured, until the change was complete. More than that if he could get away from Barbie and stay out of the moonlight. Long enough to make it back home, anyway. Barely. He had to forget about what he might have missed out on in Barbie's bedroom. He had to bypass thoughts of the anger and hurt Barbie would be feeling. Tomorrow was another day. Tomorrow, in the daylight, he'd call her. He would think of some way to explain this mess. He would plan some way to get her back. He'd offer two shopping sprees. Ten movies. Right after he got back from his scheduled PD gig.

The sound of silk ripping brought him out of thought. Christ! Another shirt was about to bite the dust. How many did that make this year?

Tearing off his coat, shoving up his sleeves, and gouging his forearm in the process with his own claws, Darin thought, Jesus! Claws! What good are they, anyway?

He inched one loafer-clad foot into the cascade of moonlight dripping past the roof of Barbie's building, winced, and drew it back. Without bothering to take the time to look up and down the street for an audience, he gathered himself and made a dash for his Porsche.

His skin began to shift as he reached for the door handle. His heart threw him a double beat that sent him reeling onto the car's shiny black hood. His shirt tore with the sound of an ocean wave hitting shore, and his pants became uncomfortably tight. With a grimace he scrambled off the hood and tried again to open the car door, his head whipping side to side in a perpetual and uncontrollable shake that increased each time he took a breath.

His hair lengthened, hit him in the face. A cough doubled him over. The skin on his face twisted painfully away from the bones and underlying ligaments as he jerked himself upright.

There went the pants, torn open at the seams. He helped the process along, ripping with his fingers and claws until he was free of them. After that, he raised his new, feral face to the heavens.

Okay, Wolf Man, Furball, Hairy-faced Hound, he thought, since he was no longer able to speak, yell, or shout. Get on with it. Enjoy.

A grating sound followed his dive into the Porsche. His claws had trailed across the glossy exterior of the driver side door when he slammed it shut. Wolfy, getting the last dig in. Damn wolf didn't have any manners at all.

Chapter Nineteen

Barbie sat on the floor with an empty cookie package on her lap, pinching the plastic pleats for crumbs, getting madder by the minute. Without the necessary chocolate fix—a girl's (and okay, Harry Potter's) best fix in times of stress or excitement—she wouldn't be able to sleep. She might not even be able to cope!

Although Angie would be on her way soon, she always took the time to beautify before heading anywhere. Beautification took Angie a while, an hour at the very least. Barbie doubted if she could hang on for an hour. Adrenaline was already surging. Her temper had risen dramatically. She shot to her feet.

Hello, Rambo Barbie!

Rambo Barbie wasn't content to sit and look at empty cookie wrappers. Oh, no. Rambo Barbie demanded action. Rash action. What would Rambo Barbie do?

Attack.

The silk camisole, the one Darin had liked, she tossed onto a chair. Donning a pair of old sweatpants and a white T-shirt one size too large, Barbie grabbed her keys, her cell phone, her socks, and her running shoes. She made two last-minute calls. The first was for a taxi, the second, to Angie's answering machine.

"Angie? I know you're in the shower, but get out. Meet me at the graveyard. Last night's graveyard. Wait by the lamppost, and don't get out of the car. Oh, and whatever you do, please don't forget to stop at the mini-mart on your way."

It took a full ten minutes for the cab to arrive. Though Barbie looked closely at the back of the driver's head, this cabbie didn't appear to be the same guy who had delivered her to the Gypsy restaurant. Thus, she couldn't grill him on where he had met Darin, or how Darin had paid. Bummer. She decided that this driver was also slightly intimidating. He wore sunglasses despite its being night and never turned his head when he spoke to her. Kind of creepy, she thought. Still, she was a woman on a mission.

She slammed the car door as she got in.

The cab driver kept talking to a minimum, foregoing any opinions on Barbie's directions. To his credit, he kept his lips buttoned about what he probably supposed was an odd choice for a jogging site. Maybe he assumed she was in search of drugs, and the running shoes were a simple alibi. Cab drivers had most likely seen it all in their checkered careers.

Barbie tipped him generously for the short trip, waved him off, and stood beneath the lamppost where she had dropped her phone number the night before. Then . . . she reevaluated her strategy, which now was cast in an unfavorable light. The night was dark. The time had to be close to midnight. She was alone on the edge of a graveyard, chasing down a defective date.

The inevitable pangs of self-doubt arose. There was a good possibility Darin wouldn't be here. Just because the guy was a graveyard keeper didn't mean he had to *live* in the grave-yard. Silly assumption, dammit. Darin probably had a very nice apartment somewhere close by. Porsche ownership showed a liking for luxury. It also suggested graveyard keeping and part-time police consulting paid better than she would have imagined.

A quick glance over her shoulder to the edges of the dimly lit parking lot produced no Porsche sighting. Nor were there any other cars, for that matter. Maybe a trip to the mini-mart herself would have been a better idea. Plenty of cookies there to take out her frustrations on. Tons of cookies. Shelves of the things. More calories, sure, but the action would have been more reasonable and far less dangerous.

"Hey!" Barbie's voice wasn't loud enough to shout down the disappearing taxi. Its taillights, like animal eyes in the dark, were fading fast into the distance. She was too stunned by her own recklessness to chase the cab on foot.

"Double duh on the darkness," Barbie whispered. "Failing grades for my behavior to date."

She glanced up. The lamp above her head buzzed softly. Bugs were skittering nearby with a connection not lost on her.

Moths to the flame.

"Now I've done it," she ranted, to cover the sound of the bugs suicide-bombing the light. She rotated slowly, sighing. "Not that I've actually ever gotten into trouble. For all intents and purposes, I have always behaved well. Maybe I have a tendency toward temper tantrums, I admit. . . ."

If this were really a temper issue now, Barbie told herself, she'd blame it on the Oreos. Those cookie packages should be larger, with at least a baker's dozen inside. A full thirteen! Spare Oreos were what was needed in today's society, along with more advanced problem-solving skills.

Damn if she really wasn't out here in the parking lot of a cemetery, despite her excuses and the blame-placing. In the dark. Alone. This merited a second sigh. The options, as

Barbie saw them, were to wait for Angie to arrive with proper medication (Oreos), in which case Barbie would have to explain why she was out here, or she could adhere to Rambo Barbie's idea and do what she'd come here to do: seek out Darin Dine-and-Dash Russell.

The prospect of facing Angie was daunting. Scary. Since Barbie hadn't told Angie about the meeting with Darin in the cemetery, hadn't even admitted to knowing the voice on the answering machine when pressed, no possible explanation on the planet would appease her friend when she arrived. There wasn't one single thing Barbie could say to make this right, except maybe, *I'll buy you dinner every week for ten years if you'll forget about this and never mention it again.* Thing was, who could afford all those meals on a teacher's salary?

Still, it really was inescapable: explanations were necessary—end of story. No matter what she did with her time until Angie arrived, she had to come clean. No matter what she did to Darin Russell.

The thought was agonizing. How could things be any worse? Well, for starters, she could listen to Rambo Barbie and make it two for two.

Edging out of the pool of light cast by the streetlamp, Barbie leaned forward as though she really would venture out alone into the darkness. Decision made. Inhaling deeply, winding herself up like a pitcher about to throw a ball and chanting "Hua!" Barbie took off at a sprint across the pavement. Up over the curb she went. Under the Forest Lawn sign, hoping there were no other extraneous party boys in the area. Three hundred rapid heartbeats later, she stood on the spot she thought might be ground zero, abduction central, huffing as if she'd run a marathon.

How to find a person in the dark, in an empty void? Shout for all you're worth.

"Darin!"

After a quick break for air, Barbie tried again. "Hey! Darin! You here?"

Startled crickets hushed for several seconds, then recommenced, rubbing their anorexic legs together in an encore chorus of whatever they had been playing. Sounded like Dvořák.

"Hey! Darin!" Barbie called. "You left something in my apartment." *Me.*

A snapped twig brought Barbie around in a frazzle of nerves. Another snap, and she whirled again. Never particularly good at directions, she lost all sense of where the parking lot was.

"Great."

She had been stupid to think this might work. She'd deserve Angie's wrath if she ever made it back to the streetlamp alive. Of course, Angie would have cookies and eventually maybe a modicum of sympathy. That was some small solace.

And, wow! There was a light up ahead! She grinned. "Gotcha, you ego buster. You . . . you . . ."

She trotted briskly toward the pinpoint of light, not giving a thought to stray heads or body parts, until something caused a hitch in her gait. A noise. Something digging in soft dirt? An animal? Coyotes? Wolves? Big dogs gone astray? Think *Hound of the Baskervilles*. There were also movies about grave robbers after gold fillings and wedding rings, not to mention certain human organs.

Barbie's feet stopped of their own accord. The puffs of her breath filled the night, joining the sounds of the crickets. The light seemed no closer. The parking lot, hidden out there somewhere, might as well have been on Mars. She was totally screwed! Her parents had once warned her about her temper, and they'd been right. Why hadn't they gotten her some help?

"Darin!" Her shout was fainter this time, less demanding.

Sensing possible disaster, mind looping half with fear, half with adrenaline, Barbie wondered if Angie had gotten her message, if her pal was already out the door in what was going to turn out to be a true rescue mission.

"Loss of will is not acceptable," she muttered to the dark. "Not for a Bradley. Besides Dad's being a judge, my big brothers are defense attorneys. I might have an ancestor or two buried close to where I'm standing. What would they think of a chicken in the family? A big chicken who's afraid of the dark?" She wasn't going to wait around to find out.

Encouraging her feet forward, Barbie scrambled through the brush, heading in the direction of the light. A flashlight would have been handy, she realized, wishing she'd learned her lesson from her last trip to the cemetery. A semiautomatic weapon wouldn't have hurt, either.

Stumbling through a thick, scratchy patch of greenery, she came up on a building so fast that she almost smacked her head on it. Backpedaling, catching herself in time to avoid a fall, she faced the building, pulse pounding.

The building wasn't wide enough or tall enough to be a caretaker's cottage, but was much larger than an outhouse. It stood smack-dab in the center, maybe, of the cemetery. Which meant it was a . . . *crypt*?

Geez. Yes. A crypt. She was so out of there.

Spinning on her heels, digging in with all the rubber left on her running shoes, she made a dash in the opposite direction . . . and belly-flopped over a gravestone.

More noise came from the bushes. Barbie wasn't sure if it was to her right or left as she scrambled onto all fours and then to her feet. There was another near miss, this time involving her left knee and a concrete urn. More cusses. Very unpious.

Bush-rustling sounds came, closer this time. Barbie's heart

leapt out of her chest, beating so rapidly that her neck actually thumped. Someone was there, in the greenery. Someone or some*thing*.

Her voice was strangled as she spoke. "Hello? Darin? You there?"

That's all she got out.

Chapter Twenty

Barbie was broadsided by a hurtling ball of energy that first knocked her to the ground, then socked the air out of her.

"Help!" she shouted when she could breathe. "Help!"

Footsteps sounded, then, "Barbie? What the . . . ? Dog, off! Come!"

The weight on Barbie's chest remained, growing heavier by the second and emitting a ferociously guttural growl.

"Dog! Off!"

The weight lifted. Barbie struggled to her feet, shaking so hard she had quite a time remaining upright.

"Barbie? What are you doing here?"

Darin's voice. Bingo. Thank God. Heaps of relief flooded Barbie, though Darin remained hidden beneath the shelter of some drippy old trees. Swaying slightly, she heard another low growl and turned her head. A blob of darkness crept into the moonlight, an obscenely huge dog. The beast Darin had called off of her. The beast that had likely ripped his Porsche's seats.

She pointed at it. "Does that thing eat people or what?"

"Dog is a Rottweiler," Darin replied. "A guard animal. He's menacing in the dark to strangers, but nice enough when you get to know him."

"You sure?" Barbie's heart continued to pound.

"Reasonably. What are you doing here, Barbie? Are you all right? I left you safe in your apartment."

Dang. Darin's voice registered concern. Barbie suffered a pang of guilt, considering his warnings of the previous night, but she recovered quickly. Why *had* she come all the way out here? So what if he happened to be the first guy she had been interested in for a long while? So what if his proximity made her all rubbery inside? The truth was, he had exited early, shaking her up, thus making this unexpected visit a necessity, because she hadn't gotten the precise time and place of her next date.

Good grief, that excuse was lame, and the only one she had.

Dog, if that's what the thing really was, being hip high and as wide as a compact truck, fussed near her feet. Uncomfortable with this, Barbie took some time to get herself in order.

"You tucked me into bed," she said scornfully. "But you forgot something."

Trying desperately to rekindle the anger she'd felt at being dumped in such a way, Barbie sensed some of that emotion reawaken, albeit in the form of a much smaller flame. An almost nonexistent flame, to be precise.

Darin stood beneath the overhang of a giant tree, branches draped around him. She could see his outline, though little else. It seemed to her that Darin might be keeping about as far from her as he could get.

"You forgot good-byes and good nights," Barbie explained, hands on hips, feet apart. "Perhaps you aren't brushed up on manners, communing out here with all the dead people."

Darin's voice now rang with relief. Maybe disbelief, too. "You came all the way out here for a good-bye?"

"My parents made sure I had social skills."

Darin took a baby step forward. "I mentioned there would

be many more opportunities to get to know each other. I left you safe and sound at home."

"Ah-ha!" Barbie snapped. "How do you know I was . . . sound?"

The moon ducked behind a cloud. Barbie blinked, once again thrown into complete darkness. This wasn't necessarily a bad thing, she told herself, since she had chosen to act like an imbecile and probably looked like one, too. Did she really want to see Darin's expression? No. Did she want him to look carefully at her, dressed in sweats and sweating? Not to mention the fact that if Darin were to come closer, she'd likely make herself an even bigger fool by throwing herself at him.

Then there was Dog.

Hearing a really fierce growl, fearing to move in case the beast had ideas of his own, Barbie fumbled mentally and tried not to whine. "You were there one minute and gone the next. I didn't know what to make of it."

"It was getting late, and harder to leave. You were so very inviting," Darin explained.

Flattery, dammit. Nice flattery. So, maybe she wasn't immune. He'd said she'd been inviting, right? Perhaps Darin's frustrating disappearance had been indeed due to a fear of diminishing self-restraint, and not because of anything she might have said or done. His vanishing act had perhaps been necessary to cover up his own needs, and not due entirely to absentee manners.

In light of these possibilities, Barbie felt truly pathetic.

"You mentioned opportunities to get to know each other," she recalled, figuring it really was too late to worry about appearing more foolish. "You didn't say when." This last bit was barely audible. The anger fled Barbie with a hiss.

"Now who's being persistent?" Darin asked, and Barbie

couldn't tell what kind of emotion backed the question. His voice was again gruff, raw, and raspy. Much like Dog's growl, which was truly menacing and overrode the seconds of silence soon after.

"Nice doggie." Barbie remained as motionless as she could, frozen with her hands on her hips while the dog circled. "It's not what you think, Darin. Not *Fatal Attraction* or anything."

"You came out here only to confirm our next date, at some possible peril to yourself."

"Yes, actually. That, and I was worried about you." Barbie shrugged and offered Darin a weak smile, though he couldn't possibly see it. Don't give in, no matter how asinine it gets, was her new credo. Stand your ground. Keep what's left of your dignity, even if it's nearly undetectable.

And please, God, let this man stay interested.

"So," Darin began thoughtfully, though to Barbie he sounded a trifle ill at ease. "How's two weeks from tonight for the next date?"

Relief was swift but short-lived. Barbie first bit her lower lip to keep from cheering, then backtracked. Two weeks? Not tomorrow night? Not Wednesday or Saturday? Didn't he want to see her right away? How could he wait all that time?

With a second bite of her lower lip, Barbie told herself not to fret, that this would be all right. If Darin could play hardball, she could too. If Darin could play hard to get, she could do it better.

"That sounds fine," she said, evidently forgetting the pact with herself she had just made in favor of game playing. She slapped her head with the palm of one hand. What about hard to get? What about hardball? He was *postponing* her, for Pete's sake! Maybe even humoring her!

"Of course," she immediately amended, "I'll have to check my schedule."

Okay. All those stories about folks and animals digging in graveyards aside, the hole she was digging for herself was now about ten feet deep. She didn't even keep a written schedule. Other than school and Angie, her social life was a wasteland.

"What time?" she heard herself ask. *What time?* Had she really said that? "If I can make it, that is."

"Nine?" Darin suggested, ignoring all her absurdity, at least to her face. He would no doubt later reevaluate this incident, Barbie knew. He might not show up in two weeks or any other time, after this. Fact was, she had come all the way out here at freaking midnight. It was *Fatal Attraction*! She had become Glenn Close.

"How about seven?" Barbie countered. "If I can make it."

"Any special reason for the time change?"

"Nope, just being contrary." *Don't want to appear too easy.*

"Split the difference?" Darin said. "Make it eight?"

"Done. That is, if I—"

"Right. If you can make it." Darin coughed and cleared his throat. "I hope you can make it, Barbie. I do want to see you again. I'd like us to start over. I suppose we have to see a movie?"

"Unless you have something better in mind?"

"I'd like to think I do."

Pitter-pat, there beneath Barbie's rib cage. She fought it by suggesting, "If it involves feeling and any sort of *tucking*, I think a movie would be the way to go."

Darin's laugh rang out, boomeranging hollowly back around through the cemetery's close buildings. Close buildings made of marble. With bodies inside.

The moon stayed hidden, as did Darin, though he had

moved. Barbie saw him as a dark outline against the light-colored marble crypt wall. By the sound of things, Darin's dog was still nosing around the brush next to her. She hoped there wouldn't be any sudden lunges.

"Look. Maybe we can talk about details later," Darin said. "It's very late. I'll walk you back to your car."

This, to Barbie, sounded quite gentlemanly in the face of her rather presumptuous escapade. Yet Darin's tone belied enthusiasm. It sounded as if he really didn't want to walk her anywhere, and might feel obligated.

"I need a minute," he said, keeping back beneath the trees and as much out of sight as was possible, it still seemed to Barbie. "Then I'll say good-bye twice to make up for the one I forgot."

All right, maybe Darin *was* being a nice guy, Barbie reasoned ashamedly. Maybe she should accept some of this blame and tuck her tail between her legs.

"Don't rub it in," she said earnestly. "I can't believe I did this either. Please do walk me back to the parking lot. Angie should be there by now."

"Angie's in the parking lot?" Darin said with audible interest.

"Hopefully. I sent up an SOS."

"Alone? She's alone?"

"Except for me, in a minute."

Darin sounded nervous. "Barbie, can you wait here, for only a moment, without moving? I need to get something."

"You're sure you can find me again?" she asked.

"Positive. I'll leave you Dog for company."

"Gee, thanks."

"Count to sixty, and I'll be back."

"One, two, three, four . . ." Barbie turned around several times in the dark, staring down at the dog. On her third rotation, a hand closed over hers. She nearly collapsed. Dog

let out a bellowing bark of recognition, and in a scene reminiscent of the night before, Darin started off at a jog with
Barbie in tow.

Over the dewy grass they went, then through some bushes
and past gravestones, cutting through the night as though
Darin knew every inch of the place, keeping beneath the
dark alley of trees lining the fence. Darin Russell, keeper of
the grounds, graveyard shift.

Finally, breath sounding irregular as he released Barbie's
hand, Darin stopped beside the big cemetery sign, also partially tree covered. Barbie, for the first time, got a load of
Dog, sitting in a pool of moonlight.

She let out a cry of dismay. Dog had to be truly the
largest four-legged animal she had ever seen. Thick chested,
wide backed, black on top, rust colored underneath, he had
a nubby tail, short downward-pointing ears, and very big
teeth—all of them bared. This was not a dog. This was a
nightmare.

"I can't go any farther," Darin announced suddenly, sur-
prising Barbie. "I'm sorry. There's something I was doing.
Something I have to attend to. Will you be okay now? Is that
Angie's car?"

Angie's car was indeed there, its candy apple–red vintage
form parked right beneath the lamppost. Barbie could see
that the driver side door was open. It didn't take a telescope
to see that Angie wasn't inside.

"She must have gotten tired of waiting for me."

Her statement brought a drawn-out growl from Dog,
which sounded like ghosts shouting from one of those
crypts.

"I told her to wait in the car," Barbie explained, both to
Darin and his dog. "Now I'll have to go and look for her."

"No," Darin said. "It's too late for that."

He whistled, and Dog ran to him. With what looked like

a tight hold on the beast's massive studded collar, Darin glanced at the empty Fiat, to Barbie, then up at the sky with such concentrated attention that Barbie followed his lead and looked up. The clouds were parting overhead. A big moon appeared, fat and silver and dripping light. The crickets again went silent. The clouds flooded back together.

"Spooky," Barbie said. "What's with the crickets?"

"They go quiet to protect themselves," Darin said, "from things that go bump in the night."

Barbie shivered.

"Sort of like you, tripping over that urn," Darin added, chuckling.

Barbie smiled and pressed the hair back from her face. He was teasing her. Surely this was a good sign?

"I'll find Angie," Darin told her. "I'd prefer it if you'd wait in the car. That way I don't have to worry about rounding up both of you."

"Yeah, and you'd give Angie a heart attack for sure. You *do* know that Dog here doesn't look much like a dog, Darin. And you'll be a complete surprise."

Silence . . . then Darin said, "Would Angie have left the keys?"

"Maybe," Barbie answered. "If she were inviting every thief in the area to come and take the car off her hands."

Darin wasn't amused. "It really would be a good idea for you to wait in the car. Dog doesn't like company, I'm afraid."

"I'd rather go with you," she replied. "Heck with Dog."

"Please, Barbie. The car. If the keys are there, start the engine and wait."

Moonlight lit the cemetery sign and highlighted a circular pattern on the ground beneath the tree where Darin stood. Barbie watched him step backward, able to see him now. Gone was the dapper suit and white shirt. Darin now wore a long coat of black fabric that fell to his ankles and hung loosely around him. His feet were encased in a pair of boots. His hair was tousled. His hands were in his pockets. His smile looked wan.

"Keep your cell phone handy in case you're disturbed by anything. You do have your cell phone?" Darin asked.

"No. Yes. Maybe—"

"Do not under any circumstances get out of the car. Do you understand, Barbie? No circumstances. No matter what you see or hear, you are to remain inside the car."

"I—"

"Go. Now. Good night, Barbie." Darin held up a single finger. Then he held up two. "Good night."

Barbie stepped off the curb. Feeling a little silly, she ran as she'd been told. She jumped into Angie's car, reached for the keys . . . and found them missing. *Crap.*

Through the small windshield she could see that no one now stood on the curb beneath the graveyard sign; Darin and his hound had gone in after Angie, losing no time. Funny, he hadn't suggested calling Angie on her cell phone. Barbie reached into her pocket for her—

Dammit! No phone. Must have dropped it.

"Man! What Karma!"

She eyeballed the sign and the darkness behind it, and envisioned poor old Angie's reaction when Darin and his doggie snuck up on her from behind. Angie wouldn't know what to make of that. She didn't know Darin, didn't know that this night's date had had anything to do with a cemetery. Angie wouldn't like the Rottweiler from hell nosing any part of her person, either.

It wasn't nice to allow your pals to have a fright two nights in a row because of you. Some friends would go only so far. Barbie opened the Fiat's door. She slid her legs off the seat and placed her feet on the pavement. The best thing, she decided—no, the *only* thing—was to go in there after Angie,

Darin, and Dog. She could soften the blow. It would have been foolish for Angie to have left the door open and the keys in the ignition, anyway. Angie loved this car. And Barbie loved Angie.

Closing the Fiat's door and setting her shoulders, Barbie headed for the cemetery sign at a walk, then picked up her pace to a jog. "Coming Midge!" she shouted.

Chapter Twenty-one

"This can't be happening," Darin muttered as he raced over the grass. "Women!"

Though Dog had a nose to the ground, Darin didn't need any help finding his prey. Angie's perfume wafted in the night as if it had been recently sprayed on, giving his own nose a twinge. Strong perfume for a strong personality? Would Barbie's friend be as hardheaded as she? Just what he needed.

Oh no. No.

Sliding to a halt, Darin stared upward. A searing pain shot through his face, causing him to flinch. He wouldn't make it. The moon was too darned bright and the trees laced too thinly. He had to let go.

With a vocalized oath, he waited for the change to transform him. Skin slid against skin. Bones creaked. His teeth slammed shut while his face rearranged. Ten seconds now to transform, he tallied. It was getting quicker.

Hugging his roomy coat tighter around himself, Darin took off again, this time able to run effortlessly, with larger strides and the joy of movement for movement's sake. Like this, as the wolf, he was able to see, hear, and sense exactly which path Barbie's friend had taken, almost as though Angie had left a trail of bread crumbs.

What, he wondered, would he do when he found her? He couldn't face her like this, in his wolf's skin. He looked like a monster! He couldn't talk.

He would have to herd Angie in the direction of the parking lot. Chase her back to her car. Make her think something might be after her, without provoking too much of a scare.

Wait! What's this?

Dropping to the ground on one knee, Darin sniffed the air. From the south came the scent of another presence, a familiar presence. He'd know this smell anywhere.

Excitement flowed through him. Angie's trail ceased to occupy his mind as he turned into the wind. Angie's trail had circled back, anyway. If she knew what was good for her, she'd be heading for her car. There was something new he had to take care of.

The beast was so easily appeased. So easily distracted.

Barbie ran as fast as her legs would take her. Dog barked somewhere up ahead. Dog would be near to Darin. Darin would be near to Angie.

Slowing to a jog as she reached the first gravestones, not really knowing how she had found them this time, Barbie listened, pointing herself in different directions like a GPS system homing in on an elusive address. But there was no sound now.

Darn.

A situation recap seemed necessary. She hadn't done as Darin asked and stayed in the car. Angie should have been bright enough to heed the phone message and stay in the Fiat. Couldn't Angie hear the tone of the message her friend had left? Didn't they teach about stress in that beauty college, and all the ways to recognize it?

The skin at the nape of her neck tingled as she took two more steps in the direction of the crypts. "Ick." One more step, she told herself, would be fine. Surely the bodies in this cemetery had mostly been nice people.

Besides, she had managed to stay on her feet this time. No belly flops. The crickets were chirping, which she hoped meant no bogeymen were around. All she had to do was cover ground, even if at a snail's pace, between the marble buildings. She had to reach Angie first, or at least at the same time as Darin and Dog. Angie's mental health depended on it.

"Dang, Angie. The rescue is now reversed," she grumbled. Wasn't it so like Angie to make everything about her?

A white thing appeared suddenly to Barbie's right, very nearly startling the pants right off of her, until she realized it was a statue of a goddess with a bow and arrow, tall and pearlescent, made of stone. Next to the statue sat a cross, ominously pale in the moonlight. Neither was altogether freaky or unpleasant when you realized what it was, but they weren't a welcome sight.

Glancing up, blinking in the bright moonlight and thinking she could feel that silver light on her face, Barbie swallowed hard and continued on. She ducked low-hanging branches, straining to hear any sign of anybody. She picked her way between the tombstones and clipped hedges, thinking that if she were to spend eternity in this place, she'd want her resting place to be out here and tree shaded, not inside of anything as closed in as a mausoleum or crypt. Those places were downright eerie. Crypts and mausoleums invited strange happenings and horror-movie scripts. The film industry could never have become what it was without them. She thought an architect might have redesigned the buildings to be more homey, like small cottages with window boxes, like playhouses with manicured yards, but no one seemed interested in changing their image.

A sound in the distance. Barbie froze. The echo of a growl reached her, followed by a bark. Another growl came, louder this time, more menacing. Had the pony-sized dog found Angie? Would Angie still be breathing after it was done with her?

Picking up her pace, Barbie skipped between the tombstones, anxious again. Still no Darin. No Angie. No Dog. Another marble crypt sprang at her out of nowhere. "Regular metropolis out here," she noted. Plus, *geez*, the crickets had stopped their silly symphony.

"Angie?" Barbie's call was soft. Goose bumps sprouted on her arms.

Did she hear a reply? Barbie darted through the surrounding shrubbery, was caught off guard by the closeness of something flying by her in the night, something big and hairy. Whatever it was, it moved at light speed beneath the trees. An animal? An animal larger than Dog? Was that even possible?

Backing up, nearly toppling over a vase of flowers propped alongside a grave marker, Barbie let out a shriek. The sound barely got past her throat as the blobby blur disappeared around the side of the crypt.

Barbie knew she had to follow, and she started out, moving her lips in a recitation of the phrase she sincerely hoped was true. "There are no such things as ghosts or zombies. There are no such things as ghosts or zombies. There are no such things as ghosts or zombies. . . ."

She was concentrating too hard to remember to shout for help.

Chapter Twenty-two

Whoever had designed a wolf's face and snout must have been drinking. It was actually quite hard to see past the nose, Darin thought as he rounded the building. Not to mention the effort it took to breathe through such a lengthy proboscis. Special focus was needed to get his eyes working together in order to see past this nose. He'd never gotten used to that.

Whoever would have imagined that a man and a wolf were a workable combination, anyway? Why not a giraffe, or a bear? Along those same lines, who was the first to suggest a man and a woman were a workable combination? Look at the obvious and lengthy list of differences between the sexes. The vast enormity of differences, in fact.

Still, he decided, vaulting over a tombstone, lumbering between two more crypts and making a sharp right turn, he supposed he should thank whoever the Creator was, because Barbie Bradley was worth giving thanks for—in spite of the suspicious quirks she exhibited. As he recalled, she had warned him about her anger-management issue. He should have listened.

Barbie crept past the trees, past a waterless fountain, and on toward more evergreens. How on earth did Angie get this far? she asked herself. Where had Darin gone? Was the hairy hide she had glimpsed yet another animal? Or maybe a frat boy coming off a bender.

Holding her breath, she slunk between two narrow buildings set close together, then loped for the trees, sure she'd seen movement beneath. What she found was a whole lot of nothing, and creepier still, the insects were still silent. Either the bugs had been seriously disturbed, or Dog had eaten them for a snack.

Beneath one of the tall trees Darin seemed to like so much, Barbie paused. Did she want to follow that thing she'd seen race deeper into the row of crypts? Not really. What she wanted to do was find Angie and skedaddle.

"What the—?"

A hand clamped over her mouth, a hand that had appeared from out of nowhere. It caused Barbie's knees to buckle. Her heart burped. Her legs wriggled as she prepared to issue a roundhouse kick and inhaled . . . Chanel No. 5?

"Don't say anything," Angie warned.

"I—" Muffled.

"Shut up, Barbie, will you please? Just look where I'm pointing."

The hand covering Barbie's mouth dropped away. Frowning, face thawing from its frozen surprise, Barbie turned around.

"Look," Angie commanded.

Barbie rotated again to peer through the bushes. More pallid buildings lay ahead. They could have been the same buildings she had just passed, and they could have been different ones. Her sense of direction was virtually nonexistent.

Nothing moved beside the buildings. She was just about to question her pal about this, when Angie nudged her in the ribs.

"Hey!"

Another nudge, harder this time. Angie was pointing. "Look."

Barbie studied those buildings harder, and with more concentration. Dimly at first, her eyes picked out a shadow. No, not a shadow. The silhouette of a man. Darin?

She almost called out. Stopped herself. A second silhouette appeared beside the first, standing close to the first. *Very* close to the first.

A curious feeling cruised through Barbie's guts. Though she had no idea if one of those shadowy forms could be Darin—after all, it was too dark to see clearly—she stared, transfixed. Her stomach tightened when one of those two silhouettes, the smaller one, leaned in toward the other . . . as in, their bodies were touching. In a flare of moonlight Barbie saw that the second silhouette was lighter, slimmer. Female.

Oh . . . my . . .

Meaning to take a step forward, Barbie stopped herself with a firm realization. She didn't know for sure if one of these was Darin. She didn't know if the smaller silhouette was a person at all. Maybe it was Dog, up on his hind legs for a good face slurp. Maybe Dog was where Darin got the idea for all that delectable licking business in the first place. Man's best friend was his dog, she'd heard.

This couldn't be Darin, she decided. Not out here with another woman on the same night he had taken her to dinner, to bed, and had then pulled off a vanishing routine. It was inconceivable that Darin could have done this to her.

However, her mind nagged suspiciously, Darin had made mention of something else he had to do. He had suggested that she get in the car and stay there. Was this cause for alarm? He hadn't wanted her to see the other female? The competition?

A great gulp of inhaled air came with hiccups as a side

effect as Barbie's insides wrenched. Who else would be out here in the graveyard besides Darin? It had to be him, didn't it? That "something" he had to attend to might indeed involve a female. Could Darin have arranged another rendezvous? Same night, but another woman at a later hour? A *twofer?*

No!

Her own hand now clapped to her mouth to keep herself from screaming. Her hiccups were like small internal earthquakes. Two weeks, huh? she was thinking, prodded on by Darin's own words. Darin Russell, all licky, touchy-feely, and then poof? Darin Russell, reappearing to woo someone else, on Barbie time?

When the blood drained from her face, she felt it. Nausea rolled in her belly. If this was Darin, then somehow she had been suckered into the guy's web of deceit. Dang if she hadn't found that flaw she'd been looking for, right smack-dab in the middle of the cemetery: the guy was a gigolo. The man she'd thought too gorgeous to be true, *was* too gorgeous to be true. He was a man with an agenda, that agenda being to see how many women he could pick up at one time. How many conquests he could make in a few hours' time?

What better way to accomplish this than to wine and dine her, emphasis on the former, ensuring they would leave the restaurant early. Seeming the consummate gentleman, he had taken her home and had come up looking like a champ. While she, on the other hand, was looking and feeling like a chump.

Tuck her in with a *T*, Darin had said. No attempt made whatsoever (not really) to get into her pants. How unlike a guy was that, anyway? How many times had this happened in her dating history? Zero. (Okay, the word *history* might suggest she'd actually had a past that involved getting very far with men, but what the hell.)

Dammit! Deep down she must have known something like this would happen. With a horrid, almost morbid fascination, she peered again through the bushes. The words *benefit of the doubt* floated by, scorned.

"Do you see?" Angie whispered.

"Yeah, I see all right."

She sure did. There were the wide shoulders and the long hair, seen glistening in another brief flash of moonlight. If that wasn't Darin, she'd eat her shoes. While the smaller silhouette, the one whose hand now rested on Darin's face, was no dog. No siree. The smaller person was a . . . blonde!

The realization struck terror into Barbie's heart. "It can't be," she whimpered.

A blonde?

All her life she had lived with this particular little problem. This particular dilemma. Blondes. And not being one.

Blondes had more fun.

Blondes got the guys.

Gentlemen preferred blondes.

Hadn't blonde Barbie always been a better seller in toy stores? More popular? More valuable with age? All little girls wanted blonde Barbie. Brunette Barbie didn't cut it. Brunette Barbie paled in comparison to the honey-haired diva of dolls.

Barbie Bradley felt herself whiten further. She was sure she might fade dead away, joining the rest of the folks in this place in a prone position.

"Isn't that the guy who just walked you to the lamppost?" Angie wanted to know.

Barbie shrugged dumbly, unable to respond, thinking she should run in there and give Darin Russell a piece of her mind. Maybe a karate chop, too. Either that, or she might cry.

"Why were you out here?" Angie whispered. "Who is that guy?"

"He's—"

"Not your *date*?" A wheeze came from Angie's throat. "That's your blind date?"

Right after Barbie's initial heart attack came a rising steam. Anger. Temper. On top of that, tears were gathering, threatening to fall. She felt shaky all over, and kind of depressed.

"The date who left you without saying good night?" Angie continued, fascination in her tone. "You came out here to spy?"

Angie asked this with not only interest, but a particular kind of empathy familiar to the female gender. Barbie looked at her as the sound of Darin's laughter carried. Angie's head came up.

"No way!" Angie said. "Is this the guy? The guy on the—"

"Yes," Barbie hissed.

"On the—"

"Answering machine. Yes, okay? There's a good possibility that he is Mr. Velvet Voice, himself. A very good possibility."

Angie looked to the two silhouettes, still sort of huddled together, and back to Barbie. She looked a little harder at Barbie. "I can feel steam rising from your body. Temper steam. Sometimes spying is a bad thing, I'm thinking. We should go now. We really should leave."

"Not before full confrontation," Barbie muttered through clenched teeth. "Confrontation is a good thing. Everyone says so. It provides closure."

"I don't think they were talking about this kind of confrontation," Angie warned. "Not the 'sneak up in the dark and surprise the heck out of someone' kind. That kind could be dangerous."

"How can he deny this behavior if he's caught in the act?"

"Honey, you need to think about this before dashing in

there. You need to give him time to explain. It might not even be the guy you're thinking it is."

"You saw him walk me to the car?"

"Sure did. I had to . . . I came into the bushes to . . . *you know*, and . . ." Angie's explanation faded. "He walked right by me. I thought I'd see what was up."

Barbie stared at her friend.

"Doesn't mean that's him," Angie said. "There could be other folks out here. Could be your guy has a brother."

"You see the hair on this guy?" Barbie asked.

"Yeah. Dark and shiny and long. I saw that, for sure."

"Did you see his body?"

"With hair like that, who needs a body?"

"That's Darin, all right. My date. He is the graveyard keeper here. No one else would be out here after dark, Angie."

"You mean, besides you and me and whoever that blonde is who's touching his face?"

Barbie's shaking got worse, knees now refusing to hold her up. Angie grabbed hold of her elbow and hung on tightly. "Come on now. Let's go home," Angie said. "I stopped at the store like you asked me to. We've got plenty of stuff to ease the pain."

"You're talking calories, Angie, not human flesh."

"Oh boy. Time to go. Really." Angie tugged on Barbie's quivering arm.

"Pain is not good enough for that man, Angie. He really had me going."

"Fine, but you can't attack now. There's a witness."

Angie was right, Barbie supposed. "Still, shouldn't this other woman be warned? Blonde or not, don't women have to stick together?"

"Not this minute they don't," Angie concluded.

Barbie stole one more glance through the bushes, heart kabooming annoyingly. The woman now had both hands on

Darin's shoulders. What was next? A kiss? A deep, drowning kiss? A French one?

Barbie's hands flew to her mouth. Her fingers moved over her lips, lips Darin had kissed. Darin Russell had gotten past the door, past Rule One, and had somehow waltzed into her bedroom on the promise of having potential. Right now, however, it seemed that Darin was a fraud. Not even remotely a gentleman. Darin was a lousy, lying two-timer. Just like Bill.

If her mother had been there that very minute, she'd be wagging her finger at her daughter for the frivolous rule-skippage that had led to this premature attachment. She'd be wagging her tongue, too, spewing remarks like *I told you so* and *You never listen to me*.

Barbie closed her eyes and swallowed a groan. She hated it when her mother was right.

Chapter Twenty-three

"Look on the bright side," Angie said as they sped through the streets in her red Fiat. "You don't know him well enough to be really pissed."

Barbie glowered at her friend, hunched over in her seat, arms crossed.

"Ooooh, you're scaring me," Angie declared. "I'm trying to help."

"Then turn around and run him over. And his little dog, too."

"That's from the *Wizard of Oz*, right? The little-dog thing?"

Barbie slunk farther down in her seat.

"Forget him, Barb."

"I liked him, Ang."

"You just met him."

"You sound like my mother."

"Go ahead, insult me some more and I'll dump your sorry ass out right here, minus the anxiety supplies."

Admittedly, Angie was right on this one. Why was she brooding, anyway? Why did it feel as though her heart had toppled off the Empire State Building? She didn't *know* the guy. It turned out to be a good thing she hadn't gotten to know the guy any better.

"I can't believe my intuition was so wrong," she said. "I lusted for him, Ang."

"Lust does not equal a relationship in any sense," Angie pointed out.

Again, Angie was right. Barbie had been gullible, that's all. Those screaming body parts looking forward to scratch-and-sniff had been hoodwinked. Duped.

"We didn't *do* anything," she mumbled regretfully.

"In my mind, this turns out to be a very good thing," Angie said. "Plus, you got dinner."

Barbie's teeth clenched tighter.

"You did get dinner?" Angie said hopefully. "I called you *at* dinner."

Barbie screwed up her face. Here came the questions, slow at first, as was Angie's way, then, *bam!* Barbie felt like opening the door and leaping out.

"I might have had a little too much wine before the actual food arrived," she confessed.

Angie shook her head. The Fiat wove back and forth across the white painted lines.

"What?" Barbie said.

"Girl, we *are* desperate. This is a very sad state of affairs, not even getting a meal out of a date."

"He used the *E*—"

"*E* as in *exit*. *E* as in *eliminated*. So get hold of yourself."

Man, this was going to be bad, Barbie knew. Angie was in good form. And Angie had seen the b-l-o-n-d-e.

"Can we eat in your car?" Barbie asked in a very small voice.

"No way. We're almost there."

"You really wouldn't reconsider running him over?"

"And scratch up my paint?"

"It was a—"

"Blonde," Angie finished for her. A minute later she added, "Goes to show that sometimes fate has a way of screwing us royally."

"Yeah."

"On the other hand," Angie suggested brightly, "I know just the thing to fix us up."

"In this bag I'm holding?"

"Not exactly."

"What else could there be?"

Grinning like the Cheshire cat, white teeth gleaming beneath the streetlights they passed, Angie said, "Three little words, I'm thinking, ought to do it."

"Injure Darin later?"

"Not those three."

"Which three, Ang?"

"Do you want to hear those three words, Barb? The ones that very possibly will change your future?"

"I'm all ears, Ang."

Angie nodded, shifted the Fiat into a lower gear, and whispered, as if the words themselves were magic, "The Dating Game."

Darin stayed as close to the building as he could, melding with the shadows. This was one strange night, for sure. Three women to contend with. You had to love that.

He was supposed to be finding Barbie's friend, but he was trapped. The moonlight had grown too strong. There had been too may close calls.

Then again, he mused almost gleefully, Barbie had looked so cute running toward that car, extra-large T-shirt flapping behind her like a sail, tight little booty encased in those baggy sweats. He'd barely gotten a glimpse, and now look at him, grounded from following her. Lassoed by the curse.

He accepted the item the woman next to him handed him with a shaky hand.

"Phone," Jessica said. "I found it on the path. Is it yours?"

Careful not to tip his head into the light beyond the overhang, Darin looked down. "It's Barbie's, I think."

"Barbie? The girl you took out to dinner tonight?" Jessica's voice held an incredulous ring.

"One and the same."

"What was she doing out here?"

"Damned if I know, Jess. She's not your average girl, that's for sure."

"Does she know?" Jess asked.

"Hell, no."

Concern crept into Jess's voice. She had been his self-proclaimed protector and confidante, his liaison to the world during his full-moon phases. Dear, dear Jessica, six years younger than he and wise enough, kindhearted enough to take upon herself some of his burden. Truly, she was a one-in-a-million woman. Like Barbie.

"What good would any average woman do me?" he asked Jess. "I'm not really an average guy, am I?"

Jess grinned. "Not even. Got to give you that. So why did she come out here, if not by invitation?"

"No doubt Barbie followed me to give me a piece of her mind. How rich is that? She doesn't think I treated her properly after dinner." He grinned, though the situation wasn't all that funny. In fact, he felt sort of sick over what had happened.

"Didn't you treat her properly?" Jess asked.

"It was a pretty strange date," Darin admitted, gesturing to the sky. "Fairly brief."

Jess nodded. After a moment she added, "You must like this girl."

"I'm that transparent?"

"Daring a date on a night like this? I know you pretty well, don't I? Do you like her as much as you like me, I'm wondering?"

"The thing is," Darin began, wanting to confide, "I *do* like her. A lot."

Jess's cool, calm hand touched his face. "How do you know?"

"Trust me, I know. Would you come out here if you didn't have to?"

"I don't have to."

"You know what I mean. You know what I am, Jess. Barbie doesn't know much about me, and doesn't seem afraid."

"Not so far, anyway." Jess sighed. "I guess it's not up to me to point out the obvious, though, is it? I suppose I have to share you sometime. So, you'll see her again, find out if your feelings are reciprocated?"

"Sure."

"You didn't scare her off tonight?"

"Walking her to her friend's car was as far as I got."

"Maybe luck was on your side." Jessica placed both of her hands on Darin's shoulders, then looked him directly in the eyes without the aid of her flashlight. "I'm a little jealous, I think, but that'll pass. Just now, you have a good excuse for calling this gal of yours back tonight, I'm thinking."

Darin cocked his head, felt his insides twist. He could barely control himself, though he didn't have to worry. Jess had seen it all. She had brought him food and clothes and made sure he was well situated on his three-day, self-imposed hibernations for as long as he could remember. She had volunteered for this job.

Jess would ride on her big brother's fuzzy shoulders and laugh joyfully as he ran. Jessica Russell never turned down a really good scare. A relationship like theirs was rare between brother and sister.

"I'm hoping Barbie is a little like you," Darin said, shoulders twitching, chest beginning its shape-shifter dance of flesh and bone.

"Then call her. See if she made it home all right," Jess suggested.

Darin hesitated, his fingers closed over the tiny metallic phone. When the moon wasn't touching him, his long coat felt baggy, cool, and rough on his bare skin. He preferred silk and softness. His skin was always tender. But it was either the roomy coat or a mess of shredded clothes. Werewolves went through piles of clothes if they weren't careful. The protocol was to remove the clothes first, then step into moonlight. Hadn't taken him long to learn this lesson.

Also, it was a good thing he had an inheritance from his grandparents for the small luxuries, and that the Miami PD paid extremely well for his unique services.

"You can tell her you found her phone," Jess said helpfully. "It's a really good excuse for calling. A very gentlemanly thing to do. A woman can't be without her phone for long without lapsing into panic. Not to mention the fact that you probably wouldn't want her returning again tonight to look for it, would you? Little Red Riding Hood alone in the woods with a wolf on the loose?"

Darin grinned, heard the scrape of his claws on the little phone, and flipped it open. His chest bulged with a faint ripping sound. His legs and tongue had thickened.

Seeing his large hands and sharp, unwieldy claws, and the diminutive size of this girl's cell phone, Jessica pried the phone loose from Darin's grasp. "Well," she said with resignation and a slight lilt in her voice. "Call out those numbers, bro. Let's shake this gal up."

Chapter Twenty-four

When the phone rang, Barbie sprang off the couch where she was sprawled. Crumbs flew.

She glanced first to the door through which Angie had seconds before exited. Having draped a cozy afghan over Barbie and placed an opened bag of cookies in her arms and a glass of milk on the coffee table, her friend had finally confessed fatigue and a dire need of beauty sleep. She also might have mentioned something in parting about too much negative energy causing premature menopause.

Amazingly enough, considering that prediction, the sound of the phone ringing sent Barbie into a bona fide hot flash, immediately doused by chills. Waves of chills, oceans of chills, all merged at the nape of her neck, where tiny curly hairs less than a quarter inch long stood on end, no professional straightening required. Had Angie had an accident?

She picked up the receiver. "Angie? Speak to me."

Faint static on the line. "Barbie?"

Feeling a second round of heat coming on, Barbie sank right down onto the arm of the couch, foregoing the cushions.

"Barbie? Are you there?"

Pressing the receiver against her chest and raising her gaze to the ceiling of her apartment as if in prayer, Barbie managed to get her temper in order and the phone back to her ear. "Yes, Darin, I'm here."

"I only have a minute. I couldn't find the card with your number until just now. I thought I'd call to make sure you got home."

"Well," Barbie replied as kindly as she could, "thanks for spending some of your valuable time on me. Yes, I got home—and with Angie, I might add."

There was a pause. "I didn't see Angie."

No shit, Sherlock.

"I'm relieved you found her," Darin said when Barbie didn't reply. "Are you both all right?"

The scoundrel. He hadn't looked for Angie very hard, had he? Certainly he had found someone, but by no stretch of the imagination could Angie be mistaken for a small, slim blonde.

"When I returned to the parking lot, the car was gone," Darin continued. "She came back to the car?"

"We're fine, Darin," Barbie snapped. *No thanks to you.*

"I was worried."

Totally grumpy, Barbie pressed one hand to the top of her head to quell the waving of her antennae, thinking she would strangle them as soon as she had both hands free. It had become quite obvious that those figurative, man-finding twirlers couldn't tell a worthy mate from a hole in the ground.

"You sound upset," Darin said. "What's up?"

"Too much static on the line, Darin. Can't hear you." Barbie made faux static sounds into her phone that sounded more like someone getting ready to spit than any technological interference.

"Barbie? Are you there?"

She gave up faking static. "What more do you have to say to me?" *That you're a lousy two-timing schmuck?*

"I found your cell phone."

Barbie rolled her eyes.

"I can't bring it to you right now."

Why not, big guy? Blondie hanging on, kissing your eyelids, maybe?

"I can get it to you in the morning. First thing."

"UPS it," Barbie said. "I know how busy you are."

Silence followed her statement. For several erratic heartbeats, Barbie's antennae beat her about the head. Again, Barbie noted, they didn't know squat. That was a fact.

"I'd prefer to bring it to you," Darin said. "It's Sunday. Maybe we could have breakfast? Make up for missing dinner?"

"You want to have breakfast?" Barbie again swatted at the top of her head. *Down, boys. Ain't gonna happen!*

This was freaking unbelievable. The jerk wanted to have breakfast. With all this in-ing and out-ing, how did he have any energy left? He had seen her, ditched her, taken up with the blonde, and now obviously planned on ditching Blondie also. The routine of a gigolo was mind-boggling.

"I'm not blonde," Barbie snapped, lapsing in concentration and composure. "I'll never be a blonde. I don't want to be a blonde. I'm not stupid, either. I don't date gigolos. I don't even know any gigolos, other than you, and you are one too many. So you can . . ." She took an oversized gulp of air. "I'm going on the Dating Game!"

She crashed the phone receiver down in its cradle; the sound split the quiet as though lightning had invaded her apartment. Barbie's heart boomed in the aftermath. She glared at the phone as if it too were an alien nuisance, sincerely hoping the crashing noise had ruptured Darin's eardrums.

She felt like crap. She really did. She had agreed with Angie to audition for the country-club version of the retro dating show. In a month she might be out there on a stage with three male contestants, asking questions, having to pick one without seeing their bods or knowing their hearts. Look how well the last semiblind date had turned out!

But there was something worse, if you can believe it. The graveyard creep had her cell phone. What if her mother called and Darin answered? How would Barbie explain that? A guy in her bed? A guy hanging around and comfortable enough to answer a girl's incomings? Mothers didn't appreciate that kind of thing, no matter how old their daughters were.

If Darin UPS'd the phone, it would take a couple days for her to get it back. That was unacceptable. Fact: either she had to go to that darned breakfast, or he would have to bring the phone to her apartment. She didn't want him anywhere near her apartment. She didn't want him anywhere near her. This was blackmail. If she hadn't been raised better, she might have had a nervous breakdown right there on her area rug. Darn it all, she was going to call Darin back and tell him what he could do with her phone—and the blonde.

She punched in her cell number. "Darin?" Had he picked up? She was sure he had. Some really heavy breathing came on the line.

"Pervert!" she shouted into the phone, then added, *"Beast!"*

"Hello?" a female voice said, and Barbie's heart stopped. "Is this Barbie?" The voice sounded very much like a blonde.

"So, you know my name." Barbie stood rigidly in the center of her living room, both hands on the phone, legs unsteady.

"Yes," the woman said into Barbie's phone. Spreading blonde cooties. "Look, Barbie, Darin's sorry he can't talk right now. He would like to meet you tomorrow for breakfast."

Too stunned to speak, Barbie's mouth went slack.

"Barbie? Can I tell Darin you'll meet him?"

"No," she snapped. The nerve of this guy, having his beach-babe gal pal arrange a date for him! Blondes. There was just no understanding the phenomenon.

"No?" the bimbo repeated.

"You can tell Darin to go to hell," Barbie replied. "After he arranges a drop-off place for my phone. Either that, or maybe you, being a card-carrying member of the female gender, can arrange to get it to me."

Silence on the line. Maybe the blonde didn't get it. Maybe she didn't know hostility when she heard it.

"I'm sure Darin would prefer to get the phone to you himself," the bimbo said. "In person."

"So, if I were to meet him tomorrow, where would *you* be?"

"At work. However, I would like to meet you sometime. Darin has told me about you."

"Oh?" *He has, has he?*

"He mentioned the café near your apartment for breakfast. Ten o'clock, he said, because you need your sleep."

"I won't meet him. I'm going to audition for the Dating Game tomorrow. Please ask him to leave the phone somewhere else for me."

"Okay, I'll tell him. I've got to go now. Nice talking to you, Barbie. Don't worry, though, Darin will return your phone."

"Glad to hear it," Barbie said. "Give him a big kiss for me, will you?"

After hanging up, Barbie stared at the phone for some time, wanting to yank her hair out by the roots.

Jess dropped the little cell phone into Darin's big hands and gently patted his hairy arm. "You sure she's the one?" she asked.

Darin held the phone up to the light and watched it glitter as they walked. He nodded his head, then cocked it again to ask Jess why she had posed the question.

"Maybe she was sleepy." Jess shrugged. "She sounded a bit agitated. I think she might possess a temper, bro. Be careful there. I have to dash. You all right?"

Darin nodded.

"She said to give you a kiss." Jess looked carefully at her brother's shaggy, wolfish face. "I think maybe she was being sarcastic?"

Darin shrugged.

"Shall I put the phone in your pocket?"

Darin continued to hold it.

"Right. Well, I guess I'll see you tomorrow night. Anything special you need?" Rising onto her toes, Jess planted a kiss on his hairy cheek. "Will you make it home for dinner before you head out of town? The parents will want to see you."

Darin nodded.

Jess clicked on her flashlight, clipped a leash to Dog's collar, gave Darin a wave, and disappeared into the darkness.

Darin returned his attention to Barbie's phone. He had trouble grasping so small an object, now that his hands were twice their regular size. He could no longer speak—not as humans know speech, anyway.

He knew from Jess's departing comments that Barbie was indeed upset, maybe even pissed, just as he had feared. He wasn't sure why. He had offered to take her to breakfast. Didn't all women like that? Romantic outdoor café, pancakes, mimosas? After a night spent as an animal, he required lots of food. In the daylight he'd be able to look at Barbie across a table. He'd hear her laugh. He'd be Darin Russell again—tired, yet up for anything.

He could stay with Barbie until dusk, but after tonight's fiasco, he wouldn't try to be with her after sunset. Even if day after tomorrow he'd be away on police assignment. There would be no lingering in Barbie's apartment. No kisses. Zero cuddling. At least, not anywhere near dark. He couldn't even listen to her voice on the phone without a jolt.

A growl escaped him. A burst of testosterone surged, making him hard in all the right (or maybe wrong) places. Talk about an odd sensation: being buck-naked and covered in fur, a creature from a horror movie, and having your willy waving in the breeze. All because of one female's voice over a cell phone! It didn't get much stranger than this.

Again, he tried to form words. Nothing but guttural sounds emerged. Nearly dropping the tiny phone in its slippery case, he grasped it even harder. The phone was the closest thing to Barbie Bradley he had. Her scent clung to it. Her lips had touched it. She'd pasted a couple of rhinestones onto the case. He did like this woman. Immensely.

He had again reached the row of crypts. Turning sideways to view his profile in shadow against the marble, Darin looked down at himself and sighed. Oh yes, Barbie Bradley was the one, all right. As his body was telling him, Darin and Wolfy both wanted Barbie.

Alerted suddenly to something other than his obscene shadow, Darin dropped to a crouch.

"Darin?" It was Jess's voice. "I found this in the parking lot." She held up a plastic carrying bag from the local mini-mart.

Darin shuddered. He could smell the chocolate from where he hunkered. The bag smelled like Barbie's apartment. Why would Barbie have left it?

And had she mentioned something about a dating game?

Christ! Although he was furry and unable to speak at the

moment, there was nothing wrong with his intuition. Barbie had not stayed in the Fiat. She had dropped that cookie bag after following him back into the graveyard after Angie. Had Barbie seen Jess? Had Barbie seen Jess and jumped to the wrong conclusions?

Scratching frantically at his throat in an effort to shout, Darin knew that was what had happened. Barbie had to have seen his sister, hence the comment about blondes. This all made an uncomfortable kind of sense now. Barbie wasn't nuts; she was just imagining the worst of him.

He bellowed out a winner of a howl and rubbed the phone against his cheek. The downside of this wolf curse was that there was no longer any way to explain anything to Barbie tonight in person. No way to clear himself. He was beyond control. He was a terrible mixture of excited, anxious, and fearful, because Barbie would go to sleep thinking him a wolf of another sort.

" 'Bye again, bro," Jess said, handing Darin the bag, then taking off again.

Another howl bubbled up, and Darin let it rip. His sister was attractive. Barbie didn't like that. He didn't want Barbie to be hurt. He had to make sure she was all right. The only way to do this was to break all of his own rules. The only way to assure himself that she was all right would be to go to her and hope he wouldn't be seen by anyone on the way. It was a dangerous undertaking. Very possibly suicide.

Just take a peek in her window, he thought. Knock on her door and leave the phone on her doorstep, along with a small token of his affection—some little thing that would make her want to show up at Café Paris in the morning. But what would ensure her presence at the café? What would make Barbie want to see him?

Yes! He had it!

Yowling jubilantly, fur standing on end, Darin looked back at the door to his second home, his moon-madness place, then at the path leading out of the cemetery. He waved a hairy fist at the moon for its rotten timing, and took off at a lope.

Next stop, Bradley Street.

Chapter Twenty-five

Sleep was elusive. Barbie sat up and rubbed her eyes. More milk, maybe? Did warm milk contain tryptophan, or was that turkey? She was always sleepy after Thanksgiving dinner.

Barefoot, she scuttled through the living room and around into her compact green and gold kitchen. Without turning the lights on, she opened the refrigerator door, took out the milk carton, and thought about calling her mother to ask about the calming effects of organic moo juice. What time was it, anyway? Three o'clock? It couldn't be! Only a couple hours had passed since her romp in the graveyard. Was it possible the microwave's clock had stopped?

Flipping the cardboard milk container, Barbie poured eight ounces into a mug that next went into the microwave oven for one minute. Leaning on the counter and tapping her fingers, she waited. Then she stopped tapping and listened.

Was that a noise?

The microwave beeped. Barbie left the milk and walked to the window, but there was nothing out there, not even many passing cars. Not at this hour. She looked to the front door, suddenly wary, scanning the flat space where her new and unbreakable deadbolt should have been, but wasn't.

Instead, the old gold chain was in place across the door, a chain that wouldn't slow down anybody with a hefty set of clippers. Nor would it stop anyone with a strong shoulder. All it might do was make a bit of noise if an attempt to break it was made. Noise that might wake her neighbors. She could add more noise by screaming.

The sound came again. A scratching noise. Mice? Not mice—it came from outside.

Stepping closer to the door, placing her ear to the wood, Barbie listened hard. The scratching sound continued. Followed by a sort of . . . rumble? Was it Mr. Meaker snoring loudly in the next apartment? Eighty-year-old Mrs. Granger sleepwalking?

"It is not safe to open this door," Barbie said aloud. "I am not Sydney Bristow, or any other kick-ass CIA agent."

The scratching noise grew louder. Her curiosity expanding beyond all tolerance, Barbie sucked in a breath and turned the knob, ready to scream. She opened the door a crack, leaving the chain on . . . and came face-to-face with a monster! A nightmare animal with black pointy ears, a gothlike studded collar, and a whole lot of teeth, looking very much like the devil himself.

It was—Geez, it couldn't be. Only one thing looked like this.

Dog.

Yelping, Barbie jumped back. Darin's pet let out a growl, sounding somewhat like a submerged torpedo, then lunged at the door with all of his bulk, which was quite considerable.

The gold chain snapped in two. The door flew open and smacked the wall behind it, the knob punching a baseball-sized hole through the drywall.

Dog bounded inside the apartment. No contest about him being the largest thing in it. Giant pink tongue extended, lips drawn back in what was either a snarl or a laugh, the Rottweiler had Barbie prone on the couch, paws on her chest, before she could count to three.

"Down!" Barbie shouted. "I am not a toy!"

Dog's breath was . . . doggy. Before Barbie could bat him away, however, her eyes locked on a shiny object dangling from the beast's spiked collar, hanging very near to her face. Her cell phone.

"Easy does it, boy. I'll take my phone, and you can go back to your master. Deed done. Nighty-night."

No movement from Dog. Nothing too intelligent in his eyes, either. Carefully Barbie unclasped the canine's collar and slid the phone free. Dog, close as he was, didn't utter another peep. At least his breath, Barbie decided, smelled like canned dog food, not human flesh.

Riiiinnnnng.

Frightening the daylights out of Barbie, the ringing device caused her to lose her grip on it. The cell phone soared into the air. Barbie pushed Dog off and made a grab for it.

"Hello?" Her voice was shaky but determined. "What do you mean by calling me like this? By delivering this huge furball to my doorstep? Why are you panting on this phone instead of explaining yourself?"

"I beg your pardon?" her mother said.

A mysterious illness settled over Barbie, causing instant paralysis. Able to move only her eyes, she found the kitchen clock. 3:10.

"It's three in the morning," her mother said. "Is everything all right? Why did you call us at three in the morning?"

"I didn't call, Mom."

"Don't be silly, dear. Of course you called. Your number is right here on our caller ID."

"I . . . must have hit autodial by accident," she lied. "I'm sorry. I dropped my cell. Can you go back to sleep?"

"My heart is racing, Barbie. How can I go back to sleep? I thought you might have had an accident!"

"No accident. I'm here at home, in my pajamas. Do you have any sleep meds?"

"Of course I do," her mother said.

"Can I come over and get some?"

"Have you been drinking, Barbie?"

"Warm milk only. I've had a strange night."

"Honey, we love you, but it's too late for you to come over. Have some turkey, or cheese," her mother suggested.

Sage advice, Barbie thought. If only she had a supermarket on the premises.

"Are you sure you're all right?" her mother asked.

"Right as rain."

"Night, then. Dad blows you a kiss."

"Right back at you." Barbie disconnected, melting down onto the couch beside Dog to eye him studiously. The fact that he hadn't eaten her yet was a plus.

"Some he-man attack dog you are," she said, since it was evident that Dog liked soft places on which to set his gigantic behind. When she reached to pat him, however, his lips peeled back from his teeth and she rescinded the gesture. With horror, she watched a great big gob of saliva drip from the corner of the beast's mouth.

Glancing first at her new beige microfiber couch, then back to the saliva, Barbie thought about her cup of now likely tepid milk, and rose to go and get it. She set the mug on the coffee table, close to the edge, and pointed it out to the humongous animal on her sofa. "Yum."

This got his attention. Of course, she'd have to trash the cup after Dog slobbered on it, and maybe a couch pillow or two. The trick was to get him to drink.

"Okeydokey, Dog. Milkfest. Tryptophan. Sleepy time."

The cell phone rang again. More paralysis struck, before the remembrance that her mother usually rang right back with a tidbit forgotten the first time around.

"Hello, Mom," Barbie said.

She encountered nothing but static on the line, followed by irregular breathing sounds. Probably not her mother.

"You can take him back now," Barbie declared with a pained glance at Dog, who now sat on the floor with his paws on the table, wrapped protectively around the cup. "Joke's on me," she added, willing to bet Darin was laughing his guts out.

What had seemed a date from paradise was in actuality the date from hell. There was a very good probability Darin could be Satan himself, and Dog his minion. But she couldn't return Dog to his master because she didn't know where Satan lived. Another truly disgusting thought . . . If Dog was this big, think how big his poop would be.

"Darin?" Desperation rang in her voice. Dog *had* to go.

There was, however, no answer from the phone. Darin had hung up without uttering a single word, leaving her helpless in this crummy predicament.

Bastard! Think of how much time she had wasted imagining him in a kilt, imagining what he wouldn't be wearing under that kilt. Imagining *herself* under that kilt.

Dog picked that particular moment to bark, making her jump a full foot. "Stop that!" she commanded. But Dog continued to bark with his head turned toward the window. The beast barked with zeal, at a decibel level even dinosaurs might have shunned.

Barbie's nerves were frazzling. How many glasses of milk would it take to bring down this pony-sized canine, anyway? There weren't any sleeping pills in her medicine cabinet. She didn't even take aspirin on a regular basis. Dog barked louder.

Oh, all right. It was going to have to be another trip to
the cemetery. She could tie Dog to a bush and let him scare
away visitors. No one would dare attempt to steal the beast,
of course, or even get close. But in order to manage her
plan, she'd have to call a cab and wait for it. She'd have to
try to stuff Dog into the cab. What if Dog didn't like taxis?
What if Dog didn't like cabbies? Remember the slasher-
style rips in the leather seats of Darin's Porsche? Would a
cabbie charge extra for repairs?

Dog was at the window, his growls sounding like thunder.
Barbie glanced over his wide back, her mind seizing with
sudden insight. What if Darin had let Dog free, then waited
around to enjoy the show? What if he was out there right
now? Could Dog know this? Could Darin and Dog be in
on this together?

Skin riddled with angry chills, Barbie sprinted to the
door, whistled to Dog, pointed into the hallway, and watched
him run. "Free at last," she whispered, slamming the door
behind the creature, then dashing to the window in time to
see Dog race past.

As the canine moved in and out of a bit of meager illumination cast by a streetlamp, a dark shape much bigger
than the Rottweiler appeared. Only a shadow, it stretched
across the sidewalk as if the figure wore a bulky fur coat.

Surely she was seeing things, imagining this. After a stern
head shake, a slow blink of her eyes, she looked again. Nothing. No big shadow, no big dog, no more barking. Only
somewhat relieved, Barbie was out the door before sanity in-
tervened.

Nancy Drew she was not, however. How did a person
search for clues in the dark on a residential street? How
could she possibly prove that Darin had been there? The
street was quiet. No wind, no loiterers, and no cars—none
other than the usual parked ones. Oh, and there were some

pretty flashing lights in the distance . . . coming closer. A cop car. And there was no time to hide.

The pretty lights seared Barbie's eyes quicker than she could have said Jack Robinson. It was the good old Miami PD, keeping the streets safe.

A window beneath those flashing lights rolled down. A head appeared. "You all right, miss?" a reproving voice asked.

"Yes, officer, I'm fine. Thanks for asking."

The head stayed framed in the open window. "Have you, by any chance, been drinking?"

Why was everybody asking her that?

"No, sir. Except for warm milk." In truth, she hadn't even had that.

"Could you be sleepwalking?"

"I don't think so. Why do you ask?"

"Aren't those pajamas you're wearing?"

Crap. Not only was she in pajamas, but pink poodle pj's. Don't act shocked, Barbie told herself. Act friendly.

"Yes sir," she said. "Got them as a gift last Christmas. From my mom."

See? Nice, friendly, all-American girl here.

Silence from the cop, then, "Do you live around here?"

"Right up those stairs behind me," Barbie assured him.

"Do you think it might be wise to go back inside, seeing as how it's after three in the morning and you're wearing pajamas?"

"Yes, sir, I do think it would be wise," Barbie agreed. "I was trying to call my dog. He ran off, chasing after something."

"Maybe you could wait inside and I'll go and look for the dog. How would that be?"

"That would be great. Terrific. Thanks." It'd give Darin a jolt, too. "The dog is a big black Rottweiler. Name's Dog. Can't miss him."

"Got it. Shall I wait to make sure you get inside?" the cop asked.

"Yes, thanks. Mind if I ask you something first?"

"What would that be?"

"Do you know Darin Russell?"

"Russell? Yes, ma'am, I do."

Uh-oh. Surely the cop was now looking at her in an even stranger fashion. What had Darin said he did for the PD? He investigated what? Oh yeah, people with unusual physical and mental problems. In that case, shouldn't Darin be investigating himself?

Barbie smiled at the cop, waved, then turned and took the steps back home two at a time. Her life, she decided in that instant, was spinning out of control.

An idea struck that came on so strongly that it sent Barbie careening into the hallway. What if Darin had put the cop up to this to keep her off his scent? What if he was still out there, chuckling? What if he and the cop were laughing now? Another conspiracy?

Darn. She just had to get her life back in order. Darin had the Miami PD on his side, and she had just loosed a really nasty beast on a public street. Could things get any worse? Yes. The truth was, Angie was right: she needed a date, any date, to cancel out the negativity and lingering bad taste of this last one. She certainly would try out for a shot on that stupid upcoming local version of the Dating Game. At worst, it was a charitable endeavor—the country club was planning on planting trees in and around the city with the money raised—and at best, she might meet someone nice. There was always a chance.

She would try out for the game, indeed. Barbie Bradley would be so darned personable that they'd *have* to choose her. The three guys vying for her attention would be drooling— much like Dog—and fighting amongst themselves to win a date. She would be queen for a day. Who wouldn't want that?

Oh yes, and as a result of this game, she would show Darin Russell what he had thrown away. Show him what a catch she was. Show him what he had missed by preferring a damn b-l-o-n-d-e.

From the corner alley, Darin watched Barbie's encounter with the cop. As soon as she had gone inside and the cop had driven away, however, he let out a howl. He howled until his insides were putty and Dog began to bark in counterpoint.

Several shades and shutters opened. Someone yelled for whoever was out there to can it.

Emotions were high. With a hand on Dog's head to quiet him, Darin wondered about this dating game Barbie had mentioned. The question plaguing him was *why* she would consider dating to be a game? Why would she do this? Just to spite him? After all the feelings they'd shared? He had those feelings still. No mistaking that.

She wouldn't meet him at the café—that was a certainty. Knocking at her door at this hour to confront her was an impossibility, too. He had changed back and forth so many times already in one night that he ached from head to foot. He didn't know which part of himself was going to be boss at any time.

Exhaustion plagued him. It was no easy feat, this bone-cracking, shape-shifting phenomenon, and there were three more hours before he could be assured of changing back into human form so that he could rest. So much for his idea about it being better to embrace your fate rather than fight it. So much for his first date with his soul mate, who now believed him to be . . . What had Barbie called him? A gig-olo? Damn.

Barbie's zest was what had drawn him to her in the first

place. Hers was a silly, crazy sort of energy, fueled by a wacky imagination. Barbie was like a hummingbird in intensity. So, what were the chances she would slow down long enough to believe Jess was his sister? How would he contact her, even in the daylight, knowing she believed him to be a liar? Would she even pick up the phone again?

He could write her a letter explaining things. That might be a good start. He could ask Jess to present herself. . . .

For the hundredth time, his mind locked on a specific question: what was this damn dating game Barbie had mentioned, and why would she choose something a werewolf with a huge distaste for crowds would be unable to play?

Darin looked up at the sky and sighed while Dog, by his side, gave a whine. Life, he decided, was too damned complicated.

Chapter Twenty-six

Tap tap tap.

"Will you quit doing that? You're making me nervous," Angie scolded, laying her hand on top of Barbie's on the card table. "Not to mention the fact that I just did your nails."

"Those three guys won't even see my nails," Barbie retorted. "They'll be on the other side of a big screen."

"That doesn't matter," Angie told her. "An entire audience of rich people will be there. Some of them have to be single. One might suit your fancy. You should feel lucky you got on this show."

Barbie shot her friend a look. "It's *strike* your fancy, Ang. Not *suit* your fancy."

"That's what I said. Strike."

"Sure you did."

Angie's hand withdrew from the table. "You, my friend, have been testy all day. As a matter of fact, you've been testy all month. Since—"

"Do *not* even go there, Ang."

"It's true, and you know it. Didn't you say he called you twice in the weeks since your rather bizarre dating event?"

"How could I talk to him after what he did?"

"You couldn't, though you should feel better he tried to reach you all the same. You might take this as a sign of your appeal."

Barbie considered that Angie might actually have something there, and that she should feel better about Darin trying to reach her. He had tried twice in that first week. Since then, however, he had given up. Which was a good thing. Right?

"Please stop with the tapping," Angie pleaded, giving Barbie a snap with a comb she was using for a last-minute hairdo touch-up.

"Why aren't *you* going on this show?" Barbie asked. "This date thing was your idea."

"I volunteered to be on the committee, remember? Committee members couldn't be considered."

"Imagine that," Barbie muttered.

Another smack of the comb, and Angie growled, "You're the one who needed cheering up. You're the one who's been in a bad temper ever since we found your guy with that—"

"Don't you dare utter that word, Angie. I mean it."

"Fact is, you need a date more than I do at this particular time. Let's leave it at that, shall we? You never know, you might find your dream guy. So don't get all snippy with me, missy. I think a thank-you is in order, as a matter of fact."

Barbie sighed heavily. "Have you seen them?"

Angie sat down beside her, a look of interest on her face. "No one has seen them. These guys' particulars are a well-kept secret."

"Great."

"Might be," Angie agreed excitedly.

"I was being facetious, Ang."

"I chose to ignore that. Anyway, all I know is that they're young, handsome, and eligible. Oh, and you'll meet them in about five minutes. Is this a kick, or what?"

"I think I might be sick," Barbie replied.

"I brought wine for the occasion. Cheer us up. It'll bolster our spirits and your confidence." Angie tugged a bottle out of her purse and held it up for inspection.

Cheap wine. The sticker said $2.99. Just what Barbie needed, when the last time she'd had wine was still on her mind. The last time she'd had wine, the world went haywire and Darin Russell had hit the road.

"Do you have a couple of glasses in there, too?" she asked.

"Nope. It was a last-minute stop to the mini-mart. Chugging is the way to go, I'm told."

Chugging from a wine bottle, from wine made in . . . Arizona? Saints above! What was Angie thinking?

But, well, why not? Maybe a swig or two would quiet her jumpy nerves. Could be that chugging this wine would make her forget the beautiful dark-haired man. Make her forget being swept off her feet, even if briefly. Make her forget the graveyard and the chirping bugs and the Gypsies. Enough of this wine, and maybe she would lose the picket-fence dream. At least, she wouldn't try to place Darin by that fence.

She brought the bottle to her lips. *Do not close your eyes. Do not see what's there waiting for you, just like every other time you close your eyes. Don't even think the word kilt.*

Barbie swallowed the god-awful stuff that tasted of raisins and cactus and dirty bare feet. Yet, damn if the stuff didn't warm her insides anyway, immediately and quite pleasurably. Surely between a few sips of wine and three handsome bachelors, she could once and for all forget Darin and his unmentionable treachery.

The dressing-room door opened. Hot, white stage light spilled across the threshold, looking a little like an invitation to some heavenly realm. Barbie stood, feeling pangs of regret about the whole deal. Angie smiled broadly and pointed the way.

"Please give a big-handed welcome for our final contestant, our high school teacher and single lady extraordinaire . . . Miss Barbie Bradley!"

It was a pleasant introduction, but Barbie had to be shoved out of the wings and onto the stage. Her black skirt, the one with no rear pleat, caused her to swivel slightly as she walked, a bit like she might be swinging her hips seductively. This couldn't be helped. It really couldn't. There was nothing whatsoever that would encourage her to be seductive while gaming for a date.

Furthermore, the wine hadn't helped her forget that this skirt reminded her of Darin and the wild Porsche ride back from the Gypsy restaurant. There was a chance the skirt was bad luck, Barbie decided belatedly. Look how that other date had turned out.

Her heels made clicking sounds on the floor of the stage. The lights, as they hit her, made her think she had stepped too close the sun. Hopefully, she thought, the wattage wouldn't cause skin cancer.

The club's audience, numbered in the four-hundred range, erupted in roars of approval—hands clapping, mouths whistling, a few wayward catcalls. Barbie couldn't see any of the people in the audience through the lights, and was glad. The lights would shield her from them. The cheap wine she had drunk would help insulate her from feeling so badly about what she was about to put herself through.

Pasting on a smile, tossing her hair behind her shoulders, and taking short steps to minimize the hip sway, Barbie toddled slowly toward the game's host. Having attended the ten-minute rehearsal, she knew that the chair on the platform to her left, the chair all gussied up like a throne, was for her to sit on. Of course, the chair, in this instance, was really more like a hot seat.

A huge screen next to the chair, made of white swirly plastic, enabled Barbie to see a hint of the outlines of more chairs on the opposite side, but nothing else. There might have been men in those chairs, but who knew? One date, she kept thinking. That wasn't so bad, was it?

No Gypsy restaurants. No ruby wine. No bangles. Not one mention of rules or shopping or . . . talking too much. Damn you, Darin.

Reminded at rehearsal not to squint, Barbie kept her eyes exaggeratedly wide, longing for a pair of sunglasses. She seated herself, offered a nod to the audience. No wiping her nose, dabbing at her eyes, or crossing her legs were the rules of this game.

"Miss Bradley, on behalf of the Buena Vienna Country Club, I would like to thank you for participating in this event. As you know, each bachelor here has put up ten thousand dollars for a chance to win your time."

Ten thousand dollars? Barbie blinked in rapid succession and kept right on smiling, teeth clenched tight. What would a man who had spent ten thousand dollars expect from his date?

More applause and cheers erupted from the obviously tipsy crowd. They'd had an open bar and dinner already. They had paid big bucks to see this show. She couldn't walk off the stage now. She couldn't fall down in an attack of nerves. She was glad she hadn't mentioned this event to her family.

The host, a perfectly groomed, perfectly tanned, gray-haired man, was grinning like the proverbial cat about to chow on the canary. His gray suit had a shiny metallic cast beneath the lights. It was obvious his silver hair had been touched up.

"This money will go toward the beautification of the land surrounding the club," he crowed at Barbie, utilizing a full range of cues to the audience, such as hand gestures, head tilts, etc. "It will enable the club to plant a hundred trees. The prizes you will receive, Miss Bradley, in addition to your date, were also donated by club members."

More cheers and applause. Loopy, Barbie decided—they were all loopy to be a part of this. Herself included.

"Remember, Miss Bradley, all you have to do is ask a series of questions, and Bachelors Number One, Number Two, and Number Three will answer. The answers you like the most will lead to your choice of one of the young men behind this screen. Are you ready, Barbie Bradley?"

"Yes."

But she was so *not* ready, of course. How was it that Angie wasn't out here instead of her? What had Angie said besides her excuse about being on the committee? Oh, yes. She, Angela Ward, was the "idea" woman.

"Could you be a little clearer, please?" the host said, smiling at her, beaming at the crowd.

"Yes," Barbie said louder. "I'm ready."

Applause. Trills of laughter from the gawkers. Easy for them, Barbie thought. None of them were up here prostituting themselves for charity.

"Wonderful." The host flashed a practiced, toothy smile and signaled for a drumroll. "Please have a seat, Miss Bradley. Do you have your questions handy?"

"I do." Barbie kept her body still, wondering what to do with her legs, since she wasn't supposed to cross them. At a loss, she finally decided on a bit of Suzanne Somers–style inner-thigh work, pinching her knees tightly together and holding with all her might. She filled her fitted lavender sweater with one last breath. Now or never. Get it over with.

"All righty then," the host announced jauntily. "Are you ready, bachelors?"

"We are," came the unison reply.

Barbie experienced a twinge of fear and glanced offstage to Angie, whose smile seemed as large and expectant as the host's. Barbie wondered randomly if Angie had done the host's hair.

"Bachelor Number One," she croaked, consulting her card and wanting to chew on it. "Bachelor One, if you were given a choice between taking a Caribbean cruise or a modest hiking trip, which one would you prefer?"

"First, I'd like to say hello to you, Miss Bradley, and that I'd like you to choose me. Then, my answer would be that I'd prefer a cruise," Bachelor Number One replied in a pleasant tenor voice. "Because I've heard the food is wonderful and abundant on a big ship, the dancing is divine, and there is romance to be found on the high seas."

Applause from the audience. Some catcalls.

Wow. Barbie held her breath and took stock. Admittedly, this was a fairly decent answer, though she would never have chosen a cruise herself. Too confining. No wide open spaces. Still, kudos to Bachelor Number One.

"Bachelor Number Two, could you answer the same question please? A cruise, or a hiking trip?"

"Nice meeting you, Miss Bradley," Bachelor Number Two said. "I would also pick the cruise. Having cruised before, I'm well aware of how romantic a ship can be. Having never cruised with the right lady before, I'm anxious to find out what that magic moonlight can do firsthand."

This was said in a deep voice with a slight British accent— an upper-crust British accent, Barbie noted. Women like herself did love the voices of sexy Brits. Clapping, cheering, stomping of many Gucci-clad feet arose from the audience over Bachelor Number Two's reply. But did this mean they liked the guy's looks, his accent, or his answer? *Hmmm.*

Barbie studied her card, said, "Bachelor Number Three, will you please answer the same question?"

"I would choose the hike, Miss Bradley."

Barbie's blood curdled as Bachelor Number Three continued. Her knees came unstuck.

"Unable to get out of doors as much as I'd prefer, I'd like to stretch my legs, feel wind on my face, and explore wide open spaces," Bachelor Number Three continued. "Even better would be to share a sunrise with a special woman, enjoy a simple picnic, and smell the outdoors. No crowds. No interference. Only she and I."

Very loud applause. A few catcalls and whistles. But Barbie was stunned and had to grip the arms of her chair to keep from springing out of it and dashing for the door. Icicles stabbed down her back in spite of the lights. Shock caused her hands and legs to tremble.

Dumbfounded, she looked to Angie, who appeared equally surprised. Would Angie also recognize the voice? How could you forget, once you'd heard it?

Yes, Darin was here, on the opposite side of that screen. Darin Russell was answering the question correctly, sending shivers of anticipation through Barbie's body. Darin Russell, whose sexy speech brought with it lightning strikes, major limb weakness, and special-effects sounds inside of her head. The rat had forked out ten thousand dollars to try to win a second date with her. But, why? So he could humiliate her again? Make her feel used and sad, and angry that she had been horny and duped?

Nonetheless, whatever the reason, here he was in front of the entire country club contributing to a charity event, making her cheeks flush as fuschia as the throne upon which she sat. And she couldn't run, couldn't hide. She had to speak.

Everyone waited.

"Th-thank you," she stuttered, completely undone by Darin's proximity. Only a bit of white plastic separated them. It wasn't enough.

With an unconscious gesture of her hand to her mouth, merely to assure herself she wouldn't start screaming, Barbie tried to get herself back in order. No sooner had she gathered her knees back up, her hands started vibrating visibly. Her cue cards fluttered to the floor. There was no way she could lean over and get those cards without the audience looking up her skirt.

She sent a helpless look at the host, and followed it with a shrug. The ever-smiling guy, fortunately oblivious to what was really going on, rushed to her aid. Barbie muttered a weak thank-you, clenched her cards, and took a few deep, yoga-type breaths. Then she slid a sideways look at Angie, and found her friend missing. Angie had deserted her in a time of need.

"Bachelor Number One," Barbie said, needing to focus, knowing the audience was waiting. "Would you please tell me what you like most about women?"

Phew. She had gotten that out, and wasn't sure how. Where was Angie, anyway? How could Darin be on this stage with her? How could he *dare*? Had he spent every penny a graveyard guy made to be here? Hocked the Porsche? Did he assume this would make a difference, and that she could be bought? How wrong he was.

"Gladly," Bachelor Number One said. "What I like most about women is their shape. Women's shapes are artistic in nature, each different, each a work of genius. Women's bodies are beautiful, sensuous, and awe inspiring. Ethereal, earthy.

I'm especially fond of necks. Graceful necks are a real turn-on."

She took no time to absorb that, and cut off the audience's reaction. "Bachelor Number Two, would *you* please tell me what you like most about women?"

The question she really wanted to ask was why Darin was here, darn it all.

"Their mouths. Lips, kisses, passion. I love kissing," Bachelor Number Two replied confidently.

Taste. Touch. Feel. If Darin responded with those words, Barbie was going to strangle him, plastic screen or no.

Again, she refused to wait out the applause. "Bachelor Number Three? . . . W-women?"

Plenty of them, she was thinking. Darin would have to reply, if he was in any way honest, that he loved being with more than one woman at a time. That he was a lousy, two-timing schemer.

I'm waiting, Darin! Let's hear it!

"What I like most about women," Darin answered from behind the screen, "is their innate curiosity and their sense of adventure. I love their sensitivity, their creativity, and their unusual capacity for forgiveness."

Forgiveness? Was he kidding?

The response from the audience to Darin's reply was deafening. Angie was back at the curtain, eyes like saucers, mouth hanging slightly open in sort of a stupefied expression. Angie had apparently viewed the stallion full-on, and she was impressed.

Barbie sent silent thoughts through the airwaves to Angie. *Okay, already, I know he's a stud, and so does the blonde babe who snuggled up to him in the moonlight. A little perspective here would be good, and some more sympathy.*

"We have a final round of questions now," the host

announced in a very good rendition of a practiced sales "closer." However, Barbie couldn't concentrate on that final question. She could feel Darin's body heat right through that flimsy screen, and was sure he was doing something magical to her, because—to use Angie's phrase—she felt her panties knotting. Moreover, she felt a wave of sultriness *down there*, as if Darin had liquified something.

This was totally unacceptable. Darin Russell was a guy to be wary of. A loser, Barbie reminded herself. A big loser. A cheater.

"Bachelor Number One," she began hesitantly, twisting the cards, squeezing her knees together so hard that they hurt. As soon as this stupid show was over, she was out of there. They could give the winner his money back. The game was rigged. No way was she going to wait around for Darin to walk from behind that screen. She'd not come face-to-face with him under any circumstances. She was too weak. He had, for all his lies and useless drivel about shopping and eternity, turned out to be bad news.

"Bachelor Number One," Barbie began anew, ditching the cards and her well-thought-out questions, winging it now. "What do you think of men who cheat on their girlfriends, wives, or significant others?"

There came a hush from the audience, then several people clapped. Women, Barbie imagined. They wanted to know the answer to the question.

Bachelor Number One took a minute to think this over, possibly thrown for a loop. Would he be assessing his own loyalties?

"I think cheating is a crime," he replied, though not as cockily as before. "If people are truly committed, their hearts should be closed to others. Period."

Much response rose from the audience. The women liked this. The men with the women had to appear as though

they liked this reply as well. So far, so good, Barbie concluded. Bachelor Number One had rallied splendidly, though
the question was really aimed at that third chair, and the
louse sitting in it.

"Bachelor Number Two, same question if you please.
What do you think of men who cheat?"

When Barbie stole a glance her way, Angie cringed. She
might even have gone pale around the lips.

Bachelor Number Two also took a minute to reply. "I'll go
along with Bachelor Number One," he said finally, somewhat uncreatively, in Barbie's opinion. "Commitment is just
what it sounds like. Cheating should, for both parties in a
relationship, be totally unacceptable."

Applause from the audience, though not as enthusiastic as
previously. Angie had her eyes closed and her hands together
in prayer. Barbie's own dander was rising. Neither of the
men had answered her question, really. The question had
been about what they thought of men who cheated. Men.
Who cheated. Words were needed, like *slimeballs*, *nitwits*.
Words like *Lord strike me down if I ever cheat on a woman I am
involved with*.

"Bachelor Number Three," Barbie said, staring at the
screen. "Would *you* please tell me what you think of men
who cheat?"

Darin answered immediately. "Tarred and feathered," he
said. "Beheaded. Strung up by their fingers or feet."

Gasps from the audience, then some scattered applause.

"Unless, of course," Darin continued, "the woman only
assumes the guy was cheating. In any case, I would hope a
woman might first be sure the guy actually was cheating before any lynching begins. I'd hope she might give him a
chance to explain his position on the matter before jumping
to conclusions. She might give him a chance to exonerate
himself if she suspects he was dishonest. Especially"——he

emphasized this—"if the woman, the accuser, knows she is prone to moments of heightened imagination."

A moan came from Angie backstage. The host's impeccable smile faltered. Nevertheless, the audience clapped again, slowly at first, then picking up steam. The men, Barbie thought. The men were applauding Darin's reply. And then, strangely enough, the women joined in, having taken the time to think this answer over, Barbie guessed. The sound in the auditorium grew and grew. It continued for a very long time.

Finally, the show's host approached Barbie, his smile back in place. He urged the clapping to cease, which took some doing, and gestured for Barbie to stand. When she had, he said very clearly, "Those were some interesting and thought-provoking questions, Miss Bradley. Having heard the answers, have you made your choice? Who is it going to be? Which of these outstanding men is going to be the lucky winner of a date with you? Bachelor Number One?"

The audience showed their appreciation for Bachelor Number One's replies, and no doubt his appearance.

"Bachelor Number Two?"

Audience response was somewhat lighter, though still fairly robust.

"Or will Bachelor Number Three be the lucky winner tonight?"

The audience went wild. The room thundered. Several people got to their feet to show their enthusiasm for Bachelor Number Three. Heads poked up above the makeshift footlights.

Barbie's heart did a somersault. Darin had mesmerized them all, men and women alike. They wanted her to choose Bachelor Number Three, but she couldn't. She could not go there. Not again. Not ever. No way. No matter how slick his answers had been. No matter how much he had paid to be there. No matter how much she wanted to take his answers to heart. She'd been sick for a month over him. A full month. She hadn't slept and had barely eaten. She'd been snappish and difficult. No one deserved this kind of grief.

"Again, Miss Bradley," the host recapped, trying to urge her on. "Bachelor Number One, Bachelor Number Two, or Bachelor Number Three? Who is to plan that date?"

Barbie's heart thundered louder than the applause. She wanted to choose Darin. Who wouldn't want to? Only Darin had answered the questions correctly. Only he made her visualize a parallel universe where picket fences and castles went hand in hand. She'd have given anything for the blonde incident never to have happened. But it had.

In addition, the guy had a seat-ripping monster dog that was bigger than her apartment. She didn't dislike dogs, but for the sake of adding fuel to an already-kindled fire, she'd try to believe she disliked them. At least *his*. Because every bit of negativity helped.

"I've made my choice," she said over the ongoing uproar, swallowing with difficulty, trying to be heard. "Though it was a very difficult decision, and I'm sure all the gentlemen are superb, I've decided on Bachelor Number . . ."

Chapter Twenty-seven

"One."

The riotous uproar faded, trickled to a near stop, then started up again as the host raised his hands in praise of her decision. Clearly they weren't going to judge her negatively, but she was going to faint. The signs were clear: ringing in her ears, lightheadedness, the room spinning madly beneath the lights.

The host had hold of her arm and was gesturing for her to look toward the screen. Barbie couldn't make herself. What if the other two guys appeared? The unpicked? What if Darin contested her choice?

"Barbie Bradley, allow me to introduce you to Bachelor Number One. John James."

Amid the lingering applause, a man walked around the screen toward her, waving at the audience, smiling. Bachelor Number One was handsome, tall, and built. He had light-brown, curly hair, nicely-proportioned features, lawyerly wire-rimmed glasses, and he wore a dressy dark suit with matching shirt and tie. A lawyer for sure. Stockbroker would have been Barbie's second guess; he had indoor-profession pale skin.

He was, of course, everything she had thought she

wanted in a male, everything she had hoped for from an early age. Looks. Security. Class. Apparently, money. Angie had always teased her about her longing for peace and normalcy, since Angie's own dream included a more take-charge type of guy. Topping Angie's list would have been someone in a dangerous job like the FBI. An animal trainer, maybe, specializing in tigers and bears.

Bachelor Number One took Barbie's hand in his and smiled warmly. His hands were soft, on the cool side, and very un-Home-Depot-ish. She enjoyed his touch, but also knew she should wait for the room to stop spinning before speaking. It didn't. She waited for a *zing*. None came.

Trying to hold it together, and with her fingers interlacing those of her chosen bachelor, Barbie faced the crowd.

"Now, let me tell you what's in store," the host announced. "First, a romantic dinner at Chez Français. After that, a shopping spree at Nordstrom. Then we have a surprise. We have you booked on that cruise! Five nights aboard the *Stardust*! Plenty of spending cash. Tons of romance on the high seas! No phones, no distractions! Come on, folks. Give it up for our happy couple!"

The audience again went ballistic, only now it all seemed like white noise to Barbie. Static. Incomprehensible sound. She was beginning to fade. There were ringing sounds in her ears. Her stomach turned over. In front of God and Miami's finest, on this very stage, she was going to pass out.

Her last thought was that she should have worn pants.

Barbie drifted, eyes closed, taking refuge in the sudden darkness. Faces with smiles dissolved. White noise dissipated. Then there was nothing.

Well, almost nothing. Barbie had a sense of cooler air on her face, and of people waiting for her to do something to let them know she was okay. Sighing, feeling depressed, she opened her eyes. A face came into focus. An unfamiliar face. A cry of alarm caught in Barbie's throat. Events came rushing back. When the clapping started back up, she supposed she might puke. Instead, she stared wide-eyed at the unfamiliar male looking down at her—the male that was fanning her with cue cards.

"Where am I?" she asked.

"The floor," the guy said, offering his hand.

Both Bachelor Number One and the game-show host quickly helped Barbie to her feet. God help her, she was still on that stage, beneath the lights. No darkness was here to be had. No wind on her face to dry the sweat on her forehead.

The audience showed their appreciation of her recovery with whoops and shouts. Angie hopped up and down anxiously in the wings, held back by the show's producer.

Looking out over the lights, Barbie smoothed her skirt with her free hand, wondering how, with a skirt this snug, she had managed to faint gracefully. Had she sagged or plunked? Only when her legs regained some feeling did she venture a glance past her date to see who else waited by the white screen.

Clang!

Darin had closed in but was unable to reach her. Bachelor Number Two, a tall, lithe Brit with spiky auburn hair, held on to Darin's arm. Both he and Darin looked tense. The expression on Darin's face could have done it for Barbie right then and there. Concern. Hurt. And something else? Possessiveness, maybe?

She clenched her jaw so hard it ached. What was up with that look of his? He wanted a harem? Girls of all hair types?

Damn him. After all this time, he was still dark and majestic in a suit that fit him as if he were in an Armani ad, his facial angles were still chiseled, his long hair lusciously shiny, his green eyes trained on her. The man was eye candy, and she was recovering from a bad sweet tooth.

Thing was, she just couldn't get over the idea that the connection they had went way beyond the obvious physical attraction, and she had only begun to discover reasons why she'd felt so strongly about him right off the bat. They'd only had one dinner, for Pete's sake, and not even that, really. Nevertheless, his expression, the way he looked at her . . . it all made her want to rush into his arms.

Remember those secrets of his? The lies? Remember the pain?

With great effort, feeling the intensity of Darin's gaze even over the lights, Barbie made herself turn. Taking a deep breath, waving her free hand toward the audience, she allowed Bachelor Number One, the man she had chosen in Darin's place, to lead her off the stage. With one more glance over her shoulder, one more twinge in her nether regions, she witnessed Darin being led in the opposite direction.

"You're all right?" Bachelor Number One asked, as if he might be afraid she had some secret and communicable disease that made fainting a habit.

"I'm fine," Barbie said as Angie finally reached her side. "That was pretty embarrassing, huh?"

"You got that right," Angie said.

"Doesn't matter, if you're okay," Bachelor Number One corrected. "Can I drive you home?"

"Tonight?" This was said by Angie and Barbie in unison.

"No time like the present to get a jump on things," Bachelor Number One said.

A jump on things? Barbie and Angie shared a look.

"I can get home by myself," Angie muttered quickly. "No need to worry about me. You go ahead, Barb. I think I have a hankering to chat up one of those bachelors you rejected."

Barbie eyed her pal with an expression that had *traitor* written all over it.

"Good," Bachelor Number One said. "Because I'd like to hang on to you"—he grinned at Barbie—"in case you decide to hit the floor again."

He made her little incident sound so charming.

"It was the heat from the lights," she told him. "I'm better now."

"In that case, fresh air might do some good. My car is right outside, and it's a convertible. Do you have everything?"

No, I most certainly do not have everything, Barbie wanted to shout. She'd lost both her wits and the man she'd once wanted desperately to get to know better. Her real choice of dates was a jerk.

"I'll get your purse," Angie offered.

"Bring it over *later*," Barbie said pointedly, glaring at her pal.

"I'll bring it over later," Angie repeated, understanding the request for backup. "On my way home. Shouldn't take me too long."

Thanks, Ang. Barbie meant it.

Barbie allowed Bachelor Number One to lead her toward the main entrance to the club, telling herself this was the perfect ending for a night that seemed totally unreal. She didn't look at the guy beside her, though, because she was still riding out the leftover internal buzz from the shock of seeing Darin. She was trying for the thousandth time to reason out why a guy she hardly knew had so gotten under her skin. A guy with personality issues. Bachelor Number One was a viable alternative, surely. Everything in the right place, concern on his face.

"I'll get the car," he told her, propping her against a pillar with a helping hand on her elbow, dangling his keys in the light from the country club's grand portico entry. "All right to leave you here for a minute?"

"Sure." Barbie tried to smile as she slumped. But as soon as her bachelor had gone, she acknowledged the lump in her throat and the unusual wetness in her eyes with real surprise.

Who was she kidding? She wasn't ready for a new guy. Bachelor Number One was nothing more than a feeble attempt at a rebound. This entire game show event had been traumatic. She'd get Angie for this. Payback, big-time. Just now, however, all she wanted was to go home and sulk. Alone.

"Hello, Barbie," a voice whispered in her ear.

Clang!

Revolving slowly, drawn to the sexy puff of air on the back of her neck, Barbie gazed disbelievingly at her angelic-faced nemesis. Her heart sputtered. Her lips parted in a silent moan.

"You okay?" Darin asked.

"Fine."

"It's good to see you."

She could not even respond to that.

"Why didn't you return my calls?" he asked.

"You didn't live up to my expectations."

"Oh? I thought we hit it off famously."

"If you thought so, you might have made an error in your reasoning."

Her speech was good, she thought, though her treacherous body was wagging all over like a lovesick puppy and already leaning toward him. She drew herself back.

"I agreed to go shopping," Darin said.

"Men often say things they don't mean in order to get women into bed."

She was, Barbie decided, being very adult about this, now that she was facing him. The anger she'd built up over the past month had flattened considerably. Darin's closeness, though sending ripples of remembered pleasure through her, was to be put into perspective.

First, there had been Liar Bill. Now Cheating Darin. The knot in her stomach was the size of a doughnut.

No karate chops were attempted, to her credit, although she had dreamed of a good sucker punch or two. She didn't yell, plead, or whine. She could hardly muster any cynicism at all. Lust just wasn't reasonable.

"I want to date you," Darin told her softly, seriously, earnestly, in a voice that caused Barbie's knees to bobble. "I want you all to myself," he added.

"That's very interesting, Darin, since you had your chance and blew it."

"I tried to explain. You wouldn't let me."

"Heavy breathing on the phone doesn't explain anything. Dog at my door didn't work either."

"I couldn't face you, Barbie, in person."

"That's flattering."

Did Darin's expression seem more tender than she remembered, as though he really missed her? As though he might also be in pain? Could she honestly dismiss the fact that the zings and the longings were piling up the longer he remained in her breathing space?

"I apologize if I've done anything to upset you," Darin said. "I'll make it up to you, if you'll let me."

Dang. This had been said with believable sincerity. Barbie's pulse pushed at her skin. Her butt, encased in her tight black skirt, was actually moving, sidling closer to Darin Russell. A moth to a flame.

She had to do something. Quick. Self-preservation.

"You fondled a blonde after you ditched me on our first date!" she charged, breathless.

"So." Darin sighed, his dark hair falling luxuriantly around his tanned cheeks. "You did see Jess, and you won't believe me when I tell you it isn't what you think? That Jess is my sister?"

"Hmmm. I'm sure women haven't heard *that* one before."

"What if it's the truth?"

"There used to be a saying about a person who cried wolf too many times, Darin."

Listen to him! Barbie's body cried.

Fat chance! her mind countered.

Darin straightened. His brow creased. "You aren't going to forgive me or let me explain?"

"Not today."

"You really don't care?"

"Not at the moment."

Liar! her consciousness shouted. Liar Barbie! You do care. You care so much that you can't be reasonable. You just don't want to be hurt like this ever again.

Darin's right eyebrow arched below his furrowed forehead. Barbie had loved that expressive eyebrow, once. His taut pecs shifted behind his shirt, causing Barbie's hands to curl into fists. She had loved those pecs, and had had absolutely no chance to touch them. Not one single touch.

Remember the pain, she told herself. Focus on how it felt to see Darin with that other woman. So what if she still had the hots for him? So what if he was absolutely the most exquisite thing she had ever laid eyes on? So what if she had felt a connection beyond those frivolous external things that she hadn't had any time to explore? Darin Russell was demented if he thought she'd be one of many women in his entourage. Lust for a man like that was a downward spiral.

"Tomorrow?" Darin said, touching her sleeve briefly, somehow understanding her fragility and her need for distance. "Will you see me tomorrow? Speak with me tomorrow?"

Barbie shook her head. "If you had a sister who had a night like mine, would you advise her to go out with a guy like you again?"

Darin looked surprised by the question. He said, "I suppose that's a tricky question, since I . . . have a good excuse for disappearing that night."

Barbie rolled her eyes. "They always do." *They* being cheaters.

"I can't tell you about it here," Darin said.

Ah-ha! A secret, is it? You're a sex fiend, maybe? With a middle name of Womanizer?

Barbie gathered herself. "You'd want your sister to sort through this instead of moving on?" she asked. "To pour salt on the wound?"

Darin remained intent, as though he was struggling with something. "I suppose not. Not on the facts you're clinging to, anyway."

Barbie nodded. "I rest my case."

But the plain truth was that she wanted Darin's arms around her. She wanted his lips and hips on hers. She wanted to believe him, meet him in the morning, hear what he had to say. Yet she had vowed not to cave. She had promised herself not to dip her toe into the pool of pain again. No two-timers. No secrets. No going back.

"Tell me now," she said simply. "Explain now."

A car pulled up at the curb. The driver side door opened with a luxurious whoosh, and the interior light came on.

"Don't go with this guy," Darin said. "Don't let him drive you home."

"Double standard?" she quipped.

Again, Darin shook his head. "A double-edged sword. If I tell you why I left, I might lose you. If I don't tell you, I might lose you. I honestly don't know what to do."

Bachelor Number One emerged from the car. Funny, Barbie thought, she couldn't even remember his name.

"We could start over," Darin suggested.

"With visions of blondes dancing in my head?"

"There is no blonde. None that affects the relationship between you and me, anyway."

"Next you'll tell me it really was your sister out there that night."

"My sister, yes. Jessie."

"Oh, please!"

"I'll introduce you. I'll arrange it."

Bachelor Number One was ten feet away, looking slightly perturbed. Darin was appraising Barbie with those expressive eyes of his. Was she nuts to turn down his offer? Could Darin have a valid excuse for his behavior? Wouldn't Bachelor One be a better option, anyway? A fresh slate? Didn't everyone always say that the third time was charm? Wouldn't this new bachelor be the third man in her life?

She smiled sadly as her new date approached. "Good night, Darin," she said and, heart pounding like there was no tomorrow, turned to face the man who'd won her.

"Don't let him in your apartment," Darin begged, voice like liquid Oreos, lips much too close to Barbie's ear. "Do not invite him in. It wouldn't be safe."

Over and above all the ridiculous zinging, Barbie wobbled forward on legs made of Jell-O, muttering to herself, "Story of my life."

Chapter Twenty-eight

Bachelor Number One's Mercedes (what else?) hummed not with the growl of Darin's Porsche, but more the sound of an overly confident cat. Also unlike her drive with Darin, Bachelor One drove slowly, taking his own sweet time, both hands on the wheel as they exited through the gates of the country club. Barbie's heart felt like granite.

"I thought," Bachelor Number One said once they were on the road, "I'd take you home to change clothes, then to my place for dinner. I had it all arranged." He glanced at her. "Just in case."

"What?"

"My place. Dinner. You and me." He grinned widely.

Barbie winced. "You don't think it might be a bit soon for dinner at your place?"

"Maybe. But we wouldn't want to go on that cruise if we're not a match, would we?"

She supposed he had a point there. And since he had no idea she probably wouldn't go on that cruise anyway, it was nice that he'd been prepared. At the same time, she fought with herself about what she really wanted. Did she really want to let this new guy take her home, to know where she lived? Did she want to go to his place? She kept hearing

Darin's warnings. Chances were good that Darin had spoken out of frustration rather than real caution, though. Right? Did Darin deserve to be listened to, anyway? He of the roving heart?

Frustration swirled anew.

"Um . . . in that case, I'm on Fifth Street," Barbie said.

What she really wanted was for Bachelor One to do a uey. She wanted to go back to the country club so that she could hear Darin's explanation of who that darned blonde really was, and what had happened to such a promising night. Only, her fragile ego wouldn't let her give the directive. By foregoing the chance to choose Darin in that game, she had opted for a different future—one with another eligible man—and at the same time had dished out a little dirt of her own, giving back to Mr. Russell a sample of what was due him. These things should have made her a happy camper. Instead, misery had settled. Instead of being sweet, revenge had turned into something sticky. Like wadded gum that she couldn't get off the bottom of her shoe.

"Second block down on Fifth," she elaborated, experiencing mental gyrations, fidgeting on the seat. She was feeling cold all over, unanimated. The fact that the man driving her home might be considered handsome no longer mattered; he'd not produced one single spark in her so far. No fireworks, no vibrations, no heat at all. In fact, he gave off a chilly vibe. Where was the storm, the lightning, the inner-thigh vibration? Where were the rips in the leather seats made by a big, slobbery dog? She seriously doubted Bachelor Number One would allow an animal in his car at all. Nor wet feet. The floor mats were immaculate. The car smelled like strawberries. He had, in fact, not even put the top down for her to get some air.

"You truly are okay, right?" Bachelor Boy asked, obviously thinking about her fainting spell.

"Sure."

In point of fact, she wasn't okay at all—not by a long shot. Something down deep inside of her hurt real bad.

"Sorry for the silence," she said, figuring she might actually look as bad as she felt. "I'll bet I'm a mess. Does this great car have a mirror?"

She pulled down the visor. Surprise! No mirror there. The huge sum this car had cost, and they had forgotten about women passengers needing fluffing? About women needing to spy—as in Barbie's desire to see if a Porsche might be following them? The only way she would know if Darin was back there now was to turn around and look. Very uncool.

Bachelor One glanced at her, frowning. "Inconvenient oversight, I guess. I'll take the car back to the dealer tomorrow and make sure they give me all the niceties."

Barbie smiled—prettily, she hoped, but not too suggestively. Wouldn't want to lead this guy on, though he *was* tall, good-looking, well dressed, polite, and drove a pricey luxury car. You know, all those things a girl in her right mind might find alluring. Attributes a mother would encourage her daughter to seek out. Believe it or not, Barbie could imagine her mom smiling right now. Maybe she was being too disagreeable by not giving this guy a chance.

"Do you own a hammer?" she found herself asking insanely, recalling his smooth, unblemished palms, and needing to get to the nitty-gritty right up front. She needed to see how he actually might compare to . . . that other person she wouldn't go so far as to name.

Obviously reticent to take his eyes off the road, Bachelor One glanced sideways again, skeptically, as though he might not have heard the question correctly.

"Are you good with your hands?" Barbie asked, rephrasing.

This drew a cagey smile. "I assure you I am."

Oh. Sexual innuendo. Typical male wisecrack. The image

of her smiling mother dimmed somewhat. In its place came a rolling sensation, a longing for something else, some*one* else, which left Barbie feeling sad, empty, and ungrounded. Dammit, she had to either admit to loving Darin Russell, in spite of his cheating, or forget him completely.

She wasn't in the mood for company of a new-guy sort. She was depressed. Her insides writhed. Action was what she wanted, some way to rid herself of the excess energy. Running? Screaming and pointing fingers? Rambo Barbie desperately wanted to make a comeback.

Then again, she'd chosen this bachelor, this person who might be expecting something other than the big brush-off for his effort. He'd forked out ten thousand bucks for charity. He had shown concern over her fainting spell, and had dinner waiting. Probably he was a nice man who deserved a little attention. Could he help it if there were no dog-ripped holes in his car's leather seats? Guilt was a terrible thing, and not unfamiliar to any of the Barbies fighting for dominance.

Small talk? She could do that at least until they got to her door. Then excuses about first-date protocol. Those rules had proven value. Darin had agreed to take her shopping, though admittedly he had been in her bedroom at the time. In her bedroom, pushing her buttons—

"I'd like to go back," she announced firmly. "To the country club. It's important. I forgot something, something I have to attend to. We can talk about the date tomorrow, okay?"

Gad! Hadn't Darin used those same words the night she'd caught him with Blondie? Something he "had to attend to"?

She about gave herself whiplash when she turned her head, and put a hand to her lips to keep from screaming. Could Darin have been giving the blonde the old heave-ho in the same way she was now intending to heave-ho Bachelor

Number One? Could the blonde have been a prior attachment? Or could the beach babe truly have been Darin's sister?

Barbie's life passed before her eyes, and not in a good way. She had been blindsided by anger, overcome by flaws in her own character. Now, all she could think about was getting the answers she needed from the only person who could give them to her. And Bachelor Number One was in the way.

He drew back in his seat, not turning the car around. His expression had darkened considerably. His knuckles were white on the wheel. "I thought we were on a roll," he said.

Huh? What to do? What to do? Apart from returning Bachelor Number One and demanding a trade-in.

If he wouldn't turn around, she'd have to get to her door and leave him outside of it. Five minutes, tops, and they would reach her street. Chitchat she could manage in the meantime, maybe with some flattery tossed in to soften the blow. Then she'd go back to the club.

"What do you do for a living?" she asked, thinking this a good place to begin a conversation. But the old song began in her head: rich man, poor man, beggar man . . . graveyard keeper!

"Attorney," he answered. "Wills and trusts."

Barbie rubbed her forehead, thinking of making a wisecrack, then reminded herself that lawyers had their own share of jokes and might be sensitive.

"That's nice," she said. "My dad's a judge."

"Yes, I know."

"Really?" She was surprised. "How?"

"I made it my business to find out who I'd be bidding on."

"I thought my identity was to be kept secret!"

"I," he said with another meaningful grin, "have my ways."

Did she want to shout *Ew*?

"Here," she said instead, with relief. "Pull over here."

The Mercedes slid smoothly to a stop. Barbie hardly noticed when the engine was switched off; she was too busy contemplating her apartment door and what would happen when they reached it. She was seeing shadows where there weren't any, and knowing deep down that hoping to see a monster dog would be futile. She had made that very clear to Darin.

"I'll get your door," her companion announced. As he slipped out of the car, Barbie gazed down the street, then at her tight skirt and heels. No way she could run. At best, she'd toddle like a glammed-up geisha. And oh boy, she so did want to run—all the way back to the club. Those pesky hairs on the nape of her neck were standing up again, each and every one of them pointing back toward Darin.

"Gosh. The dizziness is back," she announced as her door opened and she got to her feet. "I hope it's not contagious. You might want to leave me here in case it is. Thanks for the ride. Congratulations on winning. Why don't you call me tomorrow?"

Bachelor Number One's face was unreadable, pale, and perfectly smooth. "All right," he conceded, leaning in to press her up against the side of his car. "Can I have your number?"

Barbie moved her fingers, realized she was purseless, and offered up a wary smile. *Damn*. "Got a pen and paper?"

"Nope. New car. New suit. Maybe you have a pen inside? A business card?"

Double damn. Trapped.

"Sure. I'm just up those stairs," she said.

"I'll tag along to get the number. Make sure you get in all right."

He didn't back off or away, though, and Barbie had to slide sideways to get clear. With a fake smile affixed to her face, she headed up the steps as quickly as her skirt would allow.

"I'm so sorry about tonight," she called over her shoulder. "No hard feelings?"

Bachelor One, close on her heels, said simply, "Women generally don't know what they want, I've found."

Barbie would have turned her head again to address that comment, but she'd almost reached her door and didn't want to lose momentum. Once there, she reached up on top of the doorframe to find her extra key, knowing this guy's eyes were on her and she'd have to find a new hiding place, then jammed the key in the lock and heard the lock click. The door swung open.

She stepped inside, expecting her new date to follow. He didn't.

"May I come in?" he asked, back to being polite.

Don't let him inside, Darin had warned. *It would be dangerous.*

"I just need a drink of something—and that phone number," the guy elaborated. "I built up quite a thirst under those lights."

"Of course," Barbie replied, guessing at the reasons for Darin's warnings and finding them lacking. "Come on in."

Did the guy's smile have a sinister cast to it as his long legs carried him over the threshold? He stood for a full minute just barely inside of the tiny foyer.

"What would you like to drink?" Barbie asked, turning to walk into the kitchen.

"A Bloody Mary would be nice."

Barbie's steps faltered, though not noticeably, she hoped. Her heart sputtered as she groped around on the counter for a pen.

"Sorry. Tap water or juice is all I've got."

Pen and paper. Thank heavens! She scribbled her phone number down as fast as she could and started to hand it over.

"Maybe," he suggested, appearing beside her so quickly she didn't have time to set the pen down, "one good-night kiss before I go?"

She had no idea how he could have closed the distance so fast. His eyes, when she looked up, seemed to be glowing like polished lava. Black, with red rims.

As Bachelor Number One brushed a strand of hair from her neck with his cool fingertips, Barbie sucked in a breath. His touch was icy. Nothing warm or sexy about it. Before she could blink, his mouth had replaced his fingertips, resting on the skin above her throbbing carotid artery. Like some kind of freakin' vampire!

Completely horrified, and afraid she had made a huge mistake by allowing this guy anywhere near her, Barbie shoved him back, held up one finger and ran. Ducking into the bathroom, she locked the door behind her.

She'd really gone and done it now, gotten herself in a fix. Her heart raced like all get-out. Here she was, smeared against the wall of her bathroom like roadkill on the highway, breath coming in fits, afraid to move. The idiot in her kitchen wanted to . . . at the very least nuzzle her neck, and who knew when Angie might arrive to save her? It was just unbelievable that Darin could have been right about this . . . this . . . rapacious Romeo.

She should never have let him into her apartment. She should never have allowed him to drive her home. She most definitely did not want to go back out there, or have his body parts against hers in any way, shape, or form. He was a real piece of work, this guy. Her gut told her that he was not going to go away.

Escaping seemed like a very good plan—but it was also

out of the question. The bathroom had only one door and one small window above the tub. It was a window she'd never fit through, even if she could reach.

Barely perceptible scratching sounds brought her around, irritating sounds that were moving across the exterior surface of the bathroom door, as though the guy on the other side of it had sharp nails. Grimacing, Barbie scanned the bathroom for something, anything, she might use to protect herself. She found nothing but a discarded pile of clothes.

Yet, this was a start. Without her tight skirt she could at least try to make a running jump up to that window. If one could run in a six-by-six-foot space.

She rummaged through the pile, which turned out to be the discarded outfit she'd worn on her last outing to the cemetery—sweat pants, a big T-shirt, running shoes—clothes she had banned from her closet due to the bad luck of wearing them to see Darin get a kiss on the cheek from his other woman. She'd left the clothes on the floor while entertaining thoughts of burning them as an offering to the Move-on gods, but hadn't yet gotten to it.

As she stripped, the scratching on the door ceased, replaced by a steady thumping, as if Bachelor One was seeking a weak spot in the wood.

Ugh!

"Come out, come out, wherever you are," the guy said in a truly Bates Motel manner.

Again, Barbie eyed the window. She eyed her hips, which were not excessive, but certainly bigger than eight-by-eight inches. If she made it out of here, she vowed, she'd have her brothers sue the country club for not crossing sociopaths off their eligibility list. For divulging her name beforehand. For having the damn game in the first place!

The door bulged. Barbie's eyes did the same. She had to

get up to that window and out, no matter how painful! She gathered herself for a first try at that running jump.

An unexpected crashing sound drove her off course and against the pedestal sink. A sound followed of something splintering.

A muffled oath followed the crash, an oath that hadn't come from Barbie. More noises ensued, rising in volume. Growling, snarling, scuffling, banging . . . and something else breaking. Rolling-around sounds. Another oath. A long, drawn-out, batlike screech. Then silence, sudden and deafening.

Chapter Twenty-nine

Barbie opened her eyes one at a time. The bathroom door was intact. She glanced at herself. *She* was intact—and shaking. She was alone. And, enough was enough. Members of the Bradley family didn't take easily or kindly to people trying to scare them, she reminded herself. All the Bradley siblings had been raised to be strong and independent.

To be a teacher in a Miami high school, one had to be impervious to mental meltdowns and pushy personalities. Plus, didn't she have a full arsenal of help to draw inspiration from? All those other Barbies? Already she could feel the rise of Rambo Barbie inside of her. The guy out there would dare to have a temper tantrum in her apartment?

Straightening her legs, waiting a few seconds more while her alter ego took a full grip, she at last reached for the knob and yanked. No jerks lounged in the hallway. Gathering more resolve, she tiptoed around the corner, came up short, stifled a shout of dismay. Her living room looked like a battle zone. A broken lamp dangled by its cord. The coffee table had been halved and lay in pieces. Couch cushions were strewn everywhere, the fabric slashed. Foam was scattered all over the place. Feathers floated through the air. The rug was bunched. The sofa sat perpendicular to the kitchen wall. Several thin aluminum pieces of her window blinds were bent at odd angles. The front door gaped wide open.

To her relief, the scene, bad as it was, did not seem to be further complicated by any pissy bachelors with date rage. Not a single one. But as she surveyed the mess, Barbie felt her hackles rise. Who was going to take care of this? Who was going to pay for the damage? Who was going to clean up the mess?

Jaw clenched, panties again in a knot, Barbie launched herself through the open doorway. Ultimately this was Darin's fault. Rambo Barbie was going to make him pay.

Since she hadn't ordered a cab and didn't have her purse to pay for one, Barbie figured it was the perfect time to start a jogging routine. Luckily, she'd changed into appropriate clothes. Off like a shot, she mentally went over her plan: Darin would likely go back to the graveyard. She would go there, too, and confront him. She would find Darin, give him a piece of her mind, and demand answers so that she could once again breathe properly, eat regularly, and sleep through a night without nightmares of Darin and the blonde. It was called closure. Even if closure might break her heart.

The full moon that shone brightly above her head would make things easy, she hoped. She probably didn't have to worry about anyone other than Darin on the cemetery grounds. What person in his or her right mind would be there at night?

She jogged the four miles to Forest Lawn, stopping twenty times to gasp for air. When she arrived, not a single car was parked beneath the solitary light pole in the lot. This was just as she'd expected.

Over the curb and under the trees she ran, breathing like a puffer fish, certain Dog would hear, if Dog was on duty. The moon continued to illuminate everything. Barbie could see quite clearly the outlines and shadings of all she sprinted past, and decided that whoever had invented running shoes should be enfolded in a big bear hug.

The graveyard, at first seemingly quiet, was actually alive with sounds. Crickets trilled. Frogs croaked. Night birds called distantly from branches moving in the breeze. The markers and gravestones radiated heat they'd stored from the day, warming up the already-humid air.

This was the right thing, Barbie told herself. She was doing the right thing.

Deeper beneath the trees she went, without slowing her pace. As she inhaled the evergreen scent, she slowly became aware of movement on the periphery. Something running alongside?

Unexpectedly, all sound ceased—no more crickets, frogs, or birds, and only the rasping of her strained breath. She stopped, whispered a terrible thought. "Things that go bump in the night?"

From her place behind a tall gravestone, Barbie stared into the dark, listening to the silence beyond her pumping heart. She was rewarded by a faint sound. Seconds later, it came again. Barbie saw movement, a kind of sliding shadow beneath the trees.

Waiting several more pounding heartbeats, Barbie walked stealthily toward those shadows. A rustling from behind made her turn. She felt, rather than saw, the presence that glided past. Then she noted movement again to her right.

More rustling noises from her left. She whirled. No one emerged from those shadows beneath the trees. Nothing stood out. Not one single soul, Stephen King–like or otherwise, presented itself to her.

"Well," she said aloud, hands firmly on her hips. "Where are you?"

No response came at first, and then a low and almost fierce noise like a growl floated her way.

"Dog?" Barbie called, goose bumps sprouting. "Here, doggie."

The fact that Dog, if it was Dog, did not heel, gave Barbie pause.

A snapping of a twig caused her to spin again. "Darin?"

Silence. Still no crickets, no Dog, no Darin. So, what could that be beneath the trees?

Steeling herself, chanting inwardly, There's no such things as ghosts, Barbie headed forward, only to see the slinking shadow drift farther away. She trotted after it.

The shadow moved faster. Barbie moved faster. Building up speed, she dodged obstacles, hurdled small grave markers, scrambled through bushes, and cleared a hedge to land miraculously on both feet. Able to make out a dark patch not twenty feet in front of her, she continued to give chase until she slipped on a patch of dampness and nearly went down.

The dark thing she'd been chasing halted as well. Barbie righted herself, thinking of Peter's elusive shadow in J. M. Barrie's *Peter Pan*. Gritting her teeth, she resumed the chase. The dark blob also took off.

"Stop!" she shouted. The blob did no such thing. It continued on through the darkness at a medium pace, seeming simply to match her strides while keeping close to the trees, never quite outdistancing her.

They must have circled back; Barbie couldn't be sure. She had run out of breath, and slowed beside another tall, gray marker. The blob had disappeared. She saw in a full-on wash of moonlight that she stood very near to the avenue of crypts.

Hesitantly, and with a screwed-up expression, she took a step toward the buildings. Mid-second step, she was jerked backward and almost off of her feet. Strong arms had her from behind before she could say boo.

"Women," the raspy voice behind her swore, and a hand

quickly covered her mouth. It was déjà vu all over again. Barbie couldn't talk or move.

"How can I help your friend if you shout?" Darin whispered in her ear. "Really, women nowadays are too much. Stop wiggling, Barbie!"

Barbie stopped wiggling. Her heart pumped faster.

"Relax," Darin told her. "It's me. Do you and Angie have some kind of fixation with this place?"

Fixation? Breathing in Darin's oh-so-manly scent, feeling her body quiver over his nearness in a way that was absolutely not part of the plan, Barbie closed her eyes briefly to get her priorities in order.

"I went to your apartment to make sure you were all right," Darin told her. "Are you?"

Huh? He'd gone to her apartment?

She nodded, tentative.

"I warned you about James. He is quite the suitor. Actually, if truth be told, he's more like a leech. Thank God he didn't get his hands on you. Or his teeth. He was supposed to lose that damned game. Stupid bloodsucker! I'd never have allowed him close to you. He wasn't to get anywhere near you. That bathroom door wouldn't have held him back for long."

Even if it made sense, Barbie would have been unable to contribute to this conversation with a hand over her mouth, so she went momentarily limp. Darin had gone to her apartment to . . . rescue her? From a bachelor run amok? Darin had fought a giant leech over her? Were those the sounds she had heard? The reason for the mess? She really couldn't breathe. She wriggled again. Was held fast.

"I made him see reason," Darin said.

So, Barbie told herself, though her mind was spinning, maybe Darin was holding her like this because he wanted to get a few words in? The thing was, his flesh on her flesh—in this case, the palm of his hand on her lips—brought back all her latent sexual feelings. The thought of his big rescue didn't do any harm, either.

"In the meantime, right after you headed out of your apartment, your friend Angie stopped by. Not finding you there, she came this way. Fast. In her little red car. I followed, wondering why she'd think you'd be here. *Now* look at us," Darin groused. "And if you stop to demand explanations this time, you may never share little chocolate cookies with your best friend again."

Barbie twisted in his grasp. Speaking her mind seemed of the utmost importance, but being physically stronger, Darin kept the upper hand.

When no further explanation came for such a serious statement about Angie, she gave a violent heave. Bionic, even. Darin didn't budge. Barbie figured that any further struggling would be a waste of time and energy.

"I'll take my hand away if you'll listen to me," Darin told her. "If you promise to behave, I'll let you go."

The word *behave* rang in Barbie's ears. What was she— ten years old? Sadly, however, she couldn't manage much outrage. Darin's touch felt too good. He had rescued her. She didn't want him to let her go, really. Surrounded by Darin's arms was exactly where she wanted to be.

"I usually *cart*, remember? Sack of potatoes?" Darin said. "I can do that again if you refuse to cooperate."

"How could I forget carting?"

Wow! Barbie heard that. Darin's hand had dropped away. She spoke rapidly in case he changed his mind. "You're saying that Angie is out here, too?"

"Yes." Darin's fingers pressed to her lips, suggesting discretion in volume.

Barbie whispered, "Angie has no reason to be out here. Her car wasn't in the lot."

"She must have parked on the adjacent street. I'm sure she was looking for you."

"Why would Angie be looking for me out here?" Barbie asked.

"Maybe she knows you better than you know yourself." Darin shrugged. "Enough to figure you'd quickly take James's measure and end up here."

"Of all the pompous, egotistical . . ." Barbie couldn't even form the thoughts necessary to finish that statement.

"She is your best friend, isn't she?" Darin said, reminding Barbie that Angie did indeed know her about as well as anyone could. But, geez, was she so predictable?

Darin still hadn't allowed her to turn around. "This is sort of like musical chairs," he said. "You, me, Angie. Something always interrupts us from actually getting down to matters at hand."

"No time like the present," Barbie declared.

"Spoken like a true best friend."

Crap. Did he have to be right about that? "Where would Angie be, exactly?" Barbie demanded impatiently. "What was all that about never eating cookies with her again?"

Darin waved. "She's in one of these, probably."

"These?" The word hissed out. Did Darin mean one of the crypts? Had he suggested that Angie might be in one?

"If she was outside, I would have found her. It's likely one of them has her," Darin elaborated unhelpfully.

"Them?" Barbie's heart flopped. The conversation had taken on the connotations of a science-fiction thriller. "Who is *Them*?"

No answer.

Barbie turned to look at her incredibly mystifying protector. There he was: in the dark, his hunky outline shadowed by the trees, his face—what she could see of it—achingly handsome in the muted moonlight. He was dressed in the slacks he'd worn at the country club, minus the jacket. His shirt was open at the neck, showing off a triangle of muscled chest that seemed to strain at the buttons. Oh, how she'd fantasized about that chest. She very nearly moaned.

Now that she was checking him over, she hadn't recalled his shoulders being quite so wide. They had stretched his jacket at the Gypsy place, sure, yet one more bit of stretching now and he'd have to go up a shirt size.

Another quick peek at Darin's face showed his flesh white around the edges of his tan, and growing whiter by the minute. His hair hung like a lush curtain over his ears and part of his cheeks in contrast. The darkness hid most of his expression.

No true moonlight reached them beneath this old tree canopy, Barbie realized. Only the faintest of silver streams dappled the ground nearby.

"Who has Angie?" Barbie repeated, hands clenched to keep from running her fingers over Darin's exposed chest. "Where's Dog?"

"I've corralled Dog due to his inability to keep quiet. I'm about to do the same thing to you."

Barbie drew back. Didn't guys know anything about women? About female behavior? If her best friend was out here somewhere, and someone called *Them* had her, was this a time for quiet reflection? Don't think so.

Darin pulled her closer, so that Barbie had to tilt her head back to see his face. She'd had to do this before, of course, at the restaurant, but at that time Darin had only seemed several inches taller. Here, he loomed like a giant. Did her being in sneakers make the difference?

What hadn't changed was the effect Darin had on her. A totally out-of-place and unwarranted buzz ricocheted through Barbie's abdomen as it touched his. Actually, the buzz came from a bit lower than her abdomen, centered right between her not-so-charming, sweatpants-covered thighs. It didn't turn out to be any old buzz, either, but more like a call to action of female hormones—the hormones unregulated by common sense. The ones urging her to lip-lock this guy. The ones stimulated by hair-raising situations like this. Face it, she was an adrenaline junkie.

"Once again," Darin said, his breath stirring the hair on top of her head in such a way as to stir up quite a few other body parts as well. "I'd have to go into long explanations as to who this might be. Do you want to take the time for that?"

"No," Barbie allowed. "Find Angie first, explanations after." Common sense after all? Which Barbie was that?

Something else had struck her, a thought rather terrifying. What if the continuation of these lustful cravings for Darin weren't simply any old lustful cravings? What if the bells and whistles she'd experienced in his presence all along were nothing less than Cupid's incoming silver-tipped arrows? She was inexperienced, true, but what if this actually was . . . love?

"Why are you frowning?" Darin asked.

"Why are you getting bigger?" Barbie countered.

"You said explanations later."

"Then you *are* getting bigger?"

He sighed. "There's a good possibility I am."

"Brother. Those explanations had better be good."

"Oh, they will be. Now, will you please stay where I put you while I search for Angie?" he asked.

"You're kidding, right? Been there. Not going backward this time. Think of me as glue."

"I'll find Angie if you please do as I suggest."

"Sorry. Tonight I'm Rebel Barbie, so letting you out of my sight would be a stretch."

"Then I'll have to lock you in with Dog." Darin indicated the closest crypt with a wave of his hand.

Barbie searched the outline of the building and grimaced. "You're telling me Dog's in there? Inside that marble thing?"

"Yes."

"Pass."

"You don't have a choice."

"I'm a brown belt in karate and not afraid to try out what I've learned in class. Want to see?" Barbie threatened.

Darin shook his head, long hair flying in the breeze. He chuckled sort of wickedly, the sound fading into a snort that reminded Barbie of the scratch-and-sniff game and the noises he had made with his mouth against her skin. A hormonal surge happened, right there in the graveyard. Unwanted, but unquestionable. What Barbie desired most was to run her hands all over Darin's hot bod. Unfortunately, that urge was a bit impractical at the moment.

"You say 'Them' like it's a bad thing, Darin, about the people who have her." Talking kept her lips busy and away from his.

He shrugged. "May or may not be bad, depending."

"Those frat boys might have Angie, you mean?" Barbie guessed. "Those frat boys from the party have a cubbyhole out here?"

"I'm not talking about fraternity boys, Barbie."

"Hoodlums?"

Darin just looked at her.

"Wait. You don't really think I believe your 'things that go bump in the night' theory, do you?"

"Trust me," he said. "Some things go bump."

Barbie's own internal bumping increased in both intensity and tempo. Her whole body had begun to shake, one particularly potent shiver sending her pelvis right into Darin's. She got her fingers up into the wild, flying hair in record time, and pushed the mane back from his face.

"Are you one of them?" she asked teasingly.

A pinprick of light, finding its way through the overhead branches, lit her fingers and Darin's skin. She saw his eyes at last, not exactly the green she'd remembered . . . more like a piercing gray-white.

It took a full minute for her to realize that it wasn't Darin's face she was looking at between the shiny curtains of his hair. It was something . . . liquid. Flesh in transition. Like in a really scary movie.

Chapter Thirty

Barbie stifled an exclamation. Stumbling backward over the grass, she stared, riveted, as Darin's face contorted like a thing made of rubber. It was terrifying, obscene—and utterly fascinating. Although Darin shook his head trying to negate what was happening, his body began to bust out of its clothes.

Ping! A shirt button soared. *Ping!* Another. Barbie covered her eyes with her hands, saving room to peek through. No way she was going to miss this. She couldn't have run if she'd tried.

The sound of tearing silk split the night, followed by a growl so deep and guttural that Dog couldn't have hoped to compete. Darin's shirt fell in shreds to the ground, a couple pieces left to dangle from one remaining seam at his collar. His biceps bulged, sprouting Popeye-like into huge masses of flesh and muscle.

Next came forearms. Big, burly forearms, covered with dark hair. Manly hair, not anything zoological. Not yet, anyway.

Barbie crept backward until her butt encountered a solid object. A tombstone. "Oh, crap."

"Run," Darin growled in a voice that was almost unrecognizable. However, Barbie was too busy wondering if his pants would be the next article of clothing to tear away. She was considering what could possibly be underneath.

Tearing off his belt with a graceful tug of his arm, Darin repeated, "Dammit! Run!" even as he reached for Barbie's hand and caught hold. He dragged her to the side of the mausoleum and pinned her against the chilly marble. His lengthening face came close to hers. "You . . . little . . . fool!"

Without waiting for her to comment, he flung open a door and shoved Barbie inside. She spiraled backward into a mausoleum in a dance of balance (or lack thereof) and finally stopped twirling as she hit a long, low slab.

The air knocked out of her took its own sweet time to return. Only then did Barbie turn her head toward the doorway, where moonlight spilled across the threshold. In that light, she caught sight of Darin's now-bare buttocks, spotted with moonbeams.

She clamped a hand to her mouth, because above Darin's rather impressive derriere his back had grown wide in a very peculiar manner. The skin covering his backside had become a follicular miracle, as hairy as Dog's and well deserving of a horror-flick comment. As she watched, as petrified as the marble beside her, the muscles beneath Darin's newly sprouted fur coat shuddered once, then went momentarily still.

"Is this some kind of a joke?" she cried, bewildered by the turn of events. "Because I think you've made your point. I shouldn't have come out here. I should have listened to your explanations when you tried to call. Chances are I shouldn't have left my phone number on that card in the first place, or listened to Angie's client about the party."

Off-kilter, shaky, and in total denial about what had just happened, what she thought she had seen, Barbie stood tall in order to better project her voice. "You have a life apart from mine. I had no business bothering you. I had no business spying. The fact that I love you is my problem."

Oops. A slip of the tongue. Shakier than ever, she inched sideways. "Since I've apologized, don't you think you can quit the histrionics, the body bulging, and the playacting? If you leave the door open, I'll go through it and back home. With Angie, of course. You will get her, since I've more or less apologized for my behavior?"

Barbie had an even better view of those quivering naked buttocks in the doorway from her new vantage point. They certainly were great buttocks, give or take the covering of hair. Not an ounce of fat on them. Nothing to jiggle.

How long had it taken Darin to get made up like this? she wondered, again falling back on denial. This had to be a gag. He had gone to a lot of trouble when he couldn't even have known for sure that she would follow him out here. He had ruined a terrific shirt, too.

Lightning struck between her ears with that last thought. With the lightning bolt came a protest. Wait just a darned minute! How had Darin known she would return to the cemetery? She could see Angie knowing, but Darin? Barbie herself hadn't even known she would come.

Shivers rode her nerves like mini-tobogganers. A moment came and went where she was sure she might hyperventilate. Moving slowly into a karate stance, knees bent, hands up and ready, she felt raw energy course through her. She had been willing to hear Darin out, and was being made fun of.

Maybe Angie wasn't out here, taken by *Them*. Maybe there wasn't even any *Them*! This Angie-rustling bit could be nothing more than a conspiracy to throw her off guard, make her feel stupid for participating in the Dating Game. Darin was exacting his revenge by playing at being a werewolf and scaring her senseless. He merely wore a costume that came with an inflation pump inside. Technology was a marvelous thing.

Werewolves! I mean, really!

If he'd planned this, the upshot to this new turn of events remained her arsenal of alter egos, ready for the picking, that supported her biggest personality flaw: temper. Rambo Barbie. Rebel Barbie. Kick-butt Barbie. Just thinking about them all gave her a modicum of calm. For once, she felt somewhat appeased for all those years of endless teasing.

"By the way." Her voice echoed with Rebel Barbie's testy edge in the small space. "Nice ass, Darin."

His returning growl sounded something like *Lord help me.*

Of course, Barbie knew that couldn't be right, because she was the one in need of help. If Darin shut that really heavy door, she was screwed. Not only would it be incredibly dark and very probably smelly, but if Angie truly was out there, Angie would have to fend for herself.

And since Darin didn't seem to be in any particular hurry, despite his reference to *Them* and to the possibility of no more cookie consumption with Angie if they didn't find her, this had to be another game. More graveyard-keeper antics. Scary costumes and all.

Rational thoughts fled when that perfectly rounded Darin derriere moved. Thighs big as tree trunks, no longer lithe and silk clad, took a backward step. Yes, Barbie wanted to shout, Turn around! Show us what else you've got!

Evidently, he read her mind.

Chapter Thirty-one

Maintaining her karate stance was an impossibility; all Barbie's kick-boxing class time went out the window in the seconds it took for Darin to turn completely. Her eyes sprang wide. Her brain stalled. Quite probably she was staring at the most perfect body in all the world. Greek gods had nothing on this guy.

She gaped in astonishment at a heaping mass of rippling muscle and sinew, all in the right places. Industrial-strength sex appeal in a werewolf costume. Yes, it was all there: biceps, pecs, quads . . . fur, muzzle, pointy ears. Not to mention the fact that Darin's costume came with a first-class werewolf erection. It was huge! Had he gone to an X-rated costume shop? Good thing Rebel Barbie was in residence, because Barbie Bradley felt lightheaded.

"I know you're enjoying this," she remarked, hands on the cold stone behind her for support and to keep her from whimpering. After all, seeing the full splendor of Darin's mostly naked (if costumed) body in the moonlight was a shock. "It's a neat trick all right, but did you stop to think that everything else is going to pale by comparison?"

This resulted in another growl, which might have been a curse word in werewolf-speak. Hard to tell, since it must have been difficult trying to talk through the mouth hole in that mask. Barbie sympathized. Sort of.

"Sorry? Can't hear you. Come closer," she prompted, keeping hold of Rebel Barbie's enthusiasm for confrontation with only the thinnest of threads. What she needed was a *ploy*—one of her tenth-graders' vocabulary words the week before. A word described in *Webster's* as an action intended to outwit or frustrate an opponent.

She had it! *Yes, good tactical thinking, Barbie!* She would surprise the heck out of Hairball by grabbing hold of that glorious costume attachment that was supposed to be this werewolf's "all-male part." She'd feign a fondness for it . . . then rip the thing from his ridiculous costume with a hearty laugh. Afterward, she'd run like heck.

Angie wasn't going to believe this story when Barbie told her. In private they would titter. Though this escapade certainly was the oddest she'd ever encountered, it would also be the most memorable. And . . .

Dang! Determining her tactics must have taken too long. Or maybe it was all her staring. Darin moved with graceful agility, even in his costume. One hop and he was four feet from where she stood. Nothing of his usual chiseled face was recognizable behind the mask, but his dark hair was fluffed around his head like a moon-kissed aura.

Absorbing the shiver that rushed down her spine, Barbie swallowed, then taunted, "Come on. *Closer.* Nice Wolfy."

The sound of his footsteps seemed magnified in the mausoleum: padding sounds, not unlike Angie in bare feet on Barbie's kitchen linoleum.

Barbie suddenly found swallowing difficult. As was breathing. "Is your last name Chaney, by any chance?" she teased, the word *ploy* dissolving as Darin came closer. "As in Lon Chaney? You did say you liked old movies. . . ."

Darin's body, encased in its hairy ensemble, exuded a surprising amount of heat. From three feet away Barbie could feel the inferno. Two feet away, and she started fanning herself with both hands. One foot away, and she felt as if she were sticking her face into a furnace. Pure radiant heat.

Then Wolf Boy was up close and personal. In the flesh. Pressing Barbie back against the marble wall with the force of a gale. Not more than a second later she was in his furry arms, inhaling spice and musk. Another second after that, she was lying upon the mausoleum slab on her back, with a fuzzy muzzle against her left cheek.

"Down boy," Barbie gasped. "That tickles."

Rebel Barbie, don't desert me now.

"Now or never," she whispered, needing the audible command. She tried to slip her hand down between their bodies, but found him too close.

"Impressive costume—though a cheap trick," she declared, thunder rolling through her chest and slamming against her ribs, her pulse hopscotching in her throat. Further speech was impossible. Determination had been hijacked.

The wolf costume wasn't all that bad, really. In fact, it looked quite believable. This whole scenario reminded her of making out with a costumed guy in her high school days, on Halloween, on a dare.

Actually, knowing Darin really wanted her—all that hot breath and panting!—was starting to turn her on. So was the cold smoothness of the slab, pleasant on this balmy night. Heck, the mausoleum itself had become a turn-on, as sick as that might be.

All good girls had left the room.

The protrusion on the front of Darin's costume remained a joke, however. If it had been Darin, all Darin, the very large, extremely hard thing down there might have been, from everything she'd heard about the subject, a supernatural gift from God. There was no time to explore that thought, though. Wolf Boy, in two swipes of his pawed hands, had torn her sweatpants into thin strips without causing so much as a scratch on her quivering flesh. Her Saturday undies, the day written right there on the front in pink floral script, were exposed!

"You start sniffing anywhere near me, and the date is over!" Barbie warned, slightly embarrassed over being pants-free, trying to decide where she had left her wits.

Wolf Boy howled, head lifted to the interior moonlight. It was something of a Tarzan-like cry, without the pounding-on-the-chest part. The spot between Barbie's legs responded to all this animalistic maleness with a little vibration that nearly did her in with no help from Darin whatsoever.

Against her better judgment, Barbie closed her eyes and turned her head. Were people expected to be rational in a crypt?

The feel of Darin's tongue on the side of her neck set her legs to quivering. Wolf Boy braced her knees with one hand and pulled both her arms above her head with his other. The tongue returned, darting in soft downward strokes over the fabric of her white T-shirt.

Darin couldn't speak through that hairy mask, but he sure as heck could maneuver his mouth. With a very sexy purr—not too frightening; quite erotic, actually—Wolf Boy made mincemeat out of her T-shirt. With his teeth! Which left her essentially naked on the slab, save for her underthings. Cool mausoleum air mingled with all of Darin's heat. *Kowabunga!*

In the back of Barbie's mind, consigned to the farthest recesses, possible problems nagged: the fact that she was now going to have a difficult time getting home, clothes in shreds; the fact that she'd nearly orgasmed with this guy in a wolf suit just looking at her.

Another intruding thought. Had Darin stripped her so that she couldn't follow him when he ran out of here? Did he know about her shyness and assume that it would hold her back? Absurd, really, his thinking she'd chase him, since he had most assuredly made up the part about Angie being here tonight.

But, dang. Who was calling whose bluff?

What about those other explanations Darin had said he'd offer? Would those have to wait, too, given that Darin very conveniently couldn't speak through his wolf mask?

What was wrong with her, anyway? Despite being confronted by all these concerns, Barbie didn't care. She wanted more of what this big bad wolf had to offer. For sure, more nips and nuzzling. A feeling of euphoria overcame her. Too many weird things all at once, and sometimes a girl just couldn't think them all through. Darin . . . well, he just had this effect on her. In a moment of weakness, Barbie puckered up her lips and howled.

Wolf Boy drew back as if stunned, cocked his head, and answered with his own powerful howl, which might have been the equivalent of licking his chops. Afterwards, he stared down at her, his gaze riveted to her lace-covered breasts.

No way would she allow him to shred that lace. "If you go there, it'll cost you," Barbie panted, experiencing restless legs syndrome. "Even in fun."

"Hmmm?" Wolfy growled.

Had Wolfy raised a wolfish eyebrow? Naw. No mask was *that* elaborate.

"It'll cost plenty," Barbie told him. "You want to see me naked? We're talking a chick flick, popcorn, a late supper, cocktails at Sammy's, and then a fast Porsche ride through the streets of downtown with me at the wheel. All of this pending, of course, my determination of how decent your explanations are. Because you *are* going to give me some."

Wolfy hesitated, his mouth poised above her size 34-Bs. He seemed to like the lace. His throaty growls became deeper, again almost like a purr. A wolf was, after all, a wolf, right? And lacy lingerie was a bazillion-dollar business for that very reason.

"Maybe I should make you sign a contract agreeing to my demands." Barbie gulped as he continued to stare. "Got . . . a . . . pen handy?"

Darin's eyes were shining in the wolf mask—big, pale, and luminous. There was plenty of lust there, all right. He seemed to be smiling.

"No pen? Doesn't mean you get off complete—*Ohhhh,*" Barbie moaned as he began to take little nips at her flesh that felt like tiny bug bites. Only these bites were immensely pleasurable, not itchy. She remembered these bites.

"Ahhhh!" On her left shoulder, near her satin bra strap, more bites. A warm nose on her skin. Darin's proximity was like being covered in mink, that fur was so soft.

Wait! Her mind did a rewind. Hadn't she seen someone in a fur coat briefly beneath the streetlamp outside her home? Could it have been Darin, trying this costume out?

Darin made another wolfishly satisfied sound.

"That tickles!" Barbie cried out. Her voice echoed in the mausoleum. Other sounds kept on rolling after her own voice faded, too. Strange, muffled sounds. Freezing, Barbie lifted her head, listening. "What was that, Darin?"

It was hard to believe she had heard anything over her own ragged breaths, hard to believe this moment could be interrupted for any reason. But there it was again, closer. Voices? One in particular sounded familiar.

Darin's furry head lifted. As more cool air hit her, Barbie's goose bumps returned. Without the fuzz of Darin's wolf suit, the draft seemed icy. Without the close proximity of the erotic furball, she regained some approximation of rational thought.

"Darin. You *were* kidding about Angie being out here.

Right?" This was like starting their entire relationship over—in another dimension.

"Grrrr," Darin said.

"Take that mask off and talk to me. Is Angie out here? Really? This isn't a joke just to get me naked on this slab?"

"Grrrr."

She felt his hold loosen, and was off the marble in an instant, standing between Wolfy and the door. So what if she was mostly naked except for her bra, undies, socks and running shoes? So what if she never went undressed anywhere at all, except maybe from her bedroom to the shower? This wasn't the time to be embarrassed.

"I thought you were kidding." She frowned. "Is that sound coming from my friend?"

Darin, in his wolf costume, didn't answer, though he also moved toward the exit.

"This was fun," Barbie began, noticing that one of her socks was folded down while the other stretched partway over her ankle. White athletic socks. Gad, how sexy was that? "If that truly is Angie, though, we need to find her. Can you run in that hairy getup?"

"Grrrr." Darin growled louder. His tone, Barbie decided, sounded pretty darned dangerous. Perfect for saving her friend.

She smiled at a sudden thought. "You can pump that suit up whenever you want, right?"

"*Grrrrr,*" he replied.

"I'll take that for a yes." Barbie stole one more look at Darin's costume—the lower bits, especially—before setting her mind to the task at hand. "Okay. Let's get out there, Wolf Man. Let's go find my friend."

Chapter Thirty-two

The beast backed off a bit, though Darin knew it was still aroused. His stance as he listened for those sounds Barbie had heard surely allowed her a prime view of the proof of that arousal—though not on purpose.

Over the sound of Barbie's pounding heart mingled with his own, Darin perceived a cry. Was it Angie? Keep thinking, he told himself, of her. Think of Barbie's friend. The beast's needs were simple: Running. Food. And now, sex. Although Darin the man had some control left, the scent of Barbie's luscious body had a tendency to disrupt his normal brain functioning altogether. He had to keep himself focused.

"Angie?" Barbie repeated, standing there in her underwear, refusing to cower or back down.

Darin nodded, noting that while they were on the subject of bodies and how nice they were, Barbie's was better than fantastic. He felt another howl rise in the back of his throat as she ran around the slab and bent down to scoop up pieces of what had been her T-shirt off the floor. He allowed the howl to escape as she turned for the exit, tossing over her shoulder the strangest words.

"Come on, Wolfy. Sic 'em!"

The girl had bravado.

Darin was out of the crypt in two bounds, three seconds flat, with Barbie at his side. Though she tried to slip her arms through the appropriate holes of her T-shirt, tugging the remaining fabric down over her breasts as she ran, the attempt was futile.

She was so damned cute in that outfit, or lack of it, that Darin averted his eyes. He couldn't erase the image from his mind, though. Her skin was perfectly smooth, tanned, taut. She had high breasts, curvy hips, and a narrow waist. She ran like an athlete, breathing through her mouth, long limbs supple. Her brown hair floated over her shoulders in a cascade of highlighted waves that smelled like a fruit pie.

Another vocalization of lust escaped him. That pie scent couldn't mask the musk of unfulfilled sex. Barbie was ripe with promise. The heady smell trailed her like a shadow.

Do not *look at her. Bad timing again.*

As he sprinted off down the row of buildings, his emotions scrambled, Darin couldn't help noticing how Barbie managed to keep up and keep close. She was fast, nimble. Better yet, she was still here after seeing him change. She was everything a man like him could ask for, and more.

What a sight they'd present to people who might happen to visit the cemetery this particular night, he realized, as they turned another corner: nearly naked Barbie and her beast. Then again, anybody out in a graveyard at this ungodly hour deserved such a shock.

The way Wolf Boy was running, one would think a pack of animals had taken her friend. Barbie tugged repeatedly at what was left of her T-shirt as she followed him, pretty sure there'd been a fashion fad like this in years past. Shredded cotton shirts and fringed leather vests—had those Flashdance fashionistas worn anything underneath all that shredded fabric? It was a minor consideration, she supposed, when hoodlums had Angie.

She worked to keep up as Wolfy sprinted between buildings and across the marble-studded lawn, extending her stride, glad she had at least warmed up by running here in the first place. Darin was leading her in a wide arc toward a new row of mausoleums. The moon shone from high over the trees. Silver light bounced off the gray and white marble walls, presenting a dreamlike, surreal landscape that was stark, colorless, and in its own way beautiful. From everywhere came the unmistakable smell of greenery and grass. Floral smells sweetened the air.

Crickets again provided a symphony. The wind had picked up, making her ruined T-shirt even less functional. Grave markers became taller and more elaborate the closer they got to the buildings. Several fountains spurted water with soothing tinkling sounds.

Darin slowed suddenly. Avoiding a collision with his magnificent body by jumping sideways, Barbie watched him sniff the air. He then uttered a snort.

"Angie's here?" Barbie searched the area.

Another snort—one that she took for a yes.

"What do we do now, Darin?"

He turned so fast, Barbie didn't see him coming. In a flash he had the scrap of her T-shirt over her head, and had bound her hands with it before she realized what had happened.

"Kinky, and no way!" Barbie protested. "How can I help if I'm tied up? What if they circle back?"

"Grrrrrrrr."

She took that to mean something like *I told you to stay put or I'd lock you up, and I wasn't kidding.*

"You *are* a beast!" Barbie stomped her running shoe. "If it's truly dangerous, maybe we should call the police."

"Grrrrrr." Meaning, she guessed, *I don't have a cell phone, do you?*

"Geez," Barbie muttered, tugging at her soft white cotton bonds, feeling stupid for having left her purse at the club with Angie and her phone in the purse. "Sure wish somebody here spoke English besides me."

"Grrr."

"No, I don't have my cell phone!"

Darin took off again, leaving her alone beside the biggest gravestone, no doubt assuming he had disabled her for a long while. Completely forgetting about good old female ingenuity. If he thought Barbie Bradley would stay put, he had another think coming. How many times in her childhood had she been forced to play the Indian maiden that her cowboy brothers tied up, or to a tree? The exotic princess tied to the mast of a pirate ship? She was an expert in the many uses of duct tape, and if Darin assumed he'd hogtied her out of action, he was sorely mistaken.

She might not have the use of her hands . . . but she had perfectly good teeth.

Chapter Thirty-three

Free in less than two minutes, Barbie sprinted off in the direction Darin had loped, thanking her lucky stars that the moonlight was strong enough to see between buildings. Unfortunately, the moon didn't provide a view of a wolf, fabulous backside or otherwise.

Just past one particularly narrow building, Barbie pulled up. The fine hairs on her arms prickled, not as much from fear as from the exhilaration of running in her underwear beneath a full moon. The wind on her skin felt glorious. The dappled moonlight in the trees was better than anything, outside of viewing Darin himself. By all rights she should have been terrified. At the very least she should have worried about being caught, for all intents and purposes naked, and prosecuted as a flasher. What would she say to her parents if they had to spring her from jail?

Sorry, mom. A wolf of a boyfriend ripped my clothes to pieces then tossed me on a slab and licked me. He ran off. I ran after him because he said my friend was out there, too. What? Why did I believe him? Why didn't I run the other way? Good question.

Darn good question.

The words *boyfriend* and *wolf* might not go so well together in a parent's mind, especially when the wolfish persona in question was somewhat similar to Dr. Jekyll's Mr. Hyde.

Maybe she could fib and say it was a publicity stunt for the country club? No. Definitely not. She had never lied to her parents and wouldn't start now. She'd have to tell them the truth: that she had gone insane. How else could she explain Darin in a wolf costume when it wasn't anywhere near Halloween?

No, she decided, it was simply of the utmost importance she wasn't caught.

She searched for Darin among the buildings—the Darin who wasn't really a werewolf and was only playing at being one to teach her a lesson. She got that, was on intimate terms with lessons. She even deserved one, possibly, for having come out here and complicated matters. She still expected those explanations he hadn't yet gotten around to, though. She had to have them. As a matter of fact, she thought now as she paused with her nearly naked fanny plastered to a marble wall and her arms splayed at her sides, why hadn't Darin just offered those explanations and had done with it? Merely a word or two to ease her mind about the blonde would have been of benefit.

She remained plastered to the wall, thinking. Maybe Darin's costume had nothing whatsoever to do with teaching her a lesson for calling him a louse and then appearing on that stupid Dating Game stage. It could be that he dressed up like this occasionally in the cemetery to scare ne'er-do-wells. Loiterers. Gangs. Unwieldy college kids looking for trouble. She'd happened to pick the wrong time to drop in, that's all. It could be that Darin hadn't known she was coming. Maybe he had rescued her from the other bachelor simply because he was a nice guy. Because she'd told him to scram at the club, there was every likelihood he'd left her apartment after helping her out of that sticky situation, not wanting to wait around for thanks. He'd merely returned to his graveyard to get on with his job.

The costume was realistic, admittedly, but Darin wasn't a *real* werewolf. Werewolves ate people. They'd have to be locked up for everyone's protection if they really existed. The Miami PD, his other part-time job, wouldn't have hired a genetic mutant. No, Darin hadn't tried to harm her. Just the opposite. He had tried to protect her. He'd never even made love to her fully, though he'd had the opportunity. They had merely engaged in some very strange foreplay.

Eventually the wolf costume would come off, Barbie knew. Darin would show himself in the flesh. No inflatable rubber, just Darin. And the real deal would be every bit as adorable. He was even now, this very minute, trying to find Angie again. Barbie's *best friend* Angie. In light of all these rescues, wasn't he a hero? A handsome if hairy kind? One with a gorgeous body, but more importantly, one with a good sense of humor. He was a guy who exhibited a love of games and the great outdoors. A guy with loyalty to his employer and a bunch of dead folks. A guy who liked animals. A guy who liked *her*.

Barbie's heartbeat quickened. What was not to love about this guy? Er, except for the cheating part.

A sound interrupted her mental gymnastics. It came from behind her, though she saw nothing nearby except the building to which she was glued. The sound came again, probably from inside. A familiar yelp! Angie!

Flipping around, Barbie peered at the mausoleum. Sordid details of what could be going on within were trickling through her mind: Angie atop a marble slab, and not in a good way. Angie tied up. Men throwing darts. Perverts tearing off Angie's clothes.

An exuberant crashing noise echoed through the night, followed by something like the rattling of a chain link fence. Glass shattered. Another yelp. Someone's muffled shout.

"Darin?" Barbie whispered desperately, without really anticipating a reply. Darin could be anywhere. It looked to her as if she was alone.

No doubt Angie had returned to this cemetery looking for her in order to keep Barbie from making a fool of herself. Well, that hadn't worked, it was fair to say. Things were beginning to feel like the movie *Groundhog Day*, where everything kept coming back to one place. However, and on the bright side, Darin's werewolf costume would scare the pants off any poor unsuspecting hoodlums holding Angie hostage. Look how it had scared the pants off her!

Barbie looked down at herself, all seminaked. An idea appeared, gaining momentum. Maybe in her unclothed state she could help. She could walk in half dressed and cause a scene while waiting for Darin to save the day. What sex-crazed frat boy wouldn't go for that? It was worth a try, certainly. Anything to save her best friend.

"Angie?" Barbie called out. "Angie!"

The sounds inside the building ceased.

A minute passed.

Barbie definitely heard Angie's voice then. It sounded like an oath. Brilliant! Only Angie could swear like that.

Feeling around with her hands, running her palms up and down the wall to search for a door, Barbie found it in the form of a gaping hole into darkness. Appearing to be a tunnel of sorts, the mausoleum entrance was untouched by moonlight and terribly daunting, even for a Bradley with her dander up.

Stomach churning, and with a call out for her faithful rebel namesake, Barbie waved a hand and touched the void. She blinked back surprise. This wasn't a tunnel. It was a doorway covered in heavy fabric painted to resemble a tunnel, like in the old Road Runner cartoons. She narrowed her eyes. Who would seal off a mausoleum with a faux finish? Surely not ghosts, because ghosts were incorporeal and couldn't hold a paintbrush. Renegade artists? Absurd! Miami had plenty of office space. So, who else would be in a graveyard after hours besides wannabe werewolves and ghosts?

Smart-aleck criminals, that's who. Clever perverts. Wolves of a sort other than Darin, or college freshmen. *Super* frat boys might do this. Secret societies. It might be a nest, a hideout for males bent on serious trouble. And just then the idea of young men in a secret mausoleum holding Angie hostage was a lot scarier than a crypt full of ghouls.

She had to go in there. But what if they took her, also? What if one of those crashing noises was Darin in trouble? If something happened to him, what were the chances she'd ever be licked on the inside of her elbow again? Get to run through the cemetery in her underpants? See how his hair fluffed up under a full moon?

How would she find out who the blonde was?

There was a whole mess of problems if Darin vanished. Who would leave sexy messages on her answering machine? Keep Miami's streets safe? Take care of the graveyard? (It was a safe bet folks weren't knocking down the door for that job.) Who else would dress up in a wolf costume and chase her around, ensuring an entirely memorable evening? Who had the nicest behind she had ever seen on a man, was secure enough to name a dog Dog, and cared enough, showed enough promise to even suggest adhering to her stupid rules on dating?

"Wolf Boy, that's who," Barbie said aloud, pushing forward to part the heavy curtain with shaky hands.

Darin might be in there. Angie might be in there. Whoever said that women were the weaker sex didn't know squat. Think female puberty. Think dating, and learning to handle the male population in general. Think childbirth and dirty diapers. Think deciphering the world of cookbooks and shopping malls, managing to walk anywhere in high heels, wielding eyelash curlers, facing the good-old-boy club at work, and every single other thing womanhood entailed.

"Why don't you think about teaching a classroom of tenth-graders in the inner city? Yes, think about that," she muttered. "Not to mention how difficult it would be to find another really good hairdresser if anything were to happen to Angie."

That did it. Shoving her way through the opening, Barbie shouted loudly enough for even the deafest ghost or frat scum to hear. Real volume, Bradley style.

"I'm coming in!"

Chapter Thirty-four

She got inside easily enough, then stumbled down a set of worn marble stairs. Her pulse skyrocketing, eyes wide, she hauled herself up in surprise. Gaping. Mouth open. Standing there, expecting darkness, what she found instead was as mystifying as anything she could possibly have dreamed up. Something very uncryptlike. Leaning more toward the *Twilight Zone*.

The place was cavernous, with a vaulted ceiling and tall gray walls. Light flickered from candles in sconces too numerous to count, providing a hazy illumination. Twelve-foot-high mirrors in gilt frames leaned against two corners, reflecting the candlelight in an eerie glow. Gigantic tapestries, rich, though muted by age into vast expanses of diluted color, hung from branch-sized bronze rods. Oil paintings were everywhere—portraits, hunting scenes, animals, castles. Heavy antique furniture edged the room, in both light and dark wood, upholstered lushly in every conceivable shade of red. All of it was tufted, tasseled, and dripping with old-world opulence.

The place was every bit the size of the AM-PM Mini-mart, and twice as frightening in the middle of the night. Barbie stared some more.

The gray marble floor had been covered by a Persian carpet in shades of brown and gold, with twisted fringe and a few visible worn spots. The raised slab dead center of the room, similar to the one on which she had recently been stretched out—mausoleum tract homes? she wondered—doubled as a table and was covered with a swath of ivory lace.

On the makeshift table sat an ornate bronze candelabra with a bunch of candles burning. In perfect arrangement beside the candelabra were settings of gold plates and bowls, gold flatware, and crystal goblets that sparkled like rainbows. Complete place settings for two. Totally unexpected. Beyond weird.

"Barbie?"

Confused, tight-jawed, Barbie turned her head. The room seemed terribly underpopulated for a gang's crib. Too quiet. No oddballs whooped it up with lassos or paraded their stuff. No coats, hats, or boxer shorts hung from the chandelier, which was a complex dripping of crystal, candles, and solidified wax. There was not one skinny guy in a backward baseball cap. No leather-clad biker boys with shaved heads and cigarettes dangling from between their teeth lounged in the chairs or upon the several velvet cushions strewn about the floor. In fact, none of the carved chairs or stools were occupied at all.

"Barbie?"

The tone and familiarity of the voice registering at last, Barbie swept her gaze over the carpet to the farthest corner of the space. There, against the wall, chained up in Spanish Inquisition–type hardware—rusted chains and manacles—and wearing a tight black dress and a look of surprise, stood Angie Ward.

Stunned was not the word Barbie would have chosen to best describe her reaction to the scene. *Flabbergasted*, maybe.

Perhaps an even better reaction would have been a four letter cussword she had never uttered in company, and thought seriously about uttering now.

Before she could speak, however, and before she could make any reactionary sound whatsoever, a pair of muscled arms encircled her. Strong, sinewy, hairless arms. Lightly tanned.

Glancing briefly at them, Barbie recovered her senses. Slightly. Enough to realize with an intake of spicy, scented air that the arms belonged to Darin, and that he had removed the wolf costume. Also, her senses told her, it truly was Angie over there against the strange, sumptuously decorated wall, with her wrists bound in iron handcuffs.

"Angie? What is going on?" Barbie demanded, wondering why Darin hadn't gone to help free her friend. Wondering why Angie wasn't yelling. Wondering why her own feet were stuck to the floor. Maybe Angie had been shocked to silence. Relieved to the point of being completely speechless? There was a first time for everything.

Still, did she have to do everything herself?

"Let me go, Darin," Barbie said. "Hang on, Angie!" God love her, her best friend had been dragged here by heaven alone knew who, out of her Fiat and into a mausoleum that looked like it had gotten stuck in some kind of Victorian time warp. "I'm coming, Angie! I'm here!"

Struggling against Darin's hold but failing to budge him, she only then noticed what Darin must have, hence his reluctance to release her: Angie wasn't calling out for help. Angie did not thrash about in an attempt to free herself. Angie's hair cascaded in waves of black, tipped with a purple wash. Her lip gloss was in place, her lips open in an expression of complete incomprehension at seeing Barbie there. Not fright or terror, but true astonishment bordering on annoyance. Had Angie gone and lost her mind?

"Ang!" Barbie cried, if more tentatively. "Let me get you out of those chains."

Angie cocked a hip. "You do anything of the kind, and I'll dye every hair on your head green."

Barbie felt as though her feet truly were nailed down. She knew her mouth was hanging open.

"How did you find me?" Angie demanded.

"What is going on?" Barbie said.

"It seems, honey," Darin answered, mouth close to Barbie's ear, "that timing actually is everything."

"I'll second that," Angie declared.

Chapter Thirty-five

"You're chained!" Barbie shouted.

"Am not!" her friend responded, screwing up her face. "Well, maybe a little, but I can get free whenever I want, so it doesn't count." Angie casually removed her wrists from the loose metal cuffs, held them up for Barbie's inspection, then carefully stuck them back inside, smiling.

Barbie leaned back against Darin's chest, all the fight gone out of her. "Cripes, Angie! We were worried!"

"Might be better to worry about what kind of a fashion statement you've got going," her friend suggested.

As if it was the right time to remark about someone else's external presentation before answering vital questions about her own sad state of health and disposition. Nothing out of the ordinary there.

"My clothes got shredded," Barbie explained, exasperated. "What about you? What happened to you? Why don't you need our help?"

"Shredded by who?" Angie asked.

"A wolf. Long story. Now, answer my question please."

"I met the man of my dreams," Angie said, still grinning.

"Oh yes, certainly looks like it. You should see yourself, Angie."

"Might want to peek in one of those mirrors, yourself, Barb. You've been outside like that?"

Barbie nestled her nearly naked tush deeper into Darin's protective embrace. Funny how perfectly she fit inside of his arms. Their bodies cupped together like the old cliché of hand and glove. His chin rested on the top of her head.

He didn't seem too worried.

"Is he the wolf who tore your clothes?" Angie asked, alluding to Darin with a tilt of her head, her right breast nearly popping out from her skintight dress.

"Breast ahoy!" Barbie warned.

Angie looked down, removed one hand from the chain bracelet, and adjusted herself. "Thanks."

"You're welcome. And yes, actually," Barbie said. "Angie, meet the wolf, Darin. Darin, Angie. Darin was my date last month, as you might recall. *The* date."

"He was also," Angie said, "Bachelor Number Three this evening."

Gad, had that stupid game show only been that evening? Seemed like a month ago. So many things had happened. So many emotions had risen to the surface.

Barbie went on. "Now that introductions are over, what is my best friend doing here, *Angie*? What is this place, and why are you in those cuffs? The man of your dreams has cuffs?"

"Hello, Angie," Darin said in the lull that followed those rapid-fire questions. "Nice meeting you at last."

"Oh my," Angie said, eyes fixed on Darin. "Can you please repeat that?"

Darin remained quiet.

"She wants you to repeat the *hello*," Barbie prompted.

"Hello," Darin said warily, arms wrapping tighter around Barbie.

"Damn, if that isn't the voice to end all voices," Angie declared, rattling her cuffs slightly. "Maybe I should get mad at you, Barbie, for telling me you didn't know who belonged to that voice when it was on your answering machine."

"*Blind* date, Angie. The definition of which is, person without substance or familiarity until you meet face-to-face."

"That's semantics," Angie scolded. "This is the voice."

"Yes. I'm sorry. You're right." Barbie shrugged. "I should have told you. I just didn't want to go into it."

"Did the wolf get his clothes, too?" Angie queried, head tilted at a smug angle.

Only then did Barbie stop to consider what Darin's bare arms might mean. It meant that the naked arms might be an extension of a naked body. There were no rolled-up shirt sleeves on the tanned skin. She could, when she turned her head, see a bare shoulder. It sort of made sense, she supposed. Unless he had extra clothes hidden somewhere, what could he have changed into when he ditched the wolf suit? Where had he ditched the wolf suit? How had he gotten himself out of it so quickly? Velcro?

"Darin?" Barbie said, momentarily forgetting Angie.

"I'm using you for cover," Darin replied to her unspoken question. "Couldn't find a fig leaf."

"Damn," Angie sighed. "He's completely naked back there?"

Barbie wiggled a little. Sure enough, her keister was up against Darin's bare groin. Darin was utterly and completely naked.

"How did you get here, Angie?" Barbie asked, refocusing with difficulty because she was thinking about Darin in the raw. In the buff. Behind her. No wolf suit to hide behind.

Would he have tan lines?

Would any part of him resemble the wolf suit in any way?

Was it really hot in this mausoleum?

"It's not the way it looks," Angie said, bringing the focus back to her strange plight.

"I hope not," Barbie scolded, "because it looks a little like an orgy palace, Ang. I mean, how much velvet can there be in one room?"

"It's not an orgy!"

"Then what's going on?"

"I sort of met someone, like you did."

"You stopped by my place no more than half an hour ago."

"To tell you I had a date. You weren't there, so I figured you were busy elsewhere. I used your key to open the door and tossed your purse inside."

"Then you came here? For a date?"

Angie shrugged. "Coincidence?"

"Fate," Darin said from behind.

"What?" Barbie and Angie chirped in unison.

"Angie . . . May I call you Angie?" Darin began.

"You can call me anything you want in that voice," Angie said.

"Why don't you want to be rescued?"

"Yeah, why don't you want to be rescued?" Barbie echoed. "Exactly?"

"Why don't *you*?" Angie returned defensively. "You said a wolf tore off your clothes."

"I asked first," Barbie said.

"*He* asked first," Angie pointed out, waving to indicate Darin, chains clanking.

"Fine," Barbie said. "Answer him. I'll listen."

"Okay. Truth is, I like it here," Angie said without so much as a smidgen of defensiveness over her predicament. In fact, she was showing signs of agitation over the intrusion, and had started a little tap-dance routine in her six-inch stilettos.

Barbie glanced around the room a second time. "You like postmodern stuff. This is more like a haunted-castle movie set."

"I'm eclectic in my likes. I have a whole new appreciation for medieval."

"So, how did you get in here?" Barbie pressed.

"My guy lives here."

"You're kidding."

"Do I look like I'm kidding?"

In fact, to Barbie, Angie did not look like she was kidding.

"You're in fake chains. How is this possible?" Barbie had to know.

"They're real chains. They just don't work so well anymore, being antique and all. Walter collects things like this. We were playing games with them."

"Who is Walter?" Barbie asked, more confused than ever. When she felt Darin nod his head, she had an aha moment. Darin, it seemed, knew what Angie was talking about. Possibly also who Angie was talking about. He had relaxed somewhat.

"So," Darin said pleasantly, and as though they were passing on the street instead of rendezvousing for a rescue in The de Sade Museum. "You don't need rescuing, Angie. You're certain?"

"What?" Barbie cried, mortified.

"Quite certain," Angie said.

"What?" Barbie repeated.

"Walter is a very nice . . . person," Darin told her.

"You know him?" she asked.

"Yes. I've known him for some time."

"Where is this . . . Walter?"

"He's probably around," Darin said. "He is rather shy."

"Until you get to know him," Angie threw in. "Then shy is no longer an option."

Barbie tilted her head, considering this new information. "How did you meet Walter, Ang?"

"Long story," her friend replied, smiling enough to show teeth.

"Got all night," Barbie fired back.

"No, we don't have all night," Darin corrected.

"Figure of speech," Barbie said, "to get the other person to come clean with information sooner rather than later."

"I think it's fairly clear that later would be a better option for details," Darin cautioned gently.

"Amen to that," Angie muttered. "Lunch? Tomorrow? Then I'll want the details on how you left the country club with Bachelor Number One and ended up here with Bachelor Number Three."

Barbie grimaced. "Okay, I get it. Later for details—if you're positive you don't need rescuing."

Angie again slipped both wrists out of the cuffs and made a peace sign with her fingers. *All show*, she was again pointing out. And she liked it.

"Never would have figured this," Barbie muttered. "Angie Ward in bondage."

"Ain't life grand?" Angie said with an honest-to-goodness twinkle in her eye.

"Just one more question, Angie. Please. What is . . . ?"

"Walter," Darin prompted.

"What is Walter doing to you in those chains?"

"Are we nosey?" Angie replied.

"Always willing to learn, Ang."

"If you must know, it's foreplay. At least, I hope it is."

Barbie felt her eyelids flutter.

"A special kind of foreplay," Angie continued. "The kind every woman might secretly dream about."

Barbie's mouth moved. No sound came out. Pure, unadulterated excitement showed in Angie's face—that was for certain.

"Walter was feeding me before you waltzed in. You'll never guess what he's been feeding me," Angie said, slipping her bonds and prancing to the slab of a table. Triumphantly, she lifted the lid of a golden bowl. To Barbie's amazement, Angie took out a partial package of . . . chocolate fudge-covered Oreos.

Totally bewildered, Barbie laughed.

"Walter knows what a woman wants." Angie chuckled excitedly. "This here is ritual foreplay at its best."

Darin chose that moment to begin a retreat. He backed up slowly toward the doorway, dragging Barbie along.

"Dating rules can sometimes be challenged," Angie added with a little wave. "I may be all night, depending on when we run out of cookies. Suffice it to say"—she pointed up and down at Barbie's seminaked body—"that the night promises to be interesting for both of us."

"Amen," Darin whispered.

Barbie turned, still locked in Darin's arms. Her movement caused a grinding together of their frontals. Although Darin was buck naked, he sure wore a terrific smile.

"Would you mind handing me a pillow, cushion, or piece of cloth?" he asked. "I seem to have lost my clothes."

Barbie looked into his eyes. "I think now might be a good time for a bit of blackmail."

"Are you one to take advantage of such a situation?"

"What situation would that be, exactly? Oh, the one where you rip my clothes half off and that's okay, but when you lose yours, you're skittish?"

"That would be the one, all right."

"Seems to me, then, that a movie and dinner tomorrow night might be in order."

"It'd be a tall order, and maybe not so easy," Darin replied. "Unless you exchange dinner for lunch."

"Hey! You guys! Love you and all, but do you mind?"

Angie's plea was tempered by a flickering of all of the candles in the room, almost magically all at once, as though a breeze had penetrated this thick-walled, windowless space.

"What was that?" Barbie asked.

"That would be Walter." Darin's tone was confidential. "And I'm not skittish about my body. I was thinking about your reaction. If tongues aren't allowed on a first date, think what complete nakedness might do to shake things up on a second."

"Barbie!"

"Oh, all right, Angie." Barbie spoke over her shoulder to her pal. "Glad you're fine, Ang, except maybe mentally. Still, very happy you have a boyfriend prospect. We're going now. We'll leave you to it."

Whatever *it* was. With whoever this Walter guy was.

Angie sighed loudly. "Thanks. Now, there is one teensy thing you could do for me."

"You mean outside of dialing 911?"

"Yes, Miss Smarty-pants. Instead of that."

"What?"

"Do you think you could move a little so I might catch the naked show before your asses hit the road? *I'm* not skittish."

Barbie looked at Darin.

"Don't you dare," he warned.

"So, you are skittish."

"Wouldn't want to spoil Angie, is all."

Barbie grinned. "A little exposure might serve you right."

"This is not my fault, Barbie."

"Who was the blonde?"

"Jess Russell. My little sister. I swear."

Barbie cut her eyes to Angie. Angie shrugged.

"Cross my heart," Darin added.

Barbie nodded. "Okay. Promise me you'll answer all my

questions when we step outside this door, and I'll help you out of this sticky situation."

"I won't be able to answer your questions once we step outside that door."

"Barbie!" Angie was beyond impatient.

"We're ruining my friend's private party, Darin. Will you comply?"

"No."

"No?" Barbie hadn't expected this answer. Now what? Try again. "Why?"

"Because I could very easily fall in love with you. I might have fallen already. If I answer all of your questions, there's a possibility I won't be able to see you again. If we walk out that door, I won't be able to speak of this at all."

Darin loved her? There was a good chance he *loved* her?

Barbie held up a hand to let Angie know she was trying to rush things along and that she needed another minute.

"Are you a criminal? Homicidal maniac?" she asked Darin.

"Of course not."

"Barbie!"

"I'm sorry, Angie. We're going."

Though the candles flickered again, Barbie kept her focus on Darin's face. Darin said, "I think we're annoying Walter. We really don't want to get on the wrong side of him. That is a fact."

Barbie spoke loudly, for Angie's benefit. "Is Walter a homicidal maniac or criminal?"

"No," Darin replied. "At least, I don't think so."

"Is he one of those things that go bump in the night?"

"Yes."

"Yes?" Barbie was a bit taken aback.

"Afraid so."

Barbie swallowed. "Will he harm my friend?"

"Doesn't appear to be the case, as I see it. Your friend seems quite capable of taking care of herself."

"Oh, all right." With a quick smile at Angie, Barbie leaned forward to grab a cloth napkin from the elaborately set table. The napkin passed from her hand to Darin's. Their fingers touched.

Clang! It was an instant replay, for Barbie, of Darin's innate ability to beat her gongs. She felt this one from her nose to her knees and sighed heavily when it zigzagged through more sensitive parts of her anatomy. It felt *good*. In her Saturday-labeled undies and wispy lace bra, Barbie suddenly felt terribly overdressed.

"This is no more than a loincloth," Darin complained, alluding to the napkin.

"Yeah." Barbie smiled, thinking her reply sounded way too anticipatory. "On the way out," she added, smiling so widely that her face hurt, "you can pick up your wolf suit from wherever you stashed it." Oddball foreplay seemed to be ruling the day. Why the heck should she miss out?

Darin raised one of his eyebrows in that quizzical way he had. The strange interior breeze ruffled the napkin in his hand, also moving the tapestries on the walls. The candles flapped and sputtered, barely rivaling the flap and sputter of Barbie's heart.

A whoosh of cold air circled in the cavernous room, sounding like ocean waves rolling and retreating. Above those sounds, a high-pitched hum began. Barbie's smile faded.

Darin, napkin now held over private parts that were about to be not so private, turned. "Come on," he said to Barbie, making for the door.

With a shake of her head over Angie's acceptance of this kooky situation and a firm resolve not to mention some of the details of her own mental lapses, Barbie followed close on Darin's heels.

"Good night, Angie. Walter," Darin called out, gaining momentum as the door that masqueraded as a tunnel rose up in front of them.

"Good night," a bass voice returned from someplace inside of the room—and the word was followed by a squeal of delight from Angie. Either Walter actually was the man of Angie's dreams, or his hand had again dipped inside that cookie jar. Maybe both.

Though plenty of curiosity remained about Walter, Barbie was too busy keeping her eyes on Darin's backside to search for anything else. She had been right all along. Darin had a very fine behind. Though a nice male rear end had never been high up on her true list of priorities for desirable long-term potential, right now it struck her as a very nice perk.

But then . . . hey, wait just a darned a minute! Barbie backpedaled, latching onto a bit of recall. Walter's voice had struck a chord. His deep voice had resonated with a slight British accent. Where had she heard it before?

The answer came to her in her rush: the taxicab driver. On the way to the Gypsy restaurant for her first face-to-face meeting with Darin. She'd heard that voice say, *The gentleman paid*. And hold the phone—there was more! Her synapses were virtually snapping. She had heard that voice somewhere else, besides the taxi. Someplace recent.

She nearly turned back to the room, stunned by the answer coming to mind.

No. Couldn't be. Could it?

Angie was inside that wacky crypt with . . . Bachelor Number Two?

Chapter Thirty-six

Dragging Barbie along, Darin rushed out of the door and into the night. Once outside of the mausoleum, he threw himself immediately back against the wall, beneath the corbeled overhang. Grabbing Barbie, he yanked her close to him with a ferocity that knocked the breath right out of her.

"You know Walter," she accused.

"Yes."

"You knew Bachelor Number One."

He gave a slightly less enthusiastic, "Yes."

"You rigged the game!" Barbie charged. "Walter is Bachelor Number Two, right? From my Dating Game? You were Bachelor Number Three. The sociopath was Bachelor One."

"Yes."

No guilt appeared on Darin's face. Barbie tried her reasoning powers again. "Those guys were fillers? You assumed I'd choose you?"

"I hoped you'd choose me."

"You had your pals there, though, in case I didn't?"

"Whoever you chose was to deliver you directly to me."

"Like . . . *mail?*"

"Special delivery." Darin grinned. "It was the only way I could think of to see you, to get the chance to give you those answers you're so dearly in need of. It was worth every penny for the chance."

"Are you saying that you paid their way onto the show? All thirty thousand dollars?"

"Worth every penny," Darin repeated.

It now occurred to Barbie that the sociopath, Darin, and Walter were perhaps all baked in the same oven from the same recipe. The sociopath liked to dominate, Walter had his opulent, if questionable, mausoleum, and Darin had his Rottweiler, his costumes, and a bottomless bank account. That Dating Game should have taken place at a sci-fi convention.

Yet, scrambled in with all those warped eccentricities, the word *love* lingered. Angie's chirps of delight lingered. The feel of soft fur on her skin lingered. Reasoning this out would require advanced problem-solving skills that Barbie's nearly naked body, pressed as it was against Darin's nearly naked body, didn't possess.

"Love?" she said, with only her flimsy Saturday undies and Walter's confiscated table napkin to separate them. "You did say that word, right?"

"I might have mentioned it, yes," Darin confessed, feeling himself tremble, unsure whether the cause was the mostly blocked moonlight or his closeness to Barbie. Probably both. Either way, he was fairly certain he didn't have enough time or breath left to tell Barbie everything she wanted to know.

She felt so good to him, so right, that some part of himself was urging him to run. Away from her. To protect her. Because if he continued to hold her this closely, with most of their body parts touching, he wouldn't be good for anything in another ten seconds. Yet if he gave in to those feelings of escape, if he ran from her, he'd never really know if Barbie was the one. *The* one.

His secret was one to beat all secrets. He had never told anyone but his family about himself, and now he had to break that rule. He'd have to let go, become what he often became, and let her see. He had to make Barbie understand everything, know everything, so they needn't slip back to square one every time the damned moon appeared, and so she'd realize he hadn't donned any damned wolf suit.

There could be no secrets between them. Nothing withheld. No lies. He was afraid. Afraid he'd lose her. He didn't want to lose her.

"It wasn't a suit," he said, swallowing the fear that beat at him with a terrible force. "Not a wolf suit."

Barbie eyed him suspiciously, exploring that comment of his and coming up blank. To her credit and his immense relief, however, she remained close against him.

"Okay," she said finally. "Wolf *costume*, then. Semantics aside, where did you chuck it?"

"I didn't put it, stash it, or chuck it anywhere. It wasn't a costume. It wasn't a suit. This isn't a joke. It's why I had to leave you when I did on that first date. It's why I had to leave your apartment when I didn't want to after I took you home, and why I left you in the cemetery when you came after Angie. It's why I had to rely on one of the other guys to bring you to me tonight if you wouldn't listen to me at the country club."

Her lips pursed skeptically. He hurried on.

"Although I usually have fairly good control, I was losing it. You and the moon are a wicked combination for a guy like me."

Now Barbie wore a frown on her cute little face. Her hair, tousled and curling from the night's humidity, shone with drops of moonlight. Darin pulled her closer.

"Bachelor One wanted to take me to his apartment," she said. "Not here."

"I'm truly sorry about that, but I took care of it." He paused to glance up, past the overhang. When Barbie's hips slid against his again, he cussed an inward stream. Barbie's movement had allowed the faintest bit of moonlight to touch his hand. His knuckles were starting to burn.

"Please listen to what I'm saying about the wolf suit not being a suit. There's so little time to get this all in."

Barbie tilted her head adorably. Chewing on her lower lip, she said, "You're trying to tell me you are addicted to playing at being an animal? So addicted that you had to leave me on that date, on my bed, panting over *taste* and *feel*, to get back to it?"

"You're thinking I'm a mental patient?" he asked.

"Now that you mention it, is there a possibility?"

He sighed. "I wish it could be that simple. I honestly do. Would you mind if I had a screw loose?"

"No picket fences near asylums," Barbie told him. "Inmates aren't allowed power tools."

Power tools? Picket fences? Darin tried to make sense of that. Did Barbie want him to build something? Maybe he was going about this all wrong, and she was the one with a loose screw.

His burning hand stung like a son of a gun, yet if he moved it, Barbie might get the wrong idea. He ignored his rapidly rising temperature and what it meant. He had seconds only to get things in the open before the transition overtook him and he might have to run from her again. Leaving her behind, possibly for good.

"The wolf is part of me," he said clearly, hurriedly, anxiously, aware of how badly his hands shook when he placed them on Barbie's shoulders.

He watched her pouty lips part, wanting desperately to kiss them. He absorbed her shudder, wanting to get closer to her still. That just wasn't possible.

"You can't really think you're a wolf," she said eventually. "As in *werewolf*? Come on, Darin. Though I do admit it's a unique excuse for two-timing, probably the best I've ever heard as a matter of fact, I'm not that gullible."

Darin could feel his body beginning to stiffen in other places less acceptable than his private parts. He was using up his time allotment. He was struggling for one last chance to make Barbie understand.

"See that moon?" He pointed upward. "It's full tonight. When it's full, I have to hide myself away from people. That's why I come out here, and why I took this job."

Damn. Now Barbie was looking at him as if he really might be a mental patient. Take the plunge, he told himself. You're already wet.

"It's not like the old horror movies, but nonetheless a fact. I change when the moon is full. I morph from man to were-wolf. A man-wolf. I don't have to walk on all fours or any-thing. I can even postpone the transition at times, when I'm not directly in the moonlight. Clouds and roofs help with that. Nevertheless, for three days, when that thing up there in the sky is completely round, when the tides pull at the shores and the blood in our bodies moves with greater velocity, I'm susceptible to the lure. No, not even that. I am *overcome* by the lure."

"The lure of what?" Barbie's reply had a cynical quality to it, though she hadn't separated herself from him.

"The wolf," he said. "I have wolf particles in my blood. They coagulate somehow. They mingle with my more hu-man side. I'm not sure what it is they do, really, but I'm the recipient of the magic."

Barbie leaned back. Light dripped off of her forehead and onto her nose. Darin held on to her, willing her to hear him, thinking her so damned pretty and so very unique that he didn't ever want to let her go. Nor could he force her to stay. Barbie Bradley would either grasp this or not. She would believe or not. She would accept or not.

"Tell me," she whispered, "if this is an excuse to get rid of me. An excuse to meet blondes under trees. If it is, I can handle it. I'll go, leaving you to whatever it is you're doing out here."

"It's *you* I want," Darin almost shouted. "No one but you. I want to make a life with you. I've believed since the first time I heard your voice that you were the one for me, and that fate had brought you to me. However, if you take me, you take it all, Barbie. The good and the not so good. One package."

When Barbie shook her head, the moonlight scattered, drenching his left forearm. His skin crawled. He felt a snap and had a sickening hint that he wouldn't get to finish this after all.

"There's this teensy problem," Barbie said. "There are no such things as werewolves. Probably nobody other than you believes there are. If you do actually believe it."

"I was bitten while on a hiking trip through Montana," Darin told her. "I didn't find the wolf, nor did I see much of its hide. I didn't know exactly what happened to me after the bite, other than getting very sick for a while. After regaining my health, I forgot about it until the first full moon of the next year."

He grabbed at a breath, feeling rushed. The fur that covered him on nights like this was tickling the skin along his arm, ready to sprout. Jesus! Did it hide there beneath his skin somehow the rest of the time? Could an X-ray detect it down there, dormant for the other twenty-seven days each month?

A tingling sensation twitched his shoulder blades. His cheeks felt gummy.

"It's not like the movies," he said, desperately stumbling over his rehearsed dialogue, sensing now a familiar rolling in his stomach. "Some people call it a curse. Some say it's impossible. It's not impossible. It's happening to me. Whatever this is, whatever happened out there in the forest, it's who I am now three days out of every single month."

The internal roil spread to his upper back. His fingers locked to Barbie's shoulders, claws extending.

"Boy, can I understand the beastly monthly thing," Barbie confessed. "For me, it's five days at a time. However, I know the difference between acting like an animal and thinking I've become one. You're telling me you become a wolf when the moon is full, and after I've offered you a perfectly good out, you're sticking to that story?"

"Honest to God," Darin whispered, prying his teeth apart, working to keep the claws away from Barbie's uncovered skin. The fact that his legs were on fire was the final straw. Could he hang on longer? Could he postpone the inevitable if he tried his hardest? Because taking his leave of Barbie now might mean the end of any future they might possibly ever have. That was not acceptable.

"An elaborate scheme is unnecessary," Barbie repeated.

"You liked it," Darin said in reply, breath raspy, throat seizing.

"What?"

"You liked it. All of it. The dark, the moon, running through the trees. Admit it, Barbie. You liked it."

"I—"

"Liked it. What's more, you talked to me, understood me after I changed. The fact that wolves can't speak was no problem for you. You talked back. You didn't run away. You let me nuzzle you."

"The wolf costume was very realistic, Darin, but I knew you were in there."

"Yes, it is me, Barbie. If the moonlight touches me, if you touch me again in that sexy way you do, I'll change."

"Like this?" She ran the back of her hand along his cheek, softly, gently.

"Yes, and——" *Damn*.

It was too late. He was morphing from the inside out, right then and there. He could only hope for the slow version of the ten-second ordeal.

"Why me?" Barbie asked him, her fingers tracing the tight line of his jaw.

Concentrate, Darin told himself. Think of anything else, other than the light, other than the very obvious fact that Barbie has a cute little rounded belly, firm hips, and very nice breasts, at the moment still covered with the barest hint of lace.

"Darin?"

He choked, shook his head, held on for dear life. "Because I want you so . . . badly."

The wolf's sensitivities were sparking. Darin knew in that moment how much Barbie wanted to believe him. He could feel her vacillation. But she couldn't quite get her hands around the reality of such a ludicrous story. Hell, who could?

"It's only three nights," he said, his voice lowering dramatically. "This is a good place to hide."

"Sure is," Barbie agreed, wrinkling her nose.

"Admit it," Darin urged, claws now too wieldy to hold her, but hidden by the darkness.

"Admit what?"

"That you liked it all."

"I most certainly will not admit it."

Darin leaned in, face close to hers. "Admit it."

"Oh, all right," Barbie reluctantly confessed. "Maybe I did like it. A little."

"Not a little. Each bit of it," Darin pressed, feet drifting forward, body sure to follow.

"Well, not so much the scary parts," Barbie said.

"Which scary parts? The wolf? The crypts?"

With a head shake to all of those things he proposed, Barbie said, "You leaving me without a good-bye or good night. Me thinking I'd never see you again because of all those silly rules. Seeing you here with another woman."

"Jess." Darin closed his eyes, desperately wanting to kiss Barbie, the possibility of a soon-to-be-burgeoning snout notwithstanding.

"She kissed you," Barbie charged, her tone now holding a ring of possibility in it, the possibility she might heed him against all odds.

"She always kisses me," he told her. "She brings things to me. She keeps me company when I'm out here. You'll meet her. You'll like her."

"It was a costume," Barbie insisted.

"No costume. No joke, I swear."

"Then why aren't you changing now? I'm close, I'm mostly naked, and there's moonlight in your hair."

"Sheer willpower," he replied through tight teeth. "And not for much longer."

"You mean that you're about to become wolfish now?"

"Yes."

"You're saying you're a werewolf?"

"I am."

"That's what happened to you earlier, beneath the trees?"

"Yes."

"So you have to be bitten by a wolf in order to become a werewolf?"

"I . . . don't know how it works. I don't know anyone who knows how it works. Some things, I have learned, simply are."

"Montana?" Barbie said. "Not Transylvania?"

"Montana," Darin told her softly, as though it was a word he couldn't easily forget. "Outside of Billings."

Several seconds of silence followed his tortured words before Barbie spoke again. "What did you tell everyone?"

Exhaustion careened through Darin's body like one of those wayward summer lightning strikes. He was holding on so tightly to the Darin Barbie knew him to be that he'd begun to sweat with the effort. Six more seconds, he calculated, then bye-bye Barbie.

"Mainly, it's my family who knows. My immediate family," he told her. "They've watched the transformations. They know what I am. It's a part of our lives now, sort of like a monthly business trip. They've helped to keep my secret safe all these years."

"Then I'm—"

"The only other person who knows."

Barbie sighed with a soft sound. They were both shaking now. Her pink panties were tiny, soft, and silky, but he couldn't enjoy them. He wanted them off of her, and it was too late for that, too.

"If you bite me, do I become one?" Barbie asked.

"I'd never do that."

"You nipped at me before."

"Not the same."

"One good bite and you're infected?"

"I'm supposing that's the deal. I'm supposing it only works during the full moon, and if it's a serious bite. I don't know, though. I don't know how it can happen even then."

Barbie took precious time to consider this. All six seconds had passed, and still Darin held. God, he wanted this so badly. *Please.*

"What if you got mad at me? What if your teeth sort of slipped?" Barbie asked. "What about our children? Would they be born werewolves? Wouldn't nursing those children be dangerous? Oh, geez, could the female bitee have puppies?"

A laugh sprang up through Darin's distress. A human

laugh, he was relieved to note. "I believe we're way above date fifty with that last question," he told her. "Yet anything is possible."

"No other werewolves nearby?" Barbie's voice was thin.

"Not that I know of."

Could he be a mental patient? Barbie would be wondering. Darin heard this quite clearly with Wolfy's incredible talent for reading things.

"You *saw* me," Darin said with a short exhaled breath. "You've put it out of your mind. Think about what you saw."

"I saw you strip to a costume."

"Did you?"

"I thought your buttons popped off, though the pinging sound might have been my heart."

"Your heart pings?"

"Usually around you."

Please, Wolf! he begged. A minute more!

Her confession made him say, "It was the buttons, Barbie. The shirt tearing. What else did you see?"

"Your muscles might have bulged."

"What else?"

"Your face might have seemed to have altered its shape."

"It did change shape. Trust me on this."

"If I'd thought it actually did change shape, I would have run the other way, Darin."

"Maybe you didn't really care."

"I did imagine the bulging muscles, Darin. Right?"

"Do you want to find out?"

He watched Barbie bite her lip. Not so sure, she'd be thinking. She was not sure if she wanted to find out.

Darin rested the side of his face against the cool marble of the building to calm himself down. The only thing to do now, he knew, was to trust Barbie and allow nature to take her course. Let fate take her course.

Chapter Thirty-seven

Barbie slugged Darin lightly in the chest. Her mind was bombarded with thoughts, all of them running along the same lines. A life with Darin—what would her family think about her dating a werewolf? Judges were judgmental. Her brothers, criminal defense attorneys and long over their early duct-tape antics (as far as she knew), would try to protect her. Her mother . . .

Ugh. Her mother.

On the other hand, most of Barbie didn't actually care about her family's opinions at the moment. Her body, very much bigger than her brain and therefore possessed of more voting power, was all for accepting Darin's explanation at face value. Its recent *bulging face* value. Her alien antennae, apparently so crucial to finding happiness, were spinning so fast that they were creating a breeze. But with moonlight all around them, even though it wasn't exactly *on* them, Darin was still Darin.

Barbie pulled his face down to hers. He was looking at her intently, his expressive eyes blazing, his skin very hot.

"We're really talking about children?" he asked, his voice sounding strained, raw, and noticeably distant.

Didn't he like children?

"Theoretically," Barbie replied.

Trouble was, she liked children as much as the fine art of making them. Any partner of hers had to like kids as well. Yes, it probably was a dating faux pas to allow the mind to wander there, so far behind the desired white picket fence. In her defense, women naturally gravitated to these topics. Women were wired for nesting imagery.

The gist of all these thoughts was ultimately that she badly wanted to believe Darin. A werewolf excuse would be infinitely preferable to him being a lousy two-timing schemer. Hands down. No contest. Moreover, how did she *know* there weren't such things as werewolves? Who was she to argue the matter without proper documentation?

Likely, the only way to find out for sure if Darin spoke the whole truth, so help him God, would be to get him out into the moonlight. Proof, or poof. He'd either turn into a werewolf, true to his word, or she'd be gone.

If he was unable to speak when the light hit him? Well, she'd better ask some questions now, just in case.

She kept her hands on his face, needing tactile sensation, and thought he might be growing even hotter still. "So, you usually lock yourself up out here for those three days of moonshine, eh?"

"No," he replied.

"No? What do you do?"

"Enjoy the animal side of things, the freedoms."

"Such as . . . ?"

"Running naked through the dark. Feeling the wind on my skin and the night on my back. Feeling dangerously alive in a new and different way. Expanding the senses."

Barbie experienced a surge of pleasurable recollection. She had to admit she had liked those same things. She had liked chasing Darin, running with him, playing with him, in spite of assuming his wolf costume was a gag. She had actually liked being without all her clothes, liked the sensation of grass between her toes, relished the whole effect that those things produced on both her body and her soul. Who would have guessed? Most of all, though, she had relished the feel of Darin's mouth on hers. She responded to that memory with a shudder and a full-body hum.

Was any of this sane? Werewolves? For real?

Push him into the moonlight!

No, wait! her brain shouted.

"Where out here do you live during those nights?" she asked, still trying to fight off her arousal.

"Right around the corner," Darin replied, his voice very throaty.

Barbie resisted the urge to glance at the buildings. "You don't live in a crypt or mausoleum all the time, though. The other days you have a place somewhere else?"

"Yes. In the city." Voice even raspier, Darin's dual-colored eyes were hidden from her behind the curtain of his midnight-hued hair. He was clearly struggling with words. Barbie knew how he felt.

"Your digs here are like Walter's?" Her lips curled down at the thought.

"Not . . . like Walter's."

"What about Walter? You said you didn't know any other wolves, and Angie's in there with him. Why is Walter out here in a place like this? Is he in hiding for some reason, too?"

When Darin swayed slightly, Barbie could see he was in some kind of physical distress. She saw that his shoulders were once again stretching. His hips were moving. His body had heated up to a feverish temperature.

"Walter is . . . no wolf. Something else," he told her.

Prickling skin and a few wayward goose bumps led Barbie to say, "But not *criminal*. You were serious about that."

"No . . . not criminal."

"Are you saying there are other crazy things I don't know about, besides werewolves?"

Gee, did she sound kind of excited or what? Did she feel hyped over the prospect of there truly being things that went bump in the night? Maybe Hollywood hadn't gotten things so wrong after all?

Her breath caught with the possibilities. If there were werewolves for real, there was no way of knowing what other creatures might be hanging around. Get this! She had been worried about regular old perverts in the bushes!

"What is Walter, Darin? Tell me, please."

Anticipation of what Darin might say left her feeling bloodless, lightheaded, incredibly anxious.

"Angie . . . should tell you . . . if anyone. We are . . . very private."

Darin's head had begun to turn from side to side very slowly. Barbie's heart beat loudly in her chest. Unable to resist, she finally stole a glance over her shoulder at the door to Walter's mausoleum, keeping mum for the moment. Because if all this turned out to be real, and not a dream . . . If Darin was telling the truth . . .

Then, what? What would she do?

Push him!

Her inner voice was getting louder and more insistent. Thing was, she was afraid to push him. She'd know the way of it if she pushed him. This all might be over. She didn't want it to be over.

Get on with it, you coward.

Get him into the moonlight.

Quit stalling.

She released his face and placed both hands against his chest, his beautiful, manly chest that she would hate to see morph into anything grotesque. Her pulse roared in her ears as she spread her fingers wide. She felt faint, but she was going to do this. She was going to push. Wasn't she?

Bridesmaid Barbie, Bridesmaid Barbie, her mind taunted. But she was going to overcome the stigma of never making it to the altar in anything other than her dreams. This was her chance.

She slid her hands sideways over the hills and valleys of his musculature, through the baby-fine hair on his chest.

Zing.

Darin gasped. His eyes found hers.

Clang!

More moistness down under. Tons of heat. She was excited, and was also a gal on a mission who hated lies and feared secrets. Quite simply, Darin just had to be telling the truth. She had to be sure. Nerve was what she needed. Right now.

She'd count backward from ten, give herself a few more breaths of preparation.

Ten . . .

Nine . . .

Eight . . .

"Barbie." His velvet voice had gone smoky, producing waves of anticipation in Barbie that rippled outward from a trembling inner epicenter. She stopped counting, was unable to recall what number came next.

Push, her mind directed.

Pull, her body sang.

Each of her body's pulses threatened to knock her off her feet, and still questions ran rampant in her mind. If Darin was a werewolf, would he smell like a wet puppy in the shower? Wet puppies were irresistible. Did he need to eat raw food? She liked sushi.

Her fingers dipped toward Darin's navel all on their own, then slightly lower without permission. Maybe that wasn't the greatest place to apply enough pressure to get a big guy like Darin moving, especially as the intimacy of the touch brought another moan from his lips—and a matching one from hers. One millimeter lower and she could kiss the Barbie of her past good-bye. One more inch, and she'd feel the full power that was Darin Russell.

What would he say? What would he do? What excuse would she give for this bold behavior, in light of the obvious drawbacks of this maybe not being real?

Also, would she want to test things, would she want to push him into the moonlight if she were allowed to feel around some more? Already her knees were shaky. The floaty sensations that overtook her around Darin were back and shifting her into sexual overdrive. Like invisible fingers on her panties, like hot breath right on top of that embroidered *Saturday*, everything was suddenly exciting and exhilarating. Heck with pushing him—she was about to throw him to the ground and jump on for a ride. She was dealing with an immediate urge to merge.

Barbie gave in. In a deft downward detour, she brushed aside the cloth napkin that he held over his private parts without giving him time to react. The werewolf thing? she reiterated. A turn-on. Naked guy? Huge turn-on. *Darin* being the naked guy? A dream come true.

Stunned at what the back of her hand brushed behind the napkin, realizing that Darin had no pump in sight and nothing up his sleeve, Barbie fought back a moan. Wondering if any girl could handle something that large and survive, she decided she'd be willing to give it a good old-fashioned try.

"Jess?" she whispered.

"My sister. I swear."

The floaty sensations were back and wafting around Barbie's ankles. No, not the floaties; her panties had slipped down without her even noticing. In reaction Barbie leaned closer, resting her head against Darin's shoulder. Any minute now, she'd do it. She'd push him into the moonlight and see what happened. But first—

Oooh.

Darin touched her in a private place, returning her favor. Barbie's eyes sprang open in surprise. The touch, though brief, was delicious, sharp, and mind-altering. Darin's fingernails had raked the sensitive skin of her thighs, just as they'd raked her palm in the Gypsy restaurant. His hand then cupped her down there, his touch featherlight, wonderfully erotic, terribly exotic.

Barbie looked up above their heads to where the moon cast its gossamer light across the graveyard beyond the overhang. Sweet lord, they couldn't stay like this, so intimate, when the truth lay hidden. As good as this connection felt, Logical Barbie remembered her objective. For this objective, all Barbies needed to work together.

His palm was caressing her slowly, agonizingly. In another moment she'd need CPR. She was going to faint. Again.

Come on, Barbie. Speak up! Clear your mind! her brain shouted.

"Blondes should stay in their places—which is with surfers and on runways," she whispered as Darin's hands located the very center of the Land of Zing between her quivering thighs. This was round two of the foreplay they'd begun earlier, not ten minutes ago.

"Barbie." He spoke her name tenderly, urgently, with an inflection of longing and a hint of desperation. But the sheer shocking pleasure of his hand on her was nearly eclipsed by Darin's next three words.

Chapter Thirty-eight

"Don't . . . like . . . blondes," he whispered.

And she believed him.

Barbie's orgasm, arriving on the heels of Darin's three little words, made the world shimmer and all her former dreams forgettable. She had a new dream. In it, the white picket fence gleamed, then faded into a sizzling hotbed of steam and sparks. Satin sheets appeared, the color of strained ruby wine. She and Darin lay atop those sheets, sweaty, in a heap, legs tangled.

Sagging limply against Darin, she knew this climax had been too easy, and caused by a lifetime of orgasm-free living. She had finally done it, though. She had experienced bliss, and with very little help from her partner. Now, she wanted more. Much more. She wanted full participation.

She could have it, she knew. Right then. Darin and she could be together in the way that she'd never been with anyone else. She could forget about her parents and propriety—Darin was her soul mate. Yet . . . for all the rightness of their being together, one question remained. Until that question was answered, nothing had been solved for keeps. For her to know the full and final truth, she still had to see him in the moonlight.

Her heart was skidding. Her skin felt broiled. Wayward body parts were akimbo, wanting more of what Darin had to offer. More orgasms. Bigger orgasms. Orgasms caused by a true merging of flesh. Immediately. No more delay. She was teetering on the edge of the pleasure chasm, the sensations akin to biting into an Oreo for the first time. It was like being presented with an entire package of Oreos without having to worry about calories. An interstellar climax, that's what waited. It was possible, she knew.

"Is your place close by?" she asked breathlessly, her entire body a shaking, puttylike mass of nerves and need. "In case you're telling the truth?" The only thing that would stop her now was proof that he was a liar. She just didn't believe that was possible. "Step into the light," she said. "Show me."

"You're not afraid of me?" he asked as Barbie looked into his eyes.

"I . . ." she began, feeling as if she were having an out-of-body experience, nervous not about his being a werewolf, but of his not being one. Anxious to find out if they might actually have a future, even if they had to live in a zoo.

"It's your choice to make," he told her, his eyes bright with insinuation and promise. And then Darin moved sideways. Startled, Barbie stumbled along.

With a hopeful expression on his devastatingly handsome face, Darin stepped into the moonlight. For some time he stood gloriously tall and unmoving, drenched in a full flood of silver, looking like one of Forest Lawn's marble statues come to life.

Light danced off his skin, his hair, his face. Moonlight poured over every muscle, across every square inch of him, adding shadowy beauty to his contoured physique. His eyes, catching and reflecting this heavenly illumination, shone.

Barbie, staring, heard herself yip. She felt herself weaken. This was what lay underneath that imaginary kilt. Darin.

Naked as a jaybird. Darin in all his glory. The moment was so magical, tears fell from her eyes. Not daring to move, afraid of losing the beauty of the moment, she let them fall.

Darin tilted her head back with one long, pointy claw, and for no more than a second looked deeply into her eyes. Then he began to alter.

His neck widened. His biceps bulged, then his forearms. New layers of muscle piled up, mounding, rounding off into newly fashioned shapes. It was as though the moon had poured latex goo over Darin from the neck down; his chest heaved and rippled in waves, those waves rolling down his abs and onto his thighs. Second by second he unpeeled, skin ruffling and resettling, hair lengthening, first to cover his shoulders, then down to his waist. After all this, his remarkable face began to blur.

There came the sound of bones cracking. Barbie winced and sucked in a breath as Darin's cheeks expanded. His nose began to stretch and re-form. Over his naked body a full coat of fur now covered everything. Fur. No lie. There in a blink.

Barbie felt like laughing, although tears continued to spill. This change wasn't terrible at all—it was fascinating. She didn't want to run, she wanted to cry some more. Why was she crying? Because Darin had been telling the truth. Darin, it turned out, *was* a frigging werewolf!

The Darin-wolf tossed his head back, settled his massive shoulders, opened his lips and howled. As the sound echoed throughout the alley of mausoleums, he spread his fur-covered arms outward as if to say, *Here I am*. He was awaiting her decision.

How many times had he been disappointed? Barbie wondered. He had told her she was the only person outside of his family to know his secret. Some secret it was!

When she nodded, the movement felt awkward after so much stillness. Possibly she was in shock, but Darin was in that body across from her, wrapped in all that fur. His eyes gave a familiar flash of green fire, softened by a whitish glaze of moonlight, as they gazed at her from the beast's altered face. No change there. Hunger still burned in those eyes. Hunger for her.

Zing!

She reached to pull up her Saturday panties, settling them on her goose bump–covered hips that were so cold now, without Darin's nearness. She cocked her head to better see the Darin-wolf in his entirety, thinking she would have to buy a new hairbrush to accommodate all that fur. Then Barbie threw her own head back and howled.

"Ah-oooooooo!"

Weak. She tried again.

"Ah-oooooooooooo!"

Grinning, she said to Darin, "Better?"

Darin, trembling all over, held out an expectant paw, palm up. Without hesitation, Barbie placed her hand in his.

"It is you inside there?" she asked.

The wolf nodded, and shrugged his massive shoulders.

"Will you make me a werewolf?" Barbie asked.

Headshake from the wolf. No, from *Darin.* This was him in there, the man who would never hurt her, he'd once promised. The man who had mentioned the E-word in passing, early on.

Light cascaded over Barbie as she joined Darin in the moonlight. The light shimmered on her tanned skin. But she remained Barbie.

Experiencing a burst of emotion she could barely contain, different from an orgasm yet infinitely close, Barbie smiled and took a firmer hold of Darin's paw, claws and all. Darin had entrusted this gargantuan secret to her. He trusted her. This was something they would share for a lifetime, three days each month.

Only one more question sprang out of Barbie's mouth, a question requiring immediate attention. "If I'm not one, how can we . . . Because I . . ."

She reconsidered what she had been about to say and revised. "Good grief. I've waited this many years. I think I can manage to wait out a couple more nights." After a pause, she let out a moan and added, "Maybe."

Darin's laughter was a hushed and husky "Grrrr."

"Forever?" Barbie whispered back to him. "No joke? No game? The real thing, Darin? You and I and . . . Dog?"

Definitely they would have to get bigger space if Dog was part of the picture, and blankets to cover the furniture for all the animals in this family, because her dreamed-of Cape Cod house would soon have its occupants. Perhaps eventually it might be populated by a small wolf pack.

Those pictures skittered away, drifting on the currents of Barbie's exhaled breath. Her heart continued to thrum expectantly, as if there might be more to come and this was only the beginning.

"Grrr," her wolf said. Barbie knew the word he'd just confirmed was *forever.* She knew he meant it. He'd chosen her. He hadn't lied. They had a deal.

Angie's client had sent them to a singles party that just happened to be in a graveyard. Fate's intervention—the cemetery, the singles party, the moon? Fate stepping in to join two people for a lifelong adventure? Maybe four people? (That last term—*people*—she used loosely, depending on what Angie's Walter turned out to be.) Yes, that client had likely meant it as a joke. But who would have the last laugh now?

"Is there more, Darin?" Barbie waved up at the moon. "Show me *everything.*"

She grasped even tighter to his hairy paw as he turned away from Walter's lair. She trembled as his ultrasoft fur brushed her skin, realizing that she couldn't walk anywhere.

Her nerves were on fire. Her body's switch had been left in the "on" position. She was one big mass of need, and although this wolf man was truly terrific, what she had to have real soon was Darin the man back with her, in the flesh. Instead of pushing him into the moonlight, she'd have to pull him away from it.

She had her hands back on Wolfy before he knew what was happening, her fingers wrapped in his minklike chest fur. It would take a lot of effort to move a werewolf. She leaned back and tugged.

"Oooohhhhhh!" Darin barked, with what Barbie assumed might be the surprised equivalent of *Ouch!* He stumbled forward a step. One giant leap for womankind, she silently crowed.

Barbie tugged again, nearly losing her footing, but she had made it back beneath the mausoleum's overhang with the Darin-wolf in tow. Now, she only had to find that very close, relatively unoccupied crypt they'd discovered earlier. Get Darin back in the dark and out of that fur. Again.

A crypt would be a strange place to explore her sexuality for pretty much the first time, she admitted to herself fleetingly. Yet she was virtually wagging all over at the thought of forever with Darin, and she wanted it to start now. She couldn't wait one more minute. She wanted to seal the deal no matter how strange any of it was. This was love.

Darin howled his happiness over being closer to her.

Barbie howled right back at him.

They laughed together—his, a bark, and hers, a trill that kept right on coming.

"Get a room!" The shout came from inside the building at their back. Angie was never too busy to eavesdrop.

When Barbie looked back up at Darin, there he was, in man form, his luminous eyes flashing with desire. Next thing she knew, she had jumped up into his arms with her legs wrapped around his waist and her hands on his oh-so-dreamy human shoulders. He felt glorious, hard, manly, and all hers. And she could see in his eyes that he wanted to get somewhere safe to prove it to her.

She silently pleaded with him for mercy and lots of rule breaking, just this once. In her mind, Barbie visualized that big book of rules snapping closed.

"Walter?" Darin called out in his sexy, throaty voice. "I know you're busy, but could you maybe help us out here?"

Wind whipped through the branches beside them. The crickets again stopped chirping. A low rumbling noise, starting in the distance, quickly rolled in toward the graveyard and passed right over their heads. Lightning, dazzlingly white, outlined in purple, sizzled over the tree tops. And as if the lightning were a giant needle weaving the darkness together, the sky tumbled over itself and clouded over.

All moonlight disappeared.

Darin, holding Barbie close, backpedaled away from Walter's crypt. He hit the nearest gravestone and waited out a breath. It was so dark now, all the other crypts were hidden. When Darin smiled, Barbie knew it only because her lips were a mere breath from his.

"I won't even ask about that," she said, "because my friend is in there, and I refuse to believe her date could have had anything to do with a rising storm."

"Good," Darin said. "Because your mouth is going to be too busy for speech."

He proved this with a kiss so lush and deep that it needed no help from any other body parts to send Barbie over the moon. And then she was falling, locked in Darin's embrace, to the grass, where Darin proved some other things, too. Like the fact that his scratch-and-sniff theory had real merit in the dark, no visuals necessary. That internal fireworks accompanying a slow sexual coupling could easily beat out those of the Fourth of July. That grass stains on the knees can actually enhance a sexual experience, and virginity is worth keeping until the right man comes along. Oh, and she also decided that it would be a good idea for Mattel to give Adventure Barbie a hefty production run.

She had never even come close to imagining what a true sexual experience could be like. Couldn't have guessed. When the big moment came, with Darin's lips locked to hers and his body pressed in close, the ground rippled and the sky closed in. She forgot to breathe. No clanging sounds could have matched the intensity of her own whispered cry of happiness. The entire graveyard, marble and all, might have fallen, for all Barbie knew, as the rush of heat and vibration kept on quaking through her with no sign of letting up. Indeed, after sex with Darin Russell, life would never be the same again. Ever.

Incredibly, just as Darin separated his marvelous mouth from hers and her body finally rocketed to a stop, its quakes quite possibly prolonged by all those nice people underground providing an ectoplasmic things-that-go-hump-in-the-night cheering section, the three words he uttered far outdistanced everything else: the coupling, the interstellar gratification, and even the other three important words he'd used earlier.

"I love you," he said.

"I love you, too," she said right back, faintly, going dizzily interstellar again with what just might prove to be a very addictive habit. Satiated, if only for the moment, and completely out of breath, Barbie rolled out from under Darin and stretched out on her back. Eyeing the clouds beginning to move away from the moon, she felt giddily happy.

"We managed that quite well, I thought," she said breathlessly. "Considering."

"Yep. Quite proud of myself," Darin agreed in a gruff, teasing tone.

Tossing her hair out of her face, blinking at the sudden return of the silvery illumination that once again lit the area, Barbie continued, "Darin, do you know that the Barbie doll's first horse's name was Dancer? For other pets, she's had twenty-one dogs, several ponies and cats, a parrot, a chimp, a panda, a lion cub, a giraffe, and a zebra." She hesitated before finishing: "But Barbie, in all her Mattel incarnations, has never had a werewolf."

A giggle filled her body with warmth, and caused Darin to tilt his head quizzically. Well, it was the Darin-wolf's head, actually, since Darin was once again in the process of shifting his shape.

"It seems," Barbie told him, grinning widely, smiling brightly, "that Barbie Bradley has finally one-upped Mattel."

Darin nodded, growled, slurped her neck once (very sexily), and then pulled her to her feet. For a minute more they gazed into each other's eyes. Then, legs and minds in sync, they took off at a run. Together.

Was this a match made in heaven? Maybe. Perhaps even definitely. It sure looked that way to Barbie after such a promising second date. So maybe the third date wouldn't be to a movie. Maybe it wouldn't be to Home Depot for a start on that white picket fence, or even an entire evening spent in bed, undisturbed. Nope. She had a feeling the third date might be at the altar.

For surely Barbie Bradley, named after the doll, and Darin Russell, named after the singer, were the flesh-and-bone equivalent of Oreos and milk, only better.

Much better, Barbie decided as she ran with her true love . . .

Through the cemetery . . .

Totally naked . . .

Laughing.

KATHRYNE KENNEDY

Author of *Double Enchantment*

Enchanting the Beast

~Relics of Merlin~

"Really fun and imaginative." —Eloisa James

Grimspell castle. With its dark, imposing stone walls, it certainly looked haunted. As a ghost-hunter, Lady Philomena was accustomed to restless spirits. But she found the dark, imposing nature of the castle's owner far more haunting than any specter. London Society might not approve of shape-shifters such as Sir Nicodemus Wulfson, but firmly-on-the-shelf Philomena rather enjoyed the young baronet's sudden interest in sniffing around her skirts. She'd even consider giving in to him altogether if not for a murderer on the loose—a beast that might just be Nico himself.

"Simply delightful."
—*Publishers Weekly* on *Enchanting the Lady*

ISBN 13: 978-0-505-52764-6

JOY NASH

When a girl with no family meets a guy with too much…

For Tori Morgan, family's a blessing the universe hasn't sent her way. Her parents are long gone, her chance of having a baby is slipping away, and the only thing she can call her own is a neglected old house. What she wants more than anything is a place where she belongs…and a big, noisy clan to share her life.

For Nick Santangelo, family's more like a curse. His *nonna* is a closet kleptomaniac, his mom's a menopausal time bomb and his motherless daughter is headed for serious boy trouble. The last thing Nick needs is another female making demands on his time.

But summer on the Jersey shore can be an enchanted season, when life's hurts are soothed by the ebb and flow of the tides and love can bring together the most unlikely prospects. A hard-headed contractor and a lonely reader of tarot cards and crystal prisms? All it takes is…

A Little Light Magic

ISBN 13: 978-0-505-52693-9

THE
Sword
AND THE *Pen*

Love is for the mighty.

It was time. After penning ten popular sword-and-sorcery novels, Brandon Alexander Davis was ready to move on. Ready to stop hiding in his fictional world. Ready to start living a *real* life. There was just one problem: as he plotted the noble death of Serilda D'Lar, his fictional creation appeared in his study, complete with sword, skimpy leather outfit, indomitable will—and a quest. Was she nothing more than a crazy fan, or had Brandon finally cracked? This warrior woman whom he knew so well, so strong yet vulnerable, was both fantasy and reality. She was an invitation to rediscover all he once knew—that life is an incredible, magical journey and, for love, any man can be a hero.

ELYSA HENDRICKS

ISBN 13: 978-0-505-52817-9

☐ **YES!**

Sign me up for the Love Spell Book Club and send my FREE BOOKS! If I choose to stay in the club, I will pay only $8.50* each month, a savings of $6.48!

NAME: _____

ADDRESS: _____

TELEPHONE: _____

EMAIL: _____

☐ I want to pay by credit card.

☐ **VISA**   ☐ **MasterCard.**   ☐ **DISCOVER**

ACCOUNT #: _____

EXPIRATION DATE: _____

SIGNATURE: _____

Mail this page along with $2.00 shipping and handling to:
Love Spell Book Club
PO Box 6640
Wayne, PA 19087
Or fax (must include credit card information) to:
610-995-9274
You can also sign up online at **www.dorchesterpub.com**.
*Plus $2.00 for shipping. Offer open to residents of the U.S. and Canada only.
Canadian residents please call 1-800-481-9191 for pricing information.
If under 18, a parent or guardian must sign. Terms, prices and conditions subject to change. Subscription subject to acceptance. Dorchester Publishing reserves the right to reject any order or cancel any subscription.